De

To Emily,

who worked her graphic magic on this cover and who first said, "You should write this, Mama...",

and to Robert,

who untwisted every technical tangle of format and epublishing and brought a dream into reality, who for over forty-one years has been my dream and best friend,

and to my Lord,

Who is the Giver of every good and perfect gift and in Whom there is no shadow of turning.

Abby's Hope

Kathryn S. Wilkinson

Chapter 1

"When I look back over late fall of 1962 and its succeeding winter, the memory is vivid, not blurred by the passing of the years. Just the wisp of a scent of burning leaves on an autumn wind, or even the sight of dead stalks of dewberry bushes clinging to a fence line can transport me right into a moment from that time. The incidents of that fall and winter shook our little Bennington community. Perhaps the clarity of my recall is simply because of the impact and effects of its events on the people I loved. I was a child when this story unfolded. Maybe that is the real answer to why I remember so."
—Elizabeth Ann Linden Caudell

Abby Weston's House
Early November 1962

The kitchen should have had a slightly "airish" feel to it, the gift of weathering over a century's worth of years; but today in deep south capriciousness, the November dusk had settled in hot and muggy. Glancing out the window above her sink, Abby could see the stars were just beginning to peek out in the darkening skies. She wiped a bit of perspiration from her forehead with her forearm and finished swishing the dishrag around the blue aluminum cup. What had ever inspired her to buy such an impractical set of cups? They sweated like ditch diggers in the Georgia sun. And even in the heat, a cup filled with iced tea could freeze your hand. A smile played across her face. Her father had loved them. You could bounce them off the floor, and they'd never break, he'd declared happily.

Now, the plastic Tupperware—that was a different matter. They had little lids to close in what you wanted to carry with you, and they really did bounce nicely. She chuckled, the sound echoing around the room of her huge and empty home. A small sigh escaped her.

She needed to call Miz Hilton and bow out of that Tupperware party on

Monday evening. She grimaced and thought how she had already bought more bulk Tupperware than she had room in her cabinets. Abby rinsed the cup and turned it upside down with a clonk in the drain basket. Drying her hands on her apron, she stepped over to the phone and eyed it indecisively. Well, it could wait. She'd wait till after dark. The Hiltons were probably just sitting down to supper.

Abby walked to the door, untied the sash of her apron, and hung it on the hook by her father's old coat. She crossed the kitchen, then slipped off her heels and stepped into the family room in her stocking feet. Her Father's pride and joy, the big Zenith television, sat in the corner on its metal frame. She walked over and twisted the big chocolate-colored, plastic knob on the left and adjusted its volume. A small point of light at the center of the tube expanded suddenly into a blink and then a picture.

"Candid Opinion" was just signing off and she settled in on the big yellow Naugahyde couch to watch the weather, "Captain Sandy" on Savannah's channel 3. Wearing a Captain's hat and a broad smile, Captain Sandy called out a cheery "Ahoy, there, Maties!" every night. He felt like a friend of the family. She smiled a little wryly looking forward to his weather reporting helpers, Wilbur the Weatherbird, Calamity Clam and Arthurmometer. *My, my, my.* She watched another short local news show and then all the way through Huntley and Brinkley's fifteen minutes of national news.

Having heard enough of the dire headlines, Abby took the next commercial as an opportunity to feed the dogs. She opened the door to call Blue and Deacon, but they were already lolling underneath the portico and jumped up as soon as the side door to the kitchen opened. Abby had filled their two bowls with Purina, and they came tearing in like Mickie Mantle sliding into second base. Even old Blue regained his youth at the sight of a full food bowl.

Persimmon uncurled from her perch in the window, jumped down and walked slowly over to wind in and out Abby's legs. Leaning down, Abby rubbed the little cat's back. "Okay, Miss Percy. It's coming." They worked their acrobatic act across the kitchen to the refrigerator and managed a full dish of wet cat food without mishap.

She looked about her and everybody else was eating. "Ice cream!"

Time to excavate her refrigerator's small freezer. It stood in desperate need of defrosting and she literally dug out a carton of Borden's Vanilla Ice Cream by chipping at the ice with her ice cream scoop. Now for one of those great Tupperware bowls, minus its lid.

Turning seriously toward the crunching noises in the corner, she gave Persimmon, Deacon and Blue her best deep reporter's voice, "Just **two** scoops," she declared ominously, pausing to muscle in a few shovelfuls. Then, "Three! How did that get in there?"Abby hopped up on the counter, crossed her legs and joined her very wise pets in food consumption.

She was washing her bowl when the Grandfather clock in the family room chimed the half hour and brought to mind Clara Hilton's party. Moving over to the counter she surveyed her phone. It just sat there innocuously, a big, black, modern convenience, its plastic dial of holes gleaming over the order of numbers and letters circling around her own number typed out nicely in the middle. Jutting out her chin, she rested her hand on the receiver, and worked up her determination, as well as the speech she'd practiced for Miz Hilton.

They had a four-person party line, and in the past that had worked just fine. Everybody recognized their own ring and mostly stayed out of other people's calls. But with the arrival of Raynelle Abrams, all of that was gone.

She kept the phone tied up for hours and you never knew which ma... *whom* she would be talking to, *or* the subjects they might cover.

Abby never listened intentionally, although, she knew a neighbor beyond them who did. But she'd still hung up the phone blushing a time or two. "Don't let her be on here," she muttered, struggling with more than the woman's thoughtlessness. She unclipped her left earbob, dropped it on the counter; then slipped on her high heels—the better to "face" Raynelle and Clara Hilton, too. She drew a deep breath and *eased* the receiver out of its cradle. If Raynelle was on, she'd rather no one knew she'd tried to use the telephone.

"Well, he should be home any minute now." The distinctly southern voice yet held a whine. It was Raynelle alright. "He's coming in from Atlanta. But I thought I heard a car drive up a minute ago." There was a pause in the conversation as if they were waiting to see if there was a visitor.

Now there was a sharp edge of fear in Raynelle's voice, "*What are YOU DOING...*"

On the way to "re-cradling" the receiver, Abby jerked it back to her ear. There was a muffled protest and the sound of something striking an object, maybe? Something heavy must have fallen to the floor along with the clattering phone.

Abby had stood there frozen and stupid. Now, she did something even more stupid.

"Raynelle! Raynelle!! Are you alright? Raynelle!"

No one replied. But she heard the click of the other party's receiver. Raynelle Abram's line stayed open, so Abby heard the other noises. Over the phone, it sounded like something sliding across the floor.

Abby blew out an exasperated, shaky breath. She couldn't even call the police. Raynelle's phone being off the hook kept hers from being used, too. She had an extra long curling cord on her phone, her father's doing before he'd gotten sick, so she paced the kitchen, phone squeezed to her ear, right hand with a stranglehold on the wire, as she tried to listen for any other sound.

The sharp staccato of her spiked heels walking the floor in the big room jangled her nerves even more. She crossed the kitchen to the key hook by the door and noted the trembling of her hands and arms as she snatched at her keys. *What to do? Lord, show me what to do.*

Abby heard receding steps and then the sound of someone returning, but no children's voices or Raynelle's either. What if there was an intruder in the house? Would they hurt the kids?

She remembered the last time big John had brought his children into Barnes Store. She could see the Abrams' two children, Annie and Bo, their eyes filled with hope and wonder as they eyed the glass candy counter where Abby worked.

Just as she'd made up her mind to drive over, she heard a click and the dial tone started buzzing. She jolted and then turned to dial the local police.

Elizabeth Linden's House
Late November 1962

We had just come through the Cuban Missile Crisis and a subsequent surprise visit from our Commander-in-Chief. Nobody, except our small town's locals, had paid too much attention to the violent death of a young woman living up a country road not a mile away from the newly-awakened and bustling military base. In fact, I had only gleaned information about her death from conversations within my family and in our local papers, because all the other newspapers were covering JFK, Khrushchev and Castro's "High Noon".

I probably wouldn't have even noticed myself, except Raynelle's husband, John Colton Abrams was my brother's old school buddy; and Big John had been arrested the evening of her death. They lived two fields over from our house. So, we were on the same party line as the Abrams household—which meant I'd *inadvertently* heard parts of her phone conversations when Big John was away. "It was murder! Plain as day," my little grandma had said, "but John Colton Abrams didn't do it." And I had to agree.

My grandparents lived down a little two rut road from our house and a field closer to the Abrams' house. Well. I say it was the Abrams' house, but it was really my grandfather and grandmother's. The Abrams had rented— which left me to explore whatever clues I could find when my sisters and I helped my grandparents clean the house for the next renters.

"*Who*," my mother assured my father over leftovers from our Thanksgiving dinner that evening, "would *never* come. Because who wanted to live in a house recently vacated by a supposed murderer and his victim?"

My Father raised his eyebrows at my Mother and asked innocently just how Raynelle had vacated the house.

She cut her eyes at him and continued to vindicate Big John of any killing, "...even if a saint would've been tempted to do it," she'd asserted. And then she'd hushed as she'd eyed the three of us girls turning from our plates to listen.

Two blondes with identical dark blue eyes and one redhead's green ones studiously watching her turned the tide of her conversation abruptly.

"Pass the dressing, please, Elizabeth, honey," she smiled at me slightly here, "and you three, tuck in your ears."

Elizabeth. That was me. The blondes, lucky things, were my sisters, Claire and Janie. Then current carrier of our dinner conversation, and flawless handler of conversational detours, Ella Therese St. Clair Linden, continued to eye us as only a mother can. "Do not repeat anything that might have been artlessly spoken at this dinner table," she commanded while quietly reviewing just what she *had* said, eyebrows lowering perplexedly.

Our Dad, Carl Arthur Linden, having come by his name when his mother used her husband and her father's names in tandem, sat at the head of the table roundly smiling at his girls. This included my mother. But he focused in on just the three of us then.

"So, you girls are finally getting in to clean up your grandparents' house tomorrow," he mused. "I know they'll appreciate your help. *I shore* do." He stretched out the "sure" to emphasize his thanks.

So, way before I'd wanted to get up, the second day of our Thanksgiving Holidays, the three of us trudged down to Daddy's parents' home. Then the five of us rode over in Granddaddy's old red Fury along with mops, buckets, cleaners, paints, brushes and rags all "sardined" together in its trunk, as well as spilling over into the back seat with the three of us.

We had only gotten in to clean the old place up after a week of investigation by our county police. This involved everybody on our police force. That meant Sheriff Axel Arnett and his deputy Vern Starnes had tracked up every hallway and bedroom making endless rounds inside and out; and towards the end of their week of picking apart the Abrams' house, they virtually conducted tours for anyone in their respective families who was interested in the crime scene.

I know because, again, I had heard my grandma announce the fact. Of course, that statement had been made in her own home, and only for my granddaddy's ears, but mine were around when she'd said it.

My sisters, Claire and Janie, were identical twins; and stacking authority like seniority for each of the four years they had on me, had *allowed* me to tag along with them up to the Abrams' house. This they declared ostensibly, was "so that I could learn a few housekeeping skills". But at ten years old, I knew when they'd said yes to my offer of help that they were spreading out the work a little. They, in turn, having witnessed my avaricious devouring of Nancy Drew mysteries, suspected my motives, as well.

Towards the end of the first day, my Grandma asked me to take the hedge trimmers and make the Ligustrum look a little less wild along the front porch. I'd never trimmed a hedge before but could see it was supposed to look a little "boxy" and set forth to do my best with the weaponry I'd been given—a rusty pair of hedge trimmers.

I started from the outside and worked towards the steps. As time passed, the Ligustrum and I struggled mightily, and it was anyone's guess as to which of us would win. My arms had begun to tremble slightly at the halfway point and I let the hedge trimmers dangle at my side as I walked down the length of the shrubbery I'd already cut pulling out lopped off branches. Sweat trickled down my face and back, and the latter was setting up a whiny complaint.

I had reached the bush closest to the steps and was just snatching at its clippings when a reflected sparkle caught my eye. I dropped my weapon and scrambled amidst the growing pile of greenery. Underneath the bush, but away from the porch, lay a chain with something attached to it. Leaves and dirt had almost entirely covered it up. I reached in and pulled out a man's ring with a broken silver chain still dangling through its middle.

Of course, I lost all sense of hedge trimming and immediately scuttled up the front steps and inside to share my discovery with my Grandma who had just finished cleaning out the refrigerator. We washed "my find" at the kitchen sink, Grandma carefully holding it to the window's light for inspection while I clutched the broken chain in my fist. Turning it back and forth, she said it looked old.

Clare and Janie joined us and started gushing over the ring, too.

"Oh, look," enthused Janie, "it has a purple lion on it!"

"It's an amethyst, Honey," my Grandma told her absently. "It is lovely, isn't it?"

"Can I keep it, Grandma?" I wanted to know. My voice held a little too much urgency, I knew, but it was important to me. I thought it was beautiful, too.

"We'll have to make sure it doesn't belong to the Abrams family." Here she turned her eyes on me for a minute. "I'll get your Granddaddy to call the Sheriff tonight. Maybe he can find out for us."

Another slight pause and she continued, "From the looks of it, it's been there a long time, though," and she brought the ring closer to her face and then edged it out again to focus better. She clutched her chin with her left hand and rubbed her index finger up—just to the right of where her dimple liked to peek out, then continued, "This is an old place. Your Granddaddy remembers his folks saying that all this land belonged to the Feltons and was a plantation back in the early 1800's. I'm almost sure from all of the encrusted soil, it belonged to that family. The rain must've washed it up. The Felton Family's last descendants were two unmarried sisters—they died before World War II—your Granddaddy's mother went to school with the younger one. I remember her saying that Sarah Felton had...but that's another story."

She paused, reining in a slight smile and brought her attention to the matter at hand. "Well, if it's not John's, I don't see why you can't have it—unless someone claims it, of course."

This was one of the fun things about helping Grandma and Grand-daddy clean up. Unclaimed treasures usually became the finder's after all avenues of finding an owner had been exhausted.

Clare and Janie had eased outside once Grandma had begun rem-iniscing, so I, alone was left to be contemplated by my sharp-eyed lit-tle Granny. Studying my reddened cheeks and the sweat-dampened hair clinging to my temples and neck, Grandma said I could look over the ring while I rested.

"Sit down at the kitchen table for a minute," she commanded, and opened the freezer to pull out an aluminum flip type ice tray. She ran it under the water first, then pulled the lever up, releasing the fourteen little ice cubes. I guess she thought I looked a little too hot—anyway, she re-trieved one of the Dixie Cups she'd brought over and filled it with ice and water, then handed it over.

"Drink it slow, now," she advised me, "if you're still thirsty after, you and the twins come in for some iced tea—got some in the fridge," and she smiled at me like only a grandma can. "Yes'm," I mumbled, preoccupied with the piece of jewelry I held in my hand.

Turning it so it would catch the light, I grabbed up my cup, somehow managing not to slosh it on the table, and took my newfound treasure out-side. Plopping down on the front steps, I turned the ring over in my hand while I sipped.

Clare was finishing up the hedge for me while Janie, charged with piling up the clippings, poked all around the bushes in hopes of another such jewel. Stepping quietly up beside her crouching figure, I took the opportunity to ease a piece of ice down her collar as she inspected the ground around the hedge. She squealed and danced a jig to my delight. I was still snickering when she spotted my cup sitting beside the stoop. She snatched up the cup and a wild chase ensued. Just around the second corner of the house, she caught up with me and dumped her retribution down my own back.

Before our work was through, besides "trimming the wild Ligustrum", we'd swept and dusted, hauled out trash, and cleaned the only bathroom in the house. We also helped paint the walls and wash windows.

I did the trim work at the base boards, because it was easier for me to get down there with my 'little self', grandma said. Granddaddy just smiled at her bossing—of him and their three captive laborers.

We boxed up clothes and personal items that looked like they had been left in the middle of life, almost like the Second Coming our preacher liked to talk about. Granddaddy hauled it all to an old shed behind their house awaiting any relatives or hopefully a vindicated Big John to pick it all up. Only the children's clothes had been taken into Granddaddy and Grandma's house awaiting the social worker's pick up.

It took us the better part of two days to get the rental looking anything like ready to rent. And it actually took all five of us working together to do it.

I walked through the house with my granddaddy, on the last day after we'd finished, making sure we'd gathered up all the tools and brooms and brushes. While he retrieved his tool belt, I walked on through to the children's rooms for one more look. I allowed myself a little shiver at the door of Annie's room where they'd found Raynelle's body.

Now this was one of the things that made me sure that Big John hadn't been responsible for his wife's death. He would never have murdered his wife, and certainly not with his children right there.

Our family had known him since my brother's elementary school days. I couldn't remember *not* knowing him. His Uncle Burt lived across the street and he and my brother, Adam, had played football or baseball or marbles together whenever there was a waking hour free of homework. He was always over at our house and often spent the night. After he got out of the service and moved back to Bennington, he'd come over to visit my parents the first week he'd arrived and brought his wife and little Annie.

Once, Big John had even stopped his old Ford beside the road, and gotten out to take care of Ben Caudell's bullying me and Pickle, my kitty, with his new Western Auto bike. Ben Cau*dell* had just moved here, but already the neighboring kids, and that included me, called him by two names with an extra measure of stink implied on that last syllable. It has been my experience that when kids your age always call you by your first *and* last names—you're trouble. And that boy was always into something!

He'd moved here about three years ago after his Mama died, and lived with his uncle, our district attorney; but that's another story.

Big John had slipped up behind him and grabbed the seat of his bicycle. Then, he told Ben Cau*dell* that was the last time he would mess with me, or he'd tan his britches; and after that, he'd drive up to his Uncle and Aunt's house and let them know what he'd been up to.

Ben Cau*dell*'s eyes widened as he craned his neck to look up at Big John. The new kid had spluttered, and not been able to say anything except a stuttered "y-yes, sir". Big John released his hold on the bicycle seat after Ben Cau*dell*'s response, and that boy took off. His bike raised up such a dust it made me cough. But Big John got down on his hands and knees and charmed my new kitty out of the culvert.

Pickle had hidden from Ben Cau*dell*'s efforts to run over her. She was black with green eyes, and that's all you could see—those pickle-green eyes, as she'd backed so far into the dark recesses of the concrete culvert that ran the width of the road. And Big John had coaxed her out for me.

He had a deep voice, but there was such sweetness in his tones he almost had me sitting in his lap, too. Big John had a way with animals, and kids, and old people. Everybody knew him to be the proverbial gentle giant.

Shoot, he'd probably never even hurt old Ben Caudell, regardless of what he'd said. I knew he'd *never* have hurt Raynelle, even if she'd asked for it. And *I* thought she had. But if he *had* been going to hurt her, even if he'd just lost his temper; I knew he would never have done it in front of Annie's room.

She wasn't even *his* daughter, but the whole of Bennington and beyond knew he loved her just like she'd been his own. As big as John was, it was like my little grandma had said, "He has such a kindness in him—he could gentle a feral cat."

And that was a whole 'nother thing. Now, their two kids were parceled out to temporary foster homes awaiting relatives, my mother had said. I knew Big John would never have risked that—not his kids. *Uh uh.* And he was stuck in the county jail without bail and awaiting his trial.

On the night stand beside Annie's bed, I saw her Bible. My Grandma had somehow missed picking it up when she left. It looked just like the one the little church we all went to had given us whenever you turned six. Annie and her brother had walked up the road to attend by themselves when their Daddy was at work. But if he got a Sunday off, he'd go with them, parking his old Ford truck beneath the live oak at the farthest edge of the church property. Everybody parked in their same unmarked-but-nevertheless- "owned" parking space.

My mama would often look across the barbwire fenced field to the Abrams' House as we rode by to church. When Big John was working, she would let go a distressed sigh as she spotted their car sitting under the red maples. Sometimes we'd even see Annie and Bo walking the dirt road to the little church alone, Annie holding the little boy's hand. And then I'd hear Mama mumbling under her breath, "Raynelle must've slept in again."

I stepped over and picked up the Bible and, in the process, the thin pages fanned out towards the floor and away from the binder I held. A picture fell from within its folds. I picked up a Kodak print whose somewhat fuzzy color was characteristic of color photography at the time.

Zeroing in on the people, I spotted Annie. She must've been about two because January 1958 was printed on the lower white scalloped edge of the print. She still had a head full of blonde curls and big blue eyes like her mother. She was standing between Raynelle and a man with what looked to be carrot red hair whom I didn't recognize. They were standing in front of a cottage and you could see the ocean off to the side of them. I puzzled over it a bit, but replaced the picture, and determined to take the Bible to church to give to Annie next Sunday—if she was there.

An idea took hold as I turned to follow my Granddaddy out the front door. Wheeling about quickly, I placed my shooter, a blue cat eye boulder which had been my brother's, on Annie's mattress. Adam had given me the big, clear marble with the blue cat's eye inside it when he'd first taught me to play "pig eye"; and it was my favorite marble. I gave it a little short-lived spin and "high-tailed" it to the door clutching Annie's Bible under my arm. My granddaddy was a gentle man, but my Mama had taught me not to keep my elders waiting.

Monday, after school, I told Mama I'd left my shooter at the Abrams' house and was going to borrow Granddaddy's key to retrieve it. Absently working over some chewy cake batter in a big green bowl, she told me not to be gone long and let me take a finger scoop of the rich, brown sugar batter with me.

I found my Granddaddy and Grandma on their screened front porch, sitting together in the swing my Great Uncle Otis had built them. Granddaddy seemed to think nothing of my excuse to borrow his key, but it made me feel a little underhanded giving him the business like that.

My four-foot eleven little granny eyed me through narrowed lids, her baby blues fastening on my person as I shuffled my weight from one foot to the other awaiting the key. Granddaddy retrieved it from the kitchen key hook and patted my head as he handed it over.

"Be sure an' lock up," grandma offered with a slight smile gathering her lips up at the corners.

I was pretty sure she knew I was up to something, but I guess she must've trusted me enough to wait me out. I don't think I even heard the screen door bang, I left so fast for the Abrams'. I didn't want to go by way of the highways, so I climbed three fences and crossed the two fields to make it over to their yard.

The cows hadn't come in from the back pasture yet. Everything was still as I marched up the steps to John and Raynelle Abrams old house. All the official investigating done, the cleaning over, and even the breeze quiet, I began to get a little nervous. My older siblings had quite a repertoire of ghost stories they trotted out for me, on the odd occasion, at bedtime.

I stood on the front porch awhile and did a little more foot shufflin'. About that time, Ben Cau*dell* showed up on his stinkin' bike; but I was even glad to see him. He jumped off his bicycle and threw it down in the dirt driveway. I guessed it was almost three years old now and he wudn't so concerned with fine treatment. In fact, by the way his knees jutted up when he pedaled, I'd say he was due up for a new one. He walked over and looked up at me over the Ligustrum hedge. Ben Caudell stood just below the front porch.

"Whatcha' doin'?" He demanded.

I leaned back against one of the square posts that supported the wide porch roof with the keys jangling from my fingers, and nonchalantly said, "Just thought I'd take a look at the crime scene." Then I acted like I was thinking a bit and finally offered, "You seen it?"

Ben kind of swallowed hard and 'llowed as no he hadn't. His eyes travelled from me to the front door and back. He looked a little wary I thought. *Ha. Me, too.* Being there with your grandparents and sisters was a whole lot different than just yourself walking into all that quiet. Even then, it had spooked me some in spite of them noising about.

Also, if Big John hadn't done it, and I knew he hadn't, that left someone out there who *had* done it and might come back for something. There might be something they'd been searching for; how would I know if he or she had gotten all they wanted after killing Raynelle? Nervousness was fairly bubbling up in my stomach now.

I blurted out, "Andy was s'posed to meet me here, but I reckon he didn't get through with the yard work his mama made him do. He sure was lookin' forward to tellin' his buddies that he'd seen the Abrams' House." Of course, it was no such thing, and it pained me that that was the third time today I'd been deceitful. But I had to do this for Big John, I reassured myself as I waited for Ben to show interest; and Andy *had* already been in his yard working when we rode home from school with Mama today. And what's more, he *had* said he wished he could've seen it. All that didn't seem to help my guilty feelings much.

Ben kind of grimaced and swallowed big enough that I saw his Adam's Apple go up and down in his skinny, little throat. He was taller than most of the kids in our grade and growing out of all his clothes, but he didn't have a lick of weight on 'im. I probably could have beaten him in a fair fight, so I wasn't looking for protection from him—just company in a scary place—someone to grab hold to if you got startled.

He looked me straight in the eyes and asked, "You not going to sucker me in there and leave me flat, are you?"

I assured him that, of course, I was not; *but* he would have to fork over that Indian Head Nickel he kept if he wanted the complete tour. He frowned again at that and appeared to consider it while I wondered if I'd pushed it too far.

He broke into my worries with "Okay, but I don't have nuthin' but three cents with me," and he held three green edged copper coins out for me to see. "I like to keep rattlin' change in my pocket," he informed me.

"That'll do," I mumbled and quickly skimmed them off his sweaty palm. I pocketed my loot trying not to smile That was halfway onto paying for a little coke at Barnes' old store if I promised Mr. Barnes to bring the bottle back after—in lieu of a bottle deposit.

I moved over to the door then, managing to emanate calm and uncon-cern. At least, I hoped I did, because Ben wudn't anywhere near stupid and I didn't want him to know how much I wanted him to go in that house with me.

The rental's front door had big rectangular glass panes in it with a few speckles of white paint that Janie had missed wiping when she was "touching up" its coat. I rattled the keys a bit trying to slide the round one in the hole. I must've gotten Granddaddy's travel trailer key, and hurriedly tried the next on the ring before Ben smelled a rat. It slid in smoothly and worked its magic. We twisted the knob together and shoved it inwards. Ben seemed to be getting eager. Stepping over the threshold the smell of new paint greeted us warmly. It was one of those unseasonably hot De-cember days we sometimes had in the deep south that made you drink too much iced tea and seek out shade or oscillating fans. Ben's mouth had dropped open as he surveyed the house with me. I was enjoying myself by now, and relished both the next question and the way in which he asked it.

"Wh-where'd it happen?" he asked.

"Right in here," and I led him away from the den and down the hall to the back bedrooms where Big John had said he'd found Raynelle's body.

I never could figure how a person could murder someone and not wake up a'one of the young'uns sleeping right on the other side of the walls—especially since it took place right in one of the open doorways.

I pointed to the floor in front of Annie's room, and watched as Ben's chin dropped down to his chest again leaving his mouth in a rounded "O" shape. I crossed the threshold as quickly and unobtrusively as I could, made my way to Annie's bed, and smoothly retrieved my marble. This escaped Ben, as he was still eyeing the floor where I'd indicated the body had been found.

I began to search a little more thoroughly than I'd been able to with my sisters and grandparents in the house. Ben was still standing in the door-way looking stymied and staring at the floor. That suited me just fine as I checked out the shelves above the closets after retrieving a dining room chair. It was chrome with a vinyl covering, and I had slipped off my penny loafers so as not to scuff it up. Ben was following me again with curiosity winning out over the awe he felt at witnessing the scene.

"What're you doin'?" And his eyes followed me up the chair as I stretched around to feel on the shelves.

"Just checking stuff."

By the time I got to Big John and Raynelle's room, I had Ben's nose so close to my backbone I thought I might need brake lights. There wasn't a thing left to be found that hadn't been found by our two famous policemen or my little grandma. I let out an exasperated breath and huffed my way back into the little kitchen/dining room dragging the chair behind me.

Shoving it back under the table, I paused to take stock of the room. There were three chrome and vinyl chairs at the table and a fourth heavy wooden captain's chair. It looked like it might be handmade and I knew it was there to support John's big frame.

I took in the whole room down to the appliances, linoleum, throw rugs, cabinets, ceiling light, and windows; Ben's head mirroring my actions. I could see he was puzzled as to what I was looking for. Suddenly, it occurred to me that we hadn't painted the baseboards in here, because my granny had reminded us that Raynelle had Big John replace them about two months ago.

I realized I'd been twirling my hair while I had been scrutinizing the room and jerked my hand down. I almost jerked a hunk of my hair out in my hurry and temporarily forgot about the baseboards. With watering eyes, I realized I needn't have worried—Ben was still looking around the room as if he, too, thought to find something amiss.

I stepped closer to the baseboards and began to examine them. I'd read through a bunch of the Nancy Drew and Hardy Boys novels in our town library during the past summer, so I got down on my hands and knees to employ my "sleuth skills". I noticed Ben mirroring my movements. He seemed to be looking, too. There wasn't a matchbook, or a gold toothpick, or a thing to be found.

I was beginning to revise my ideas about Sheriff Arnett and Deputy Starnes' investigating. At least they'd seemed to be thorough. By the time I'd concluded that there was nothing to see, I'd made my way so far under the table I had to shove at the chairs to back out, as Ben had blocked the way I'd intended to exit with his own searching.

The chair closest to the wall got jammed against it and caused the baseboard beside it to pop out at the miter cut a little. I crawled over once I'd extricated myself to shove it back, when I noticed the other mitered end was not twelve inches from the cut jutting out from the wall.

I wiggled it a little because I liked to fiddle with things, and having watched a lot of carpentry between my Daddy and Granddaddy, I wondered why Big John would cut such a short board and not hammer it in right. The short baseboard edged out a little further away from the wall, too.

I fiddled a little more, but by this time a roughened freckled hand just a bit larger than mine was wedged in the crack and working at pulling it away from the wall. I didn't even pause to tell Ben to cut it out. I was some excited and I wanted his help. It slid out pretty easily with the two of us working at it. We kind of gasped together.

It was really a small drawer about twelve inches long by almost three inches deep and attached to the twelve-inch baseboard. Big John had made room for the little drawer by cutting into the drywall behind it to accommodate the two or three inches it took up inside the kitchen wall.

We dragged it over to us, Ben having a little trouble seeing it as he was wedged between the chair and me. We scooted out away from the table and took a better look.

Inside was a small key, some rolled up papers, and a small slip of paper with a Louisiana address on one side and some numbers on the back. Ben and I kind of sat there just a minute and paused to look up at each other. Then almost synchronized, we grabbed at the roll of papers. We stopped just in time to keep from tearing them.

"Look," I said eyeing Ben Caudell, "this house is my granddaddy's. I should unroll this and take it to him."

Ben eyed me pugnaciously, then let go of the papers reluctantly and waited for me to unroll them unassisted. A wad of bills fluttered to the floor.

I'm sure we both gulped then and started grabbing paper. It looked like someone had just stuffed it within the "scroll". Ben and I counted the lot and came up with $1,250 worth of cash mostly in fifties, with a few tens and ones. We looked at each other bug-eyed. It was a fortune.

"Put it back in the drawer," I commanded. "It's not ours and we've got to read the papers."

Ben looked like I'd gutted his Christmas stocking, but he shakily put it back and 'llowed as how he wouldn't a'took it anyways.

I unrolled the papers again. It looked like names. A couple of them I recognized. But the rest, I had no idea. I stopped to smell the paper. It had a new wood and paint smell still clinging to it, but I could also detect the pervasive smell of Raynelle's favorite scent.

I'd once heard Miz Delia at the 5 and 10 talking to herself after she'd rung up Raynelle's order. She was mumblin' under her breath and sneezing, but it sounded like "I Swanee. That woman must douse herself in that perfume before she leaves her house!" Then she'd grabbed up the local paper and started vigorously fanning the air around her. All I knew was that I didn't like to walk behind Miz Abrams in a store. It was really too much.

"This paper had to be Raynelle's." And I shoved it under Ben's nose.

He immediately crinkled up the offended member, and exclaimed, "Pew! Get that away from me!"

Ben and I rummaged through everything in the little miniature drawer. I pulled a small unused address book from my pocket, and began to copy down all the names and all the numbers and anything else I could find written in what we assumed must be Raynelle's handwriting.

"She sure wrinkled up that money some shoving it in there," Ben noted as he watched my quick copying.

"Reckon she must've been in a hurry."

I took the pad and began fanning my face. It was beginning to get unbearably hot in the old house.

"I don't think Big John knew she'd put this in here. He'd just come in from driving his truck on a Savannah/Atlanta route my daddy said. If she was hiding it from him, it had to be temporary, because he knew about this hiding place—probably having built it himself."

Ben scratched his head and nodded at that, agreeing. "Yea, I heard Miss Abby picked up the phone to call Miz Hilton and Raynelle was on it already. And Miss Abby heard the murder. She said Big John hadn't come in yet."

"I heard my folks talking about that, too. But the sheriff said since Abby hadn't actually heard the intruder's voice, and Big John was there when Abby drove over to check on Annie and Bo, he had to arrest John Abrams. I hope this stuff will help clear Big John. I wrote down all of the names and numbers in my notebook. Maybe we can figure out who really did it."

I took a last look at my notes and showed Ben, too.

"Let's take it to my granddaddy's. Can you leave your bicycle here and go with me over the back fields? I really don't want to carry this down the road."

Ben agreed to that, and while I relocked the door, he walked his bicycle behind the house and away from the frontage of the road.

"Good idea," I told him.

For the longest time, nobody in our neighborhood had ever locked a door when leaving their homes. Our family had just begun that practice; and that was only because someone had stolen my mama's Sunday ham right out of her oven while we were at church.

The little drawer wasn't heavy, but it was difficult getting it over the fence, so we handed it off to one another while we scooted under the barbed wire. The cows didn't pay us a bit of mind. They had gathered up in the shade of the live oaks that ran down the fence line and the whole herd was lying about chewing their cud. Only a couple of calves pushed up from the ground and ventured closer to see what Ben and I were up to.

We headed for my Granddaddy's hurriedly while trying to keep the contents of the drawer hidden. I don't know who we were hiding it from because my granddaddy's Herefords were the only ones about.

Chapter 2

"They's a whole lot I been ponderin' on and I ain't got no unnastandin' of it. Like why pure meanness seems to prosper and lovin'kindness bears the hurtin'. I reckon evuhbody gots heartache and joy all wrapped up to-gethuh-like. I jess hang on to that 'yet a little while...and it came to pass'."
—Rennie Esther Jones Baker

IT had taken twice as long to tell Granddaddy and Grandma, because Ben and I were so excited we tried to talk over one another. They'd had to hush us both and start us over.

"One at the time now," my Granddaddy had said as he and Grandma both examined the little drawer now deposited in his lap.

Every now and then Grandma Lelah would say, "My lands!" and "Mercy!".

They were still sitting in the swing on the front porch. After a bit, he got the story straight in spite of us and my Grandma. Granddaddy walked inside to the phone, trailed by the two of us with Grandma Lelah bringing in the drawer. As he picked up the phone, he motioned for us to be quiet. We knew of course that he was calling Sheriff Arnett.

About thirty minutes later my granddaddy turned "the evidence" over to Axel Arnett after he pulled up in our yard in his big, black and white Galaxy. Then they had a long, heated discussion.

After the dust had all settled, the Sheriff seemed to think that this sealed his case against Big John. He seemed a little reluctant, but he reiterated to my Granddaddy that Big John had obviously found out about all Raynelle's—he'd paused at this juncture and stretched his eyebrows up to his nonexistent hairline to indicate a few things I've mentioned I already *accidentally* discovered about Mrs. Raynelle Ann Abrams over our party line. Then he'd shrugged his shoulders, resignedly and guessed as how Big John had lost his temper.

"He was always as strong as an ox. I doubt he even knew his own strength…" and here he'd trailed off sadly.

Everybody in the county thought a lot of Big John. He was that kind of man. He was a regular visitor at our house during his school years, and I once heard my Daddy say to Mama, *"He didn't come from much, Ella, but he's turned out to be a fine man,"* then he continued pointedly, *"and he's always covered the ground he's stood on, too."* My Father didn't hand out too many accolades, so I knew he thought Big John was something special, and I did, too.

The good sheriff turned to go, and paused to lift a small manila envelope from his front shirt pocket.

"Here, Mrs. Linden," he said. "Big John said this ring didn't belong to him or anyone else in his family. Must'a been left there a good while ago—some other tenant or maybe further back. It looks pretty old and probably valuable. I'm sure anyone renting from you would've gotten in touch with you by now."

He smiled and said he'd had a talk with Paul Miller, our town's only jeweler, who seemed to think the ring must have belonged to the Feltons based on its heraldry. Sheriff Arnett hitched his pants up and said he had to get back to town.

He turned to my Grandma once again and doffed his hat with a "Miz Lelah," and a nod to my Granddaddy, "Carl."

Lastly, he turned to Ben and me and said, "This is some great detective work. I'd be remiss if I didn't say thank you, but you kids be careful. Could be someone else might be involved other than who I think. Oh, and I'd take it as a favor if you wouldn't mention it to anyone else, The less that know about it, the better."

"Good evening," and he slapped his hat back on his head and headed out.

Granny in turn gave the ring to me.

"Don't lose it, Ellie," using her pet name for me. "Like the sheriff, you could ask Paul Miller if he can tell you anything about it," she suggested. "Oh, and I'd get another chain since the one it's on is broken, that is, if I wanted to wear it—wear it round your neck," and she'd smiled.

My Granddaddy was scratching his beard and still pondering his and Sheriff Arnett's conversation. But he was half listening to us, too, and said, "That's a good idea. He might be able to tell us how old it is."

I smiled. Everybody knew Mr. Miller. He was the town jeweler and knew a lot about antique jewelry according to the lady at the county museum. He had helped them acquire and compile information about their small collection of colonial jewelry on display. When we visited the museum on a field trip, she'd given a long talk on each piece, and the Mr. Miller part was one of the things I managed to remember.

Christmas came. We sang carols at church and home, made all sorts of Christmas goodies, and had a program at our church that Ben and I and a few others in our neighborhood took part in.

Normally, I loved the Christmas Season and everything about it, but Big John's situation was bothering me. And especially the fact that I'd seemed to have helped the prosecutor's case. I wished I'd never gone over there that afternoon with Ben. Also, Annie and her brother had not come back to church. Our Sunday School teacher told Mama that a family member from Alabama had come to get Big John's kids. I wondered and worried about Annie, and Bo.

Added to all that, Ben had been appointed to play Joseph's part, and I had been asked to play Mary's for our manger scene. Why they wanted a kid with curly red hair to play Mary's part, I don't know.

I really tried not to scowl. Ben and I had seemed to call a truce during our joint investigation of the house that day. We'd gotten along even on the bus rides to and from school. I don't remember Mrs. Warren, our bus driver, once having to speak to either of us, or even eye us in her mirror. But playing Mary to his Joseph? That was the outside of enough.

That night Mama and I had a real "heart-to-heart". I accepted the role of Mary with alacrity via our phone. Miz Benny, short for Miz Bernice, took the news without surprise, thanked me, and said she'd have my costume for me come next Sunday.

The evening of the program, we were all a bundle of nerves and pretty much riotous joy. After all, nothing was better than Christmas. But Ben and I were stuck up in front of the whole church through the entire service—me seated beside the manger with Miz Benny's cousin's black wig on, whilst Ben stood beside me—with as much room between us as Miz Benny would let him get by with.

All around us were squirming angels and shepherds and wise men. Claire and Janie had gotten to stand off to the side with the older class comprising a small and boisterous choir. They got to perform their part with very little lighting, surrounded by the anonymity of shoulder-to-shoulder classmates; and only stepped to the front to read their portion of the Christmas story behind a lighted lectern.

We'd gotten through the program without a hitch other than my not knowing whether to stand or sit on the last hymn. Should I stay in character and remain seated as Mary looking down on the baby Jesus, or stand as Elizabeth Linden respectfully taking part in the hymn singing?

In the middle of "Joy to the World", I finally stood. I never would've sat it out if I'd been sitting beside my folks within the confines of pews and congregation I reasoned. I don't know why it got to me so, but I was blushing six ways from Sunday; and as soon as the pastor finished praying and blessing our congregation, I practically ran out the back entrance on my way to the privacy of the primary age restrooms.

I bolted smack into Vince Caudell, Ben's uncle—our DA, and Jerry Bigham, a rookie policeman on the city force. They were standing right at the church's back entrance, caught up in some angry verbal exchange. The strange thing was that Jerry had his big hands on Vince's shirt—and it was an expensive shirt, too. So, the verbal had led to physical aggression, and said shirt was all bunched up in his fist and Vince kind of looked like a catfish hanging off the hook on a cane pole. I almost felt sorry for him. His face was all red and twisted.

When I piled into the two of them Jerry dropped his hands quick-like and they both jumped away from each other and me. Ben's Uncle Vince seemed to be too relieved to say anything, I thought, but Jerry Bigham gave out an angry, "Hey, you little runt! Watch where you're goin'!"

I made myself scarce posthaste and forgot all about my embarrassment at the end of the program as I busily pondered over the altercation I'd interrupted between the two men. Once inside what I considered the safety of the girl's restroom, I changed back into my Sunday dress and shiny patent leathers. I was glad to have outgrown the crinolines I used to have to wear.

"Now, what would Jerry Bigham have to do with Vince Caudell in the first place? And where would he get the nerve to mess with the county prosecutor?" I mumbled to myself.

On the afternoons that my mother worked at the local grocery store in Carverville, I rode the bus home to Granddaddy and Grandma's house if Claire and Janie had afterschool activities. After I got my homework done, we'd ride up to the little country store at the edge of Bennington.

Barnes' had opened in the mid nineteenth century and had been run by family ever since; but in recent years they had hired a young woman, Abigail Weston, to help out. Mostly they carried a huge line of soft drinks, jaw breakers, bubble gum and the biggest cookies in jars you've ever seen. They also had some household items which I considered inconsequential. Barnes' had a line of glass counters that curved in a u-shape all around the back walls of the store. The cluttered candies and novelty items both within and atop those counters was "the stuff dreams are made of"—at least for a kid. Barnes' also served as our post office, and Miz Abby could handle the mail for you, too, if Mr. Barnes, our postmaster, was busy with something else.

Today, I accompanied my granddaddy to Barnes' to collect the mail. There wasn't a soul in the store, except Miz Abby, and she was reading our local paper at the counter. Her hair was pulled back in a French twist, and she looked like she'd dressed up. Her outfit was almost the color of a peach and reminded me of Jacqueline Kennedy complete with a small string of pearls—only Miz Abby was prettier I thought. But her eyes were red and she was busily employing her delicate lace handkerchief underneath her nose. Man. I hated colds. I sure didn't want to catch it.

Our steps on the old heart of pine floor must've alerted her to our approach, because our opening the door sure hadn't. She kind of jerked up and quickly folded her paper closed. Miz Abby gave one last swipe to her eyes; and attempted to bring the corners of her mouth up in the semblance of a smile. It never reached her eyes, though.

I'd made an effort to notice the article she'd been reading. It was the front page, so I was pretty sure it was the paper's coverage of Big John Abram's trial. Miz Abby had testified at Big John's trial because John's phone was on both our party lines and one other house. She had picked up just in time to hear the murder and set the time at just after 7:30 PM. Granddaddy said she'd tried to tell the DA that it wasn't John who did it, but the judge had shushed her and "cautioned the witness" to just answer questions. I remember Granddaddy telling my Grandma that Abby had seemed real upset-like. Well, those weren't his words, but it's what he meant.

Miz Abby had lived in our "neck of the woods" in Bennington all her life, but we didn't see much of her except on the bus, when she was still in school. She was a couple of years younger than my brother, Adam, and Big John. When her father had died a year or so after her graduation, she was left with their homeplace, as she was the only child Mr. Archie and Miz Elizabeth had. She didn't even have any cousins because her parents were the only children from each of their parents. I often felt sorry for Miz Abby and only very rarely envied her.

Her "homeplace" consisted of several hundred acres of pasture and woodland with a large two-story house resting at the front of the property. It was an old place, no longer supported by cattle, horses or farming, and had to be hard for her to afford. It was often the subject of our supper conversations—how she managed to work and pay for the upkeep on that big, old house. My Mama would just click her tongue and hope that Mr. Archibald Lewis Weston had left her some money, as well as that big, old, lonely house.

Granddaddy called out cheerily as we marched right up to Abby's counter, "Hey, Abby girl. Got any mail for us?"

The red-nosed clerk smiled a little sheepishly, I thought. I backed up a little, feeling sorry for her all the same. At least she wasn't sneezing.

"Sure, Mr. Linden. How's Miz Lelah?" she let it float back over her shoulder as she turned to check the boxes for our mail.

"She's fine," he smiled.

Miz Abby was the daughter of my grandma's best friend, Elizabeth, who'd died before I was born. Grandma Lelah had told me that Abby looked a lot like her Mama, and she'd said it kind of wistful like. My granddaddy and I knew that Abby's asking after her would please Grandma.

"Here you go," she said with a smile. "Oh, and you've gotten a late Sear's Christmas Catalogue. I know Miz Lelah will enjoy that."

My grandma had been fussing for some time about her missing Christmas catalogue. It was after Christmas and she still wanted it. Finally, my granddaddy had placed a call to the Sears and Roebucks headquarters and requested one. They had agreed to send one out; and he grinned widely as Miz Abby handed some envelopes and said catalogue over the counter to my Granddaddy.

Miz Abby paused a little before adding tentatively, "Mr. Linden, what did you think of J—Mr. Abrams' trial?"

Granddaddy halted and searched Miz Abby's face as he seemed to ponder her question. Then he tugged at his short beard a little and offered, "I think Big John got a fair trial. But if you're asking if I think justice was served—then, no. I don't think John Abrams could kill anyone, whether he was mad or not. Someone else out there murdered Mrs. Abrams. Is that what you meant, Abby?"

She lifted her chin slightly and thrust her shoulders back and looked intently at Granddaddy. "Yes, Mr. Linden. And that's what I thought, too, exactly what you said," and her voiced dropped low on the last few words. Then her cold must've taken hold again, because she started reaching for her handkerchief. "Oh, Elizabeth," her voice was husky as she eyed me over her handkerchief, "don't forget to get you and your grandma a couple of pieces of that bubble gum. It's on me. I know how she likes it," and she smiled even as she patted her eyes and nose.

"Yes, ma'am," I enthused.

My granddaddy broke out another grin and trailed my "Yes, ma'am" with his "Thank you."

Abby had always been a "quiet, gentle soul", my granny once said. Grandma studied people and would often share with me if her reflection was to note some strength or beauty. I smiled now because Miz Abby was loved by every kid in our small community, including me. I already said she was only a little younger than my brother and Big John, but Mama and Grandma would've skinned me alive if I'd left off the "Ma'am" or the "Miz". She was Barnes' clerk, and I'd better show some respect.

I almost took off, when that little fact hit me. "Thanks, Miz Abby! Grandma thanks you, too. I know!"

We always halved the bubblegum which was pink and thick and rectangular. It had a slight perforation down the middle and was easy to tear in half. Then we'd read the cartoon from its inner wrapper together. It was our tradition. So, today, even though we had a plenty, we still halved the one piece and read our cartoon together and saved the other piece for later.

Abby waited until Mr. Linden and little Elizabeth had shut the narrow front double doors behind them. She took a moment to blow her nose thoroughly, brushed a bit of dust off the jacket of her dress, and placed the paper under the counter with finality. Mr. Barnes had taken his wife to Savannah to celebrate their anniversary, trusting Abby to lock up that evening.

She absently rubbed her temple with her forefinger as she thought over the events that had colored the fall. Her thoughts were in turmoil as she stepped to the back room to wash her hands. Regaining the front counters, she turned back to the store's broom and duster. Abby sniffed and determined to get a little clean up done. She would not look at one more article about Big John...well not until she'd gotten home for the evening.

The wind rattled the long hurricane shutters and even the windows. Winter had set in with a vengeance it seemed. She would be glad to get back home to the little beagle she'd acquired two hunting seasons ago, and old Blue, her Daddy's pointer; and Persimmon, the little tortoiseshell cat who seemed to "rule the roost" and, no doubt, was even now waiting on the windowsill, watching for her.

Even though the house her parents had left her was empty except for her small trio of pets, she longed for its shelter with its wide surrounding porch and dormered roof-line and rooms full with memories and love. She would build a fire to help the furnace and make a cup of hot tea.

She wouldn't watch Chet Huntley or David Brinkley tonight. She didn't think she'd even bother to watch Cap'n Sandy and his weather report. And maybe she would not read any more articles about Big John Abrams and the blond-haired wife he'd brought back from Louisiana.

Abby Weston had been shocked at John and Raynelle Abrams' wedding announcement in the paper four years ago. Two years later she had been even less prepared to meet a very pregnant Raynelle in Mr. Barnes' store. Big John, his calm, gray eyes serious and unreadable, had introduced the two of them.

It had been her first week of work at Barnes—a fine, clear January day in 1960, and she had stuffed her feelings down in an all too familiar pattern where John Abrams was concerned, and greeted his wife with as much cordiality as she could muster. Spying the bounce of a cluster of blonde curls peeking out behind Big John's long legs, Abby arched her brows inquisitively at the couple while pointing at the cookie jars.

John grinned and nodded; so, Abby had reached around and gotten a big sugar cookie out of one of the mammoth glass jars Barnes' kept on its counters. She handed it over to the little one offering her a smile along with it. The young clerk had the distinct feeling that the very pregnant Mrs. Abrams had hardly taken note of her or the cookie passing into her little girl's hands; but little Annie ventured out from behind her big stepdaddy's frame and looked up at Abby with her heart in her eyes.

Big John's wife had given a brief nod to the exchange, and then her eyes had wandered the store and come to rest on Vince Caudell, who was just being handed his stepmother's mail by Mr. Barnes. While John Abrams had offered a thank you and urged his little Annie to add hers, Abby caught the spark of interest that seemed to flare in Raynelle's eyes. Abby watched their journey up and down the length of Bennington's smartly turned out district attorney.

She knew that Vincent DeLand Caudell was not a young man, but he still seemed to retain the vigorous good looks of a man in his prime; and the uncharitable thought occurred to her that the appearance of affluence might outweigh his age in Miz Abrams' eyes. Abby hoped the gold band on Vince's left hand's third finger would attract her attention, as well.

At this juncture, Mr. Barnes had taken the opportunity to announce in near stentorian tones, "Tell Miz Eulee that we've gotten in more of her snuff."

You could see Vince's whole body cringe, and Abby knew without looking that Mr. Barnes' expression could rival Da Vinci's most famous painting. Caudell snapped out an about face, and rebuttoning his expensive trench coat along the way, gave Big John, Raynelle and Abby a curt nod as he made his exit. Abby who had found out the three-year old's name was Annie, quite mirrored Mr. Barne's expression after little Annie blurted out, "Daddy! I nebber seen a man *dat* purty."

The gust of wind rattling the deep green storm shutters outside brought Abby back to the present. She snatched up the duster and began going over the counters and shelving crevices.

There was no help for it now. There never had been. Big John had been collared to disaster the first moment he'd set eyes on Raynelle; and it felt like Abby, herself, had been sucked into their downward spiral, sinking in the mire of their marriage just as surely as they had.

The thing that tore at her heart was that Big John had never had any idea of her feelings for him. She'd seen John Abrams a lot when he'd ridden the bus home with Adam Linden on Friday afternoons; then, of course, in the hallways at school in passing; and then after his uncle had been given custody of him at twelve, he'd come to live across the street from the Linden's and not a quarter of a mile from where she and her father lived. If he saw her, he always spoke, and she would nod her head and smile back at him.

She'd heard whispers about his folks and an occasional adult's thoughtless comment about his "no 'count parents". She was almost sure he must've heard some of those comments as he'd walked by the people unwisely dispensing condemnation with their gossip.

Once, she was sure she had seen the back of his neck and ears flush in embarrassment or anger after he'd passed. She'd hurt for him, and felt like lashing out at the adults for making his troubles worse. How could anybody add to a boy's troubles with indiscriminate words too easily overheard?

And how could a parent not appreciate a son like John Colton Abrams? How could anyone have let him stay in foster care so many different times when he was just a little one? She knew that was true because she'd overheard Mr. Burt talking to her Daddy late one evening on the front porch.

That was before she'd ever met John, but she figured he was in real trouble the way Mr. Herbert's voice had cracked over his sister and brother-in-law's little boy. So, she'd started praying for him at night before she went to bed. And after all those childhood prayers, how had he ever willingly chosen to marry a hard-hearted woman like Raynelle Ann Abrams?

One big tear brought her out of her thoughts. *Oh, mercy!* Anyone could've come in and seen her losing control. Mr. Linden and Elizabeth *already had.* She drew herself up from her slump, dashed away the tear, and turned back to her cleaning.

Abby had been dusting the counters like a car that was running out of gas. She'd spluttered into flourishes of cleaning, then her arm had slowly seemed to relax, and she'd squished the duster against the glass so many times that she thought she might have to buy the Barnes a new one.

Just so, she limped along through the last half hour of her shift. As soon as she realized she was caught up in worry, she'd jolt upwards and go into action again with a vengeance. After she'd swept the floor, cleaned the glass counters with vinegar solution and helped a few more customers, the store clock had finally edged over past six.

She quickly barred the front doors, counted up the money in the register, and placed it in Mr. Barnes' open safe. Remembering the two feral tabbies who'd turned up last week, Abby put two bowls of cat food on the back stoop. She shut the safe and hung out the closed sign. Gathering her belongings, she edged through the back door, scattering the tabbies as she did so. She cooed her apologies and locked the exit.

Abigail Faith Weston stood for a moment, a lone figure against the backdrop of the store, then, hunched her shoulders against the wind and headed for her car and home.

Barnes stood at the junction of two highways, and on a windy day the cold fairly howled up the roads to the store. The moisture in the air gave it the ability to cut through to your bones, Abby thought. She trudged over to her black '59 Volkswagen and opened the door, remembering the evening her father had driven it home.

She'd been home for a few days between the winter and spring quarters at her junior college just a few months before the doctors discovered Archie's cancer. She had just hung up the phone after confirming her departure time at the bus station the next morning when the distinctive sound the car's little motor made attracted her attention as it approached their driveway. Making her way to their front porch, she was just in time to see her Dad pull the little bug over the cattle gate and down their driveway with a smile bigger than the curve of its hood.

He'd bought it from a military officer who was going overseas with his family in the next few weeks. The man had wanted to get rid of their second vehicle, and her father assured her he'd "gotten it for a song". It was a funny little vehicle, not more than a couple of months old. Abby had loved the manual transmission, and laughed at the little six-inch mechanical arms that had extended from the door frame whenever she'd flicked her blinker on.

She eased into the car now, and gratefully shut the door against the whistling coldness of the air. The evening star shone to the left of a pale moon high in a sky drained of warmth. Remnants of clouds, swirled in tones of silver and rose and blue, hung at the edge of the horizon. "Mare's tails" scudded across the rest of the sky.

The car was cold and everything around her seemed so still and quiet except the wind. She was glad to hear the burbling of the motor at the back of the "bug" once she'd started it. Her hands resting on the chilly wheel, she widened her eyes in thought. What kind of sign was it when you felt like your car was an old friend?

Earl and Rennie Baker's Home

Earl had just walked out to the clothesline to talk to Rennie, who was busily snatching the clothes off the line, throwing them in the basket she dragged along beside her, and shivering. He'd caught a ride home from the paper mill with a coworker.

He stretched his thickly muscled arms out and let out a loud half yawn/half holler. Rennie jumped, as he knew she would, and smacked him with the jeans she had just unfastened from the line. He laughed and reached out his big chocolate-colored arms once more but, this time, Earl grabbed her round the waist, pulling her to him so that he could plant a quick kiss before she smacked him again. They laughed together, and she turned to hug her man.

Rennie had gotten in from cleaning and cooking at the Caudell household a little after three, and she was tired; but it amused her how Earl could lift her spirits and energy just by cavortin' around with his big self. Who could help but grin at such a man. She hugged him again before turning back to her workload.

"I'll tote that for ya', Miz Rennie," simpered Earl, as he grabbed her basket and ambled toward the house.

"Humph," snorted Rennie and snatched the clothespin bag off the line before following her man. She began to click her tongue at his backside.

"Put a little back into it, man," she chortled.

"Come on up hyeah, and tell me that, woman," he let fly over his shoulder.

Suddenly Rennie stopped, and smacked her forehead. "Aw, Earl. I forgot. I heard tell, we gettin' a' early freeze after all that heat the last few weeks. I was hopin' it'd at least last till after New Yeah's. S'posed to be down in de teens, Miz Caudell's stepson say—jest 'fo I left."

Earl waited for Rennie to catch up. "I reckon we better go up ta Miz Abby's 'fore suppa, then," he mused.

"Yeah, I reckon so," and she smiled up at Earl. "I know Mr. Weston sho' set some store by that girl. And he wuz good to us, Earl."

Earl nodded, "Sho wuz, baby."

She smiled. "You a good man, Earl. Been 'most three yeahs now, and you nevuh missed a freeze helpin' out little Abby. I know Mr. Weston would'a been so thankful. He sho' loved his baby girl some."

"Put on your coat, Rennie. I done tole you 'bout walkin' out to that clothesline without it," Earl commanded.

Rennie snapped the sleeve of his tee shirt in response, "Like you can talk, big man. You didn't even finish changin' shirts 'fo you came out heah!"

Earl laughed and 'llowed as how they'd better get a move on. "We'll walk over right after I put yo' basket in de house."

He hadn't finished the sentence before the two of them heard the little Beetle rumbling up the dirt road that went by both Abby Weston's and Earl and Rennie Baker's home. They smiled at each other.

"It'll be good to see dat chile this evenin'," and Rennie turned quickly to retrieve her coat, pausing to hold the back door open for Earl.

She chuckled up at him trying to heave the basket through the door at the same time he squeezed his big frame through it. Thankfully remembering the cornbread in the oven, she grabbed a few quilted scraps and pulled the big pan out, placing it at the back of the stove top. She enjoyed the sight and the smell of it. It was golden and had risen up in the center just like she'd intended. Rennie didn't make her cornbread to soak every bit of moisture from your body at one bite. Hers had been made with a good mixture of flour and corn meal and it was light and a perfect place for a pat of butter.

It was one of Earl's favorite things. Earl maintained that she cooked like nobody's business and the thought bringing out a smile, she turned to grab an old baby quilt from her closet along with a galvanized steel bucket. She wrapped the quilt around the inside of the bucket and placed the pot of stew in the middle. She cut up the pan of cornbread and placed it all in her biscuit warmer using it as a lid for the stew. It all worked pretty well to hold in the heat.

She placed a sack of Tea Cakes she'd baked according to Elizabeth's Grandma's recipe to one side of the stew pot. Abby got home so late, she mused worriedly. Maybe she couldn't make up for her Mama and Daddy not being there, but she could sure have her a bit of warm supper waiting on her and some company in that big old lonely house—if little Abby wanted it.

Rennie tended to use "little" as a term of endearment. But in this case, Abigail Elizabeth Weston stood at a petite five feet four inches. Ever since she had come to take charge of little Abby, Rennie had bemoaned the fact that Abby hardly ever sat still.

"How I gonna' put any weight on yo' skinny little self, chile?"

And she and the little girl had just smiled at one another and laughed. She looked so much like sweet Elizabeth, Rennie thought— dark brown hair with the sparkling red that showed up in sunlight and eyes the most unusual color of green she'd ever seen.

Rennie sighed; Abby had been so quiet amongst most folks, white or colored, from the time she could say anything. It was only when the two of them were at home or Mr. Archie was there, that her eyes "came alive" and her laughter rang through the house. Rennie had watched those beautiful dark-lashed eyes taking in everything. That one never misses a thing, she'd laughed to herself.

Buttoning up her coat, she turned to lug the heavy pail outdoors. Earl had gone to the back of the house to get a shirt and a coat, but Rennie had wanted to look at the last of the day. It was a bit windy, and she would be glad when Earl was beside her.

There was still some light from a now absent sun, but Earl grabbed his old military flashlight anyway. He wriggled into an old Eisenhower jacket and then buttoned it all the way up, even turning up the collar. By the time he and Rennie walked back it would be dark; and though the woods might cut some of the wind, it wouldn't keep out *all* the cold.

Rennie handed Earl a big slice of cornbread that was hot enough to have a few wafting swirls of steam curling upwards. She watched the smile spread across his face. Rennie kind of figured hers looked the same. Earl finished the cornbread in three bites making "mmm" noises throughout his eating.

They set out together arm in arm; she swinging the flashlight and he toting the heavy pail—their gate easily synchronized. It didn't take much studying to walk together smooth-like after thirty-odd years of marriage, she thought as they traipsed the wide path together.

Abby had had a pony cart when she was a little girl, and had helped to keep the path wide and weed-less between her daily rides to see Rennie and her Papa's mowing machine. Now Earl kept the path clear for Rennie and Abby.

Archie Weston had given Earl a job at the paper mill right after Earl had left the military and just after they had married. Her husband had been a young man then, and Rennie smiled at her remembrance. He'd bought their land from Archie with his savings and severance pay; and Archie had given Earl a great price on the property. It had really helped in setting up their household.

Some of his brothers came up from Darien and helped him raise a small house. She'd been so proud of them and it. Archie and Elizabeth, who insisted Rennie drop the Mr. and Miz, walked over with house warming presents. Elizabeth brought some fruit and a pound cake, along with a quilt she'd made "for just such an occasion" she'd said.

Rennie started working for Abby's Mama, Elizabeth, not long after the Weston's "House Warming" visit. As the years passed, became close friends. They talked about everything, while working side by side—family, their backgrounds, and even politics. Their favorite was talking about the Lord. Archie told them they had more church than cleanin'.

Rennie had shared troubles that she and Earl sometimes encountered with their three children, Earl Jr., Louise, and Chester. She and Elizabeth prayed for each one many times, and they prayed for Archie and Earl Sr., too. For that matter, they did a mite a prayin' for each other.

Archie and Elizabeth had despaired of ever having children, until late one summer Elizabeth came home from Dr. Prescott's overjoyed. She and Archie were going to have a baby! Elizabeth had joked with Rennie that she and Archie were going to name their baby "Isaac" if it was a boy.

So, Rennie worked for the Westons until Elizabeth died on the night Abby had been born. Dr. Preston had come early to the Weston household on an icy February morning, and left late with his shoulders hunched from more than tiredness. It should have been a celebration, but the wee baby girl had lost her mother, and Archie his long-time friend and wife; and to Rennie's way of thinking they had lost a very great lady.

She stayed the night, and Mr. Archie insisted that Earl stay, too. They slept in the room across the hall from the little nursery. Mr. Archie abandoned the master bedroom and took a guest bedroom downstairs. He said he just couldn't face their room without his Elizabeth.

They lived at Archie's in the upstairs room for over a year, Earl continuing to catch a ride with him in the mornings, while Rennie kept little Abby. After Abby was off the bottle, they moved back to their little home and she came over in the mornings to clean and cook and take care of Elizabeth's precious baby.

When Mr. Archie got home around six, she headed home to cook Earl's dinner. Some days, she and Abby rode the pony cart over and Rennie got an early start on dinner. Either way, Archie hadn't cared—only that his precious little Abby was loved, and Rennie excelled at that, he knew.

In the years that followed she raised Abby almost as if she were her own, while Archie kept the paper mill running down at the coast. Their lives intertwined for years with a mutual respect and appreciation for each other. Indeed, Abby's childhood was one of love and security marked by an amazing cordiality and dependence between the two families.

The road had been fairly smooth after little Abby's rough beginning until Archie's annual checkup, a little over three years ago, had revealed a tumor. By late fall of 1960, Archie was gone and she and Earl and Abby sat together as family for Archie's funeral.

The south was a strange place in those days—folks, both black and white, where relations were close, attended weddings and funerals together, unless one had to work the kitchen. On the one hand, there was a wall between the two worlds—erected in doctor's offices and dentist's and school locations; and there were places where Earl and Rennie would never go, but on the other, as with Abby and the now-growing-elderly couple, there was deep connection and love. They celebrated and they grieved together.

Earl and Rennie managed the walk through the woods without using Earl's old flashlight, but they knew they would need it on the walk back. As they followed the trail together, she could see the moon atop the black silhouettes of oak and pine and sweet gum trees.

At the end of the path now, they spotted Abby's car pulled up under the side portico originally cut for wagons and buggies. It was the perfect size for her little Bug.

Rennie's Mama-Heart knew when a chile of hers was upset. She hadn't watched Abby grow into a young woman without noticing the way her eyes followed Big John whenever he was in her vicinity. She patted Earl's arm hurriedly.

"You go 'head an' open the back do' an' mind, you put that on the stove to wom. We be right in."

They separated then, Rennie hurrying over to the little black Bug. "Oh, Baby," she blew out air in a whooshing noise through her teeth, "Oh, Baby. Lord, hep 'er," and she shook her head back and forth with her words as she approached the little car.

She could see Abby's head pressed against the steering wheel, her face wet with tears. She should've come sooner. The chile didn't have nobody! Bad enough she'd had to testify and the DA twisted it to harm Big John, but then Earl told her yesterday that the court proceedings would be in the paper today.

Last time she'd seen little Abby like this was the day that sorry ol' newspaper article 'bout John's marriage in Louisiana came out.

Abby must've sensed her presence and though a little startled, she jerked open the door and fell into Rennie's arms.

"There, Baby, there. You be awright. The Lord'll see you through, Honey. Bless yo' sweet, sweet heart."

Many times, Rennie had missed Elizabeth through the years, but never as much as this evening, with the cold wind whirling around the two slight figures in the gathering darkness; her holding sweet Abby, and the deep, silent sobs wracking the chile's frame so hard they resonated into Rennie's shoulders.

Oh, Elizabeth, she thought, *I only wish you wuz heah tonight, to help yo' chile. Oh, Lord, Lord, help this baby.*

"Sing, Rennie."

She heard it strong and clear in her mind. She almost looked around. She'd never heard the Lord's voice audibly. She'd heard of people who had—besides Moses, and Samuel, and all. Rennie didn't doubt that it was so.

Elizabeth used to say, "God can do anything, anytime, anywhere, any way He wants to." Rennie didn't think she'd heard Him out loud then, but it was just so clearly not her voice or thought, and peace sang through it. A tear rolled down her warm brown face, too, as she looked skyward, smiling at the way He always provided.

She started in humming then, rich and low in her contralto voice. Nobody could sing like Rennie.

"Mm-mmm. Mm-mmm."

She hummed hurt and longing to the Lord like words couldn't cover. Her Earl called it the Holy Spirit praying through her like it talked about in Romans 8. She kept holding Elizabeth's sweet baby girl and feeling the Love of God flow through her and out to Abby in her humming and in her arms.

She could hear Earl walking around the house, wrapping the outside spigots and turning them on so that they would drip all through the night. The pipes wouldn't freeze up that way. Earl kept out of sight and as quiet as he could.

Rennie just kept holding on to her Abby and humming more. She didn't know how long they hung on to each other and wept, only that the two of them were stiff with cold. Rennie began to feel peace in her spirit and an ending for her song. She eased down to the tonic home note softly. Abby suddenly lifted her head from Rennie's shoulder ruefully.

"Oh, Rennie, you're so c-cold. Oh, my. We ought to go in the house. I'm so sorry."

They began to walk stiff-legged and sniffling up the steps under the portico. They ended up having to help each other up each step.

They could see Abby's small beagle stretching up above the windowsill and nosing the kitchen window. Rennie and Abby could hear his impatient whining, and beside his bobbing face, Abby's little tortoiseshell sat on the sill looking askance at Deacon's gyrations. Persimmon raised a velveted paw and 'pap-papped' on the top of his head to remind him of his manners.

Even in the midst of her heartache Abby had to laugh with Rennie at their antics. Blue, her father's aging bird dog was a pointer, and almost never joined her welcoming committee except when she approached the stove or fridge. They knew without seeing that Blue, would be resting beside the gas heater at the back wall of the kitchen.

They reached the top of the stoop then and Abby shoved the door inward ushering the only mother she'd ever known inside. Rennie was never so glad to see her girl smile.

"O, my, thank you, Jesus," her heart uttered as she scooted over the threshold making room for Abby.

Earl had also made it in by that time and they met him in the kitchen putting on a pot of tea. Abby stepped around Deacon to set up the percolator after Earl moved toward the table. Earl and Rennie loved their coffee.

"I got all dose spigots drippin', Miss Abby, and you jez need to 'member to leave de kitchen sink drippin' tonight. Oh, and I fed yo' troublesomes there."

He grinned and pointed towards her dogs whose tails were currently wagging their bodies as they shadowed her movements beside the stove. Then he waved further to include the little cat who still sat sedately in the window watching her people. Abby smiled and lifted the toe of her pink pumps to scratch underneath each dog's chest whilst she spooned coffee into the strainer.

"Hey, boys," she crooned as she slipped the glass coffee strainer into the carafe, placed the small wire protector over the burner, and eased the glass percolator down.

She nodded gratefully up at Earl as she took Rennie's and her coats to the pegs by the side door and hung them beside Earl's. She patted her Daddy's old long woolen coat that still hung on its peg. She'd given away almost everything else of his clothing, but somehow, she just couldn't bring herself to give away that coat by the door. He'd put it there himself before he was confined to bed in those last days.

Earl watched Abby patting the old coat. He and Rennie smiled wistfully at each other, then at Abby. He could see that both Rennie and Abby were red-eyed and Abby's nose and cheeks were red, as well.

"Oh, Rennie. Earl. I don't know what I'd have done if y'all hadn't come over. I've never been so thankful to see anybody."

Rennie patted her arm and walked over to dish out their meal from the stove where Earl had kept it warming.

"I brought supper to eat wit' you, Honey. Dat is, if you want comp'ny?" Abby nodded again. It was as if the years had rolled away, and she was little again. Rennie waved her to sit and rest while she got the bowls and dished up the stew. There was an air of comfort that always surrounded Rennie, and Earl, too—but especially Rennie. She'd always made Abby feel like everything was going to be alright. Tonight, her singing felt like someone had reached in to save her from the mire and literally pulled her out. *Oh, God. Do that for John tonight, too.*

Chapter 3

*"When I came to the Caudell House, I was really just a girl, but after
marrying Vincent it didn't take a fortnight to grow up."*
—*Alice Camille Winslow Caudell*

The Caudell Household

G ranny Caudell had had a *bad* night. Young Ben could hear it in
her voice. He had hardly finished his breakfast before she'd started
ringing her bell.

She was upstairs and it took awhile to get there—she had to know it;
but still she screeched, "Be-en! Ben! Boy come heah!"

His Aunt Camille winced and mouthed "Sorry" at him. He didn't know
why she didn't just say it out loud. His granny was upstairs and between
that and her being hard of hearing, they wudn't no chance of her knowin'
anything they said at their breakfast table. But his aunt would always care
about those kinds of things, he knew. How she ever got suckered into tying
up with his Uncle Vince, Ben would never know.

The swing door to the kitchen cracked open enough for Rennie's head
to peep through. She was busily wiping her hands on a dish towel.

"Miz Camille, you need me to see 'bout Miz Eulee?"

Ben let his fork rest on his plate where once his pancakes had been.
He rose from the table while slurping down the last of his milk.

"It's okay, Rennie. I'm goin'. She'd a'called you if she'd wanted you
upstairs."

And he gave her a big grin. Rennie was right up there with his Aunt
Camille. She was one of three people in this world he knew really cared
about him, and when you'd had a shortage on that kind of thing, you no-

ticed. He started to wipe his milk mustache with his shirt sleeve, when he spied his aunt's amused grimace.

"Oops," he smiled again, and reached out for his fancy linen napkin, wiped and tossed it on the table. "S'cuze me," he offered, "I'll put my plate in the sink when I come back down."

Rennie reached over and picked up his plate and utensils, "I got it, Ben. See to Miz Eulee."

Ben rolled out his best smile, said thank you to Rennie, and trotted upstairs—which made him miss the smile that passed between Rennie and Camille.

"Dat boy. He gettin' better evuh day, Miz Camille," declared Rennie before turning back to the kitchen.

Granny was working the clapper on her little bell again when he made it to her bedroom. She had the bell in one hand and her coffee cup in the other. Neatly fitted around her was a lap table, with a bowl of oatmeal and scattered slices of half eaten toast. Beside her plate was a full glass of juice, not touched, rejected in favor of her beloved morning coffee.

The local paper lay in a mess beside her, partially covered by her quilt.

"There you are," she announced.

His Grandmother accompanied her statement with a wave of her coffee cup, which Ben noted thankfully was almost empty, and she made a little satisfied "uh" noise under her breath.

"G'mornin', Granny," Ben ventured.

"Humph, boy. Wait and see," the old lady returned. "Come heah. Come close. I wanna talk to you," she commanded.

And she began to look warily at the door he'd just shut behind him. Ben stepped quickly to her side. He knew his Granny. This morning was not a morning for patience by the looks of her.

"Ben. I need a favor," she almost hissed.

Ben tried to hide his dawning smile. Mostly she called him boy, and he didn't mind because she always had love in her eyes. She was a tough old lady, but he knew she loved him; so, she could call him what she would. But when she called him "Ben", he knew good things were in store.

The old lady leaned over and opened the top drawer of her night stand. She withdrew a notepad with writing on it, tore off the top page, folded it, and handed it to Ben.

"Heah. Give this to Mr. Barnes or Abby."

She watched as the boy folded the paper once more and stuffed it in his blue jean pocket. Ben heard another soft "uh" under her breath.

"Now, get my pocketbook from underneath the dresser," she clipped.

Ben had sprung to get it at the first syllable of "pocketbook". He knew right where it was. Once retrieved and handed over, he leaned against the bed and watched her handle the big black purse.

It had a silver clasp that clicked loudly when being shut and took a strong hand to unclasp again. Mrs. Eulee Barton Caudell unclasped it with another satisfied "uh". She dug around for a minute, and then reached out from its inner recesses with a piece of Dentine gum, which she handed over to Ben. Then she tugged out a little black coin purse and pulled out "folding money".

While she counted, he unwrapped his treasure and stuck it in his mouth and continued to watch. He made sure his lips were together when he chewed because Ben knew she'd get him if he smacked.

His Granny snapped the little coin purse closed and it was duly swallowed up by the handbag that Ben thought closely resembled and served as a small suitcase. She snapped the gleaming black pocketbook closed, too, then handed the bills to Ben.

"Heah, now, Ben. You know what I need, right?"

"Yes'm," he affirmed with an added degree of assurance by shaking his head vigorously up and down.

He had done it before and was looking forward to doing it again. He'd pedal his bike up to Barnes' Store and make her purchases. He was allowed to make purchases for himself with the change or pocket it for a

later purchase. Ostensibly, he'd bring back his granny a Red Rock Strawberry Soda, or some such, from Barnes' Store, for which she would claim
to have a hankering; but in the bag, he carted upstairs to her bedroom,
there would also be three cans of Levi Garrett Snuff.

Most of the time his Granny got Rennie to bring a few little tins of snuff
along with her to work. She'd pay her a little extra "for her trouble" if she
could get Rennie to take it. But sometimes, she'd run out inconveniently.

In the past, she got his Aunt Camille to bring the snuff, but his Uncle
Vince had caught her at it and "put his foot down". Under no circumstances was she to bring his mother snuff. No woman kin to him—even if only
by marriage—was going to be caught publicly buying or using that vile excuse for tobacco. An infuriated Vince had snatched the bag from Camille,
pulled out the cans, slung the bag down as he turned to march out of the
house.

Ben had watched his aunt tremble at his uncle's outburst, and he had
wondered about it long after the altercation.

"Well, boy," Granny's voice brought him back to the task at hand, "get
a move on!"

He heard her chuckle lightly as he "scatted" out the door. Ben took the
stairs two at a time, and barely stopped to whisper to Camille that Granny
had sent him to Barnes'. He knew Vince wasn't about, but you couldn't be
too careful, he thought.

It was still bitterly cold from the big freeze three mornings ago, but
things had warmed up a mite. He didn't much care. He had on a thick
woolen jacket and new boots from Christmas. He shoved his cowboy hat
down on his head and tightened the strings under his chin. Barnes' was
a little less than a mile down the road. He grinned and headed his brand-
new bike down Sweet Gum Road, glad there wasn't much wind.

He liked to keep his hat shoved down against the chill. His uncle
always had Ben's hair clipped short, no matter the season, so, the hat
helped to keep the cold out—besides, it was *cool*. His aunt had bought it
for his Christmas. It was black just like Paladin's, complete with the silver
conchos on the band.

If it had just been his Aunt Camille and Granny he lived with, the last
three years would've been happier than he'd ever known life to be. But

when you threw in Uncle Vince, it was edged by uncertainty and darkness. Still, Vince wasn't as bad as Ed Norris, yet.

Ben's mama had been a Caudell. In fact, when she'd died she had still been a Caudell, and he was, too. Ben hadn't minded that so much when he thought of Granny and his mama and Aunt Camille, but he sure didn't like sharing his surname with his uncle.

He didn't exactly know how Mama's life had gotten so tangled, but he knew he had something to do with it. She could play the piano and sing like nobody's business, but the places she had to sing weren't anywhere he'd brag about. And he'd never even seen his Granny until his mama's funeral.

She came, and Aunt Camille, too, but not his uncle. From listening to his granny and Aunt Camille, he surmised that a lawyer had called his Granny about his mama's death. Until then, she hadn't had any idea where his Mama was. He didn't think she'd had any idea that there even was a Ben either.

He often wondered how they'd managed to come to the funeral, but he figured his little granny had had something to do with it. She could be formidable when she put her foot down.

They had just showed up in Tallahassee at the funeral. Ben had watched them take care of the bills at the funeral home, the hospital, and their apartment.

The apartment. That was another thing that had puzzled him. He and his mother had lived with an older couple—the Jensens. His mother had in some way been indebted to them. She never went out without one or the other of them. And right after they'd gotten word of his mother's death, J.C. and Della Jensen just packed up and left—within the hour.

He'd only been seven when she died, and that couple had always been around. They'd never mistreated him, but he'd never felt like they cared about him either—there was no connection akin to grandparents or anything like that. It had never seemed odd to him before, because they had always been there from the time of his birth until the night his mother had died.

After the funeral and a few days in foster care, Social Services let him stay with his grandmother and aunt at their motel. Aunt Camille sorted through his Mama's stuff with him and picked out the keepsakes he wanted; then had a neighbor haul whatever was good to a local church.

They talked to him and his foster parents, and the social worker in charge of his case. They hadn't been able to talk to the lawyer because he'd been killed in a hit and run a few days before the funeral.

After a day or two, they'd taken a seven-year-old bewildered boy home to Georgia.

Back then, his granny could walk with the aid of a cane. And they'd hugged him and made him comfortable in the big shiny '59 Cadillac Eldorado. It was the one Vince drove around.

Aunt Camille had inherited his '54 Bel Air when he'd bought the brand-new-off-the-showroom-floor convertible. Vince had traded in his Aunt Cammie's 1948 Chrysler Town and Country Convertible for the Cadillac. It was the last car her Dad had bought her.

The Cadillac had big shiny fins and a convertible top. Ben figured Grandma's foot stomping must've registered on the Richter Scale to make Vince let them use the Cadillac. It hadn't taken Ben long to understand that Granny had a whole lot of money—inherited money from her husband, Vince Caudell, Sr., and inherited money from her folks, James and Mary Nell Barton of Savannah. It mostly sat in the bank, but ever since Vince Caudell, Jr. had acquired power of attorney when Granny had had her first debilitating stroke, *he* spent it. But today, Vince was at a two-day conference in Atlanta, and apparently Granny felt it was a perfect time for *her* to do a little spending too. Ben smiled at the thought.

He personally thought that snuff was a nasty habit, too. Granny kept a little cup hidden in the drawer of her night stand to spit in and he'd seen her do it. Not to mention, poor Rennie came in daily and emptied it for her—only to return it spotless and shining. He'd lived with his granny for two months before he'd worked up the nerve to ask Rennie on the sly why Granny had black spit.

He thought Rennie would fall down she laughed so hard. "Chile— chile—," she couldn't talk for wiping her eyes and sucking huge amounts of air between laughing fits, "she don't have no black spit. Aw, haw haw haw." And she was off again. I finally got it out of her about the snuff and then after some more guffawing, what snuff was and how you used it.

'Well, yuck.' I'd thought, ignoring my own wish to try a little chaw of tobacco like my heroes, Roger Maris or Mickey Mantle; and I still thought dipping snuff was nasty. Nevertheless, I'd have faced jungle cats without Tarzan's help to make sure my granny got what she wanted.

I'd reached Barnes' by this time and walked my bike up to the front porch leaning it against one of the built in wooden benches. It was too cold for the old men to "set and talk a spell" so I felt comfortable doing it. Opening one of the double doors, I walked in proudly, remembering to take my hat in my hands while indoors because Granny and Camille were kind of strict about that rule.

Abby was sorting through the mail, and Mr. Barnes was helping a customer. I sidled over to Miz Abby. Every kid in Bennington knew Miz Abby. She had a smile as warm as sunshine, and always treated you with the respect she would have given an adult customer. And besides all that, every now and then, she'd gift you a piece of candy that she paid for.

"Miz Abby."

I caught her attention and handed over the note. She unfolded the sheet and read it quickly accompanying her perusal with one of those sunshine smiles.

"Okay, Ben. I'll pack a double bag for you. Seems like today's supplies might be heavy."

She got out two of the largest size brown paper bags Barnes' carried and lined one with the other, shaking them out with a good deal of noise. I smiled waiting to see what extra things my granny had bought.

"Let's see, now."

And Miz Abby began to gather up things I never dreamed Granny would need. She named each one as she retrieved it.

"A sack of crystal marbles, a sack of jaw breakers, two Red Rock Colas, a package of caps for someone's six shooter," and she paused to smile at me, then continued with "eight sugar cookies."

She wrapped these in a separate paper bag before placing them on top of the heavier things; then said, "Ben, I think I'm coming home with you."

I smiled up at her as I began to lean in on the glass counter, relaxed now. I threw my new Paladin hat over my head and let it hang on its string down my back, then spread my forearms out over the edge of the counter. I rested my chin on the knuckles of my hands. My grin just kept spreading out, too.

"Oh, yes," she continued, "a package of poppers, a box of sparklers— what color you think your Granny wants?" she asked me.

I pulled out another keyboard grin, "Reckon she'd like *BLUE*, Miz Abby, and thanks."

She returned my grin and went on down the list, "Doublemint Gum, a package of Dentine, the January 18, 1963 *Life Magazine*"—which she pulled out of the magazine rack from behind her and then slid it in the side of the bag. I noticed it had a picture of The Trojan Horse on the front cover and thought I might want to read that one.

She paused for a breath, then finished with a flourish the last three items on the list, "a *Savannah Morning News*, three lace cotton hand-kerchiefs, and this." Here, she quietly packed in five cans of Levi Garrett Snuff.

"What a load! Can you carry all that on your bike?"

"Yes," I assured her, "I got a new basket for Christmas! Granny bought it."

She smiled and winked at me, then added, "Wonder what your Granny's gonna' do with a pack of marbles and a bunch of caps and poppers?"

We both laughed then. Not counting my Granny, Camille, and Rennie, and a *stubbornly resistant friend* down the street, Miz Abby had to be my favorite person. She always had a smile for me. I fished Granny's money out my pocket and put it on the counter. Miz Abby brought over her receipt book and Granny's bag of goods to ring up. I figured I at least had a dollar and some rattlin' change comin' to me. I was some kind of happy with the loot in the bag and the treasure soon to be in my pocket.

When I got home I planned to take my poppers out near the road and sling them down one by one as hard as I could—but only if Vince wudn't at home. It was real satisfying, the way those little paper wads blew up. I pretended they were gunshots or bombs going off.

Miz Abby was still writing down items in her receipt book and adding up figures. While I waited, I remembered the last time I'd gotten to come to Barnes' for Granny. It had been just before Halloween and Vince had been watching me close ever since. Seemed like someone must've told him about me and Granny's deal, and I figured I knew who.

All of a sudden Uncle Vince started to call home when I was out of school at odd times during his work day, and after making sure that Camille was there, he'd ask where I was, often insisting that I come to the phone. Then he'd give me some odd chore he wanted done or ask about my schoolwork. On the face of it, this sounds like a nice concerned uncle, but I'm telling you, Vince was slick. And darkness followed him.

All of this strange behavior started just after the last time I'd gotten Granny's snuff. That last time, I'd had to wait behind Big John. His wife was still alive then—even so, Big John had had both children in tow, and no Raynelle in sight. But, then, you didn't never see the two of them together. Leastways, that's what my granny had said—and she'd still been able to get her own *stuff* when she'd said it, or what rhymed with that word, back then and she got as much as she wanted, too. *Back then.*

Annie, the oldest of the children, had turned while we waited and showed me the missing tooth that had come out only that morning. She was three years younger than me, and was looking forward to the tooth fairy's visit. I grinned and wished her a rich tooth fairy.

Oh. I meant to say—Big John and I hadn't always been on good terms. Once when I'd first come, he'd caught me pestering 'Lizbeth Linden and her ol' cat. I still felt a little sheepish about that. I knew I hadn't ought to have done that, but she, 'Lizbeth, could be so smug sometimes. I wouldn't'na really hurt her ol' Pickle.

Anyway, Big John had stopped me in my tracks by grabbing the seat a' my new bicycle. But we had made our peace a few months after he'd straightened me out.

When I'd first come to Bennington, I missed my Ma. My life hadn't been too much in some ways before I come here, but at least I'd known where I stood and that my Ma loved me. So, yeah, I missed my Mama something fierce.

Somehow, I didn't much want to admit to that, so whenever stuff twisted up inside me too much, I'd hit the road with my bike. Sometimes I'd ask my Aunt Camille and sometimes I didn't. I never could figure why she hadn't let my uncle know what I was doing. She'd talked to me about it, but that was before I knew her very well or Uncle Vince either. Mostly, I was just angry as I could be and sick of everything. But I knew she hadn't told her husband or he'd a'skinned me alive.

Anyway, as I was sayin', Big John and me come to an understanding. One afternoon while I was on jest such a ride, I come across a broken coke bottle before I could stop. It slashed right into my front tire, because of the way the bottle was wedged into the dirt road. Big John come along on his way home from work, and pulled over when he come to me. I looked up at that very big man and felt my heart sink. The last time he'd really talked to me hadn't been good.

"Hey, Ben," he spoke like he respected me and we wuz friends or somethin'.

I looked up at him feeling just a little less uneasy and rose from my kneeling position beside my bike.

"Looks like you might need a new tire."

Still I looked up at him, searching for somethin' to say.

"I'm s'posed to take the children to Western Auto to pick up a wagon. I could take you along if you want—you know, to get a new tire. We could stop by and talk to your aunt. See if you could go?"

It was more of a question put to me than a statement. I hesitated and gathered my courage. This guy seemed pretty nice today. Not a'tall like the big man who'd promised me "what for" if I messed with persnickety ol' 'Lizabeth. I thought awhile on my sometimes friend. I was a little miffed with Elizabeth just now, so my thoughts on her weren't too pleasant momentarily, because I figured she'd been ashamed to play Mary with me as Joseph. She lit out of there before the preacher had hardly gotten out the "Amen" and she hadn't ever said why; so, I figured I *knew* why.

But back to my discussion with Big John.

I had finally replied, "Well, we could try. I shore would like that," I told him, then added forthrightly, "Not sure if my aunt would let me go though, *or* pay fer it."

Big John reached for the bill of his old red baseball cap and held it above his head while he scratched his scalp with his unencumbered ring and little finger.

"Well," he speculated, "we'll just ride by and see. Hop in the truck, boy and I'll throw the bike in the back."

Didn't nobody much have seatbelts back then. Most people didn't know they was such a thing 'cept in racing cars and such. I knew we'd find a way to pile in all three skinny kids and one big man.

I leaned into his cloth seats and smiled. The wind felt good blowing in with both windows down. It had been a very hot summer's day. He swung by and picked up Annie and Bo.

Miz Raynelle didn't seem to be at home. I thought that was a little bit odd 'cause Bo was mighty young to just have Annie takin' care of him; but nobody said nuthin' about it, so I didn't neither. They didn't seem surprised to see me, but the two of them gave me a big "howdy".

Big John let Annie and me ride in the back with my bike, but kept little Bo up front with him. I guess the pleasure of ridin' 'side his daddy kept him from complainin' 'bout not gitten to ride with me and Annie in the back much. Me, I'd never ridden in the back of a truck before and I wuz some excited to do it. He took all the back roads and went kind'a slow I thought. But it was the best fun I'd had in a long time.

Big John drove the four of us over to my Granny's house, where Camille and Vince lived, too. He told the kids to wait in the truck, and Annie got out and sat in the cab with Bo while he and I went to the door together. The upshot of all this was that my Aunt Camille said yes, and then had to insist John take the money to pay for the new tire and tube. Big John and the kids picked out a shiny, red Radio Flyer Wagon, and then he'd paid on some layaway he had in the store.

Big John had given my aunt's money to me in the truck before we came in along with getting me to read off and remember the "numbers" on my bicycle tires. He told me to tell the clerk what I needed, then, watched as I fished the money out of my pocket. So, he let me purchase the tire and tube with my aunt's money myself. Made me feel kind'a grown and important.

On the way home, he stopped and got us all a popsicle from the freezer section of the small garage and gas station located on what was then Highway 82, just outside of Bennington. His kids sat on the tailgate, while I stood beside him licking my popsicle as he pulled my bike from the bed of his truck. Big John turned the bicycle upside down, loosened the bolts with an adjustable wrench and whipped the wheel off the front of my bike. He removed the tire from the rim and then ran his finger along the inside of the metal to make sure there were no rough spots to puncture my new tire. He worked the tube and tire around my bike rim; and as I'd finished my popsicle by then, Big John let me fill the new tire with air from the compressor by the gas pumps.

It was pretty easy to do after he showed me how. After we got the air pressure just right he gave me the wrench and held the bike frame while I reattached the tire. I felt we wuz pretty much buddies after that.

Oh, yeah. I was sayin' about the last time I'd gotten snuff for my granny. Big John was waitin' on his mail from Miz Abby, who was turned around gettin' it. He had this funny look in his eye. It kind'a reminded me of when my Mama and I used to go to ride in the Jensen's old Chevy of an evenin'. Course, we always had Miz Jensen with us when we rode. She drove while we sat in the back. We never went anywhere without that woman. If she had the time for us to go to ride, we'd go through the section of town with the old houses, and along about dusk—just when people started cuttin' on indoor lights and all.

We'd ride real slow and sometimes, we'd see a family together on the porch, or a well-lit dining room with a family round the table; and my Ma'd get that same look that Big John had while he watched Miz Abby get his mail. Big John continued to watch her close-like until Miz Abigail Faith Weston turned around and handed him his mail with that smile I spoke about. But as she handed the mail over, her hand kind of trembled.

I know'd she was too young to have the palsy like old Mrs. Fulton back in Tallahassee; but since I was worrying about her a little, because you sure can't afford to lose people like Miz Abby, I noticed her face looked kind'a flushed, and her eyes looked too bright. I began to wonder if she'd caught that flu that was going around.

Big John, seeming not to be as observant as me, had said thank you and turned to go; but not before she told him to get those kids their pick of candy. He turned back then and offered, "Aw, I almost forgot," in a husky voice, and here he laughed softly, "but I know they'd remind me. I wanted to get them a sack of jaw breakers—no hot ones, though. They don't like those."

She gave me that sweet smile then, and said, "Hang on, Ben. I'll be right back."

I didn't mind a bit, 'cause I enjoyed watching people—especially people like Big John and Miz Abby. So, I watched as she piled that bag up high with jawbreakers—all colors, because Bo was yelling for blue. Annie had just smiled and said that she did like blue, but she was kind'a partial to the pink ones, too.

"'Cides, Bo," she reminded him, "they turn other colors after you suck on 'em awhile." Then she looked at Miz Abby and assured her, "Any color's fine. Thank you, Ma'am."

Then Miz Abby had given them a cookie for each hand. You could'a filled out two piano keyboards with the white showing from those wide smiles. She wouldn't take John's money. Said the store offered "free treats to all its neighboring kids at least once a year—a thank you to customers," she'd added.

Big John's eyes had kind'a narrowed then as he looked at her, but he had smiled and urged the kids to add their thanks to his and began to herd them out the door. About that time, Harve Whitcomb popped open one of the double doors and sidled into Barnes. As soon as he saw Big John, Harve looked like he'd lost every last bit of color in his face. He backed out'a that store so fast I thought he was gonna land on his fanny on the threshold.

I couldn't see Big John's face so I don't know what had happened between the two, but I could see around him out the door and Harve Whitcomb's ol' red truck was spitting up dirt like a mud dobber beside a spring puddle as he lit out'a that parking lot. I turned back around as Big John and the children left, and caught Miz Abby adding some money to Barnes' big cash register.

He still had one of those big old fancy metal registers from way back. Shoot. They still had an ol' time gas pump on the front porch along with the benches. None of those fancy, squared-off, digitized, new-fangled models for him! I knew she'd been paying for the kid's treats. I'd seen her do it before with first one family and then another.

The Abrams family had hardly gotten out the door, when Dennis Hilton walked into Barnes' just as Miz Abby was packing the Red Rock Strawberry Sodas in the bag. She followed that with three cans of Levi Garrett Snuff as quickly and unobtrusively as she could. I still wasn't sure Mr. Hilton hadn't seen or at least suspected.

Dennis HIlton's wife, Clara, was my Uncle Vince's legal secretary She was my Aunt Cammie's distant cousin, too, but I thought sure there must've been a mistake there somewhere. and besides all that, she prided herself in knowing everybody's business and broadcasting her findings unless it pertained to Uncle Vince's proceedings.

I swallowed the word on my lips that Miz Abby didn't need to hear, and according to Granny and Camille, I didn't need to say ever again.

"I'll see you, Miz Abby. Thanks a heap. Oh, and Aunt Camille and Granny say hello."

She seemed to understand as I avoided Dennis Hilton and offered a distraction with her "Hi, Mr. Hilton. You and Miz Clara got a bit of mail today." I slid out the door with the goods on the opposite side of me that was closest to him. He was using his superior height, which wasn't much, to arch his neck and look in that bag anyway I noticed. *The rat.* Then he looked toward Miz Abby as he greeted her.

I shut the door with a solid thump, situated the package in my basket, and walked it as quickly down the steps as I could without jarring the Red Rocks none. I had never been so glad to be on the road to Granny's.

But that had been back in the fall when Big John's wife was still kicking up a fuss. This time nobody disturbed our transactions, and I'd gotten away smoothly with my very large bag of treasure and five tins of Levi Garrett Snuff. I laughed. Me and Granny would both be happy tonight. I wudn't always right, it seems.

This had all taken place on Friday afternoon, late, and it was fast closin' in on evening. Uncle Vince wasn't due back from Atlanta until late Saturday night. But, Vince came home way early from his trip. He stalked in the house like a dark shadow.

From my viewpoint at the top of the stairs, I saw Camille's head jerk upwards through the open dining room door and figured she had heard his footsteps. She was making a pair of fancy church pants for me for next Sunday, I think. She and Granny kept saying my legs wuz going to grow out my bed and through the window any night now. And then they'd go on about how they wasn't a slim that was slim enough.

Camille stilled at her sewing machine, but when she spotted Vince making for her, I could see her hands started to patting here and there at the pattern pieces and material. They never seemed to still or accomplish anything either after she'd spotted my uncle. As Vince reached the table and towered over her, she brought them together and looked like she was squeezing the blood out of 'em. I had eased down a little closer, and could see they looked pure white around the knuckles. Vince looked at her disgustedly; scowled further at the pile of sewing; and swiped the pattern cuttings and fabric off the table with his left hand.

His right hand remained fisted precariously at his side while he yelled, "You know I don't like you making the place look like a dang fabric shop! Get this stuff upstairs! What if someone came by?"

He turned sharply and took in the fact that I had been coming downstairs and had frozen there with my mouth open.

"Why are you looking at me like that, *boy*?"

He didn't say that word anything like my granny, and it kind'a run a chill down my back. I jerked up and headed back upstairs. He turned and headed for his study. When I heard the door slam, I ran back down the stairs and helped Aunt Camille gather up the mess Uncle Vince had made as quick as I could.

She was trembling again, and I could hear the sounds of glass clinking from within his study. I recognized that sound. I looked worriedly up at Camille. She'd managed to box the sewing machine. I whispered that I'd carry it upstairs for her. She seemed befuddled and let me take it easily from her hands. I fairly ran upstairs with that cumbersome sewing machine and shoved it in the hall closet.

I could see her standing with all the sewing paraphernalia held tightly to her chest, her eyes glued on Vince's study.

"Come on!" I hissed.

She seemed to come to, then, and scurried up the stairs after me. I took her hand at the top of the stairs and pulled her into Granny's room. Although, I'd never seen my Uncle Vince this mad, I figured my granny's bedroom would be safe. I'd heard him use light sarcasm on Granny, but he hadn't ever raised his voice in her vicinity—at least, not in the three years I'd been living there.

As I'd hurried Camille into the room, I could tell by Granny's face that she had heard some of the commotion.

"Pull those two chairs up to the side of my bed and drag that small table over here; then sit," and she pointed her finger at the chairs and then the area she wanted them.

I dragged them both over after pulling the table up first. "Uh," I heard the familiar satisfied ticking-off-the-list grunt she liked to utter under her breath.

Then she turned to Camille and spat out, "Get a move on, girl. Put that sewing stuff in my bureau drawer."

Camille seemed to do a little better with Granny at the helm. She tottered over and stuffed the materials in like Granny had said. Then we both sat down for a seeming visit. "Uh," I heard again. Granny lifted her covers and pulled out the cans of snuff I'd delivered earlier to her. She placed two of the tins in the top drawer of her night stand.

"Boy," even *her* voice shook a little. "Take these three cans over to that wardrobe. Open the right door."

She waited.

"Uh. That's good," she encouraged. "Pull the top drawer out. All the way, Ben!"

She was getting a little out of breath now.

"Hurry."

I pulled the drawer out and set it on the floor. The "Uh" came so softly from Granny, I wondered if Camille had heard the peculiar way my Grandmother Caudell had of showing satisfaction, but Camille just sat there watching everything like you would a television show.

"Look in where the drawer was," Granny commanded. "There's a notch at the back to pull the sliding board to the side. Slide it to the left."

She waited in between each instruction to see that I'd done it and forgot for once to utter any more "uh's". Sure enough, that little board slid to the left and revealed a small space just large enough for small things like cash or in this case, snuff cans. I couldn't help but smile to myself in spite of my nerves, and I shoved the three cans in the little hiding place and slid back the door before she told me what to do.

Picking up the drawer, I asked if she didn't want the other two cans in there.

She responded with an exasperated "NO. Put the drawer back in now and hurry."

I pondered that some, but let it lie. I knew better than to tangle with my granny.

"Now, listen, boy. If Rennie is still here, tell her to bring us some tea. Don't let your path cross Vincent's. Understand me?"

"Yes'm," I answered and turned to do her bidding.

"And be quiet and careful," she added.

I was out the door, but still heard her quiet adjuring. Sure didn't sound like my granny right then. The door to Vince's study was still closed. I could hear murmuring from within and thought I'd heard him say he'd like to speak to Judge Connors; then I heard some more of those clinking sounds like glass on glass. I figured he was squeezing the receiver between his ear and shoulder, and pouring himself "another one" while he waited for Judge Connors to come to the phone.

Judge Connors was Vince's uncle on his mother's side. She had died in the Spanish Flu epidemic of 1918. My Grandpa Caudell had met my Granny five years later and married her after almost a year of courtin'. But my Mama had told me repeatedly, if I ever ran into her half-brother, my Uncle Vince, or his Uncle Julian, not to trust either one.

I slipped on past and into the kitchen, where, thank God, Rennie was still stacking dishes from supper. I knew she must've heard everything downstairs, because I thought I'd heard her praying under her breath when I'd come in. That wudn't nuthin' new for Rennie, but her tone of voice was stressed and earnest-like. I thought that prayin' business might be a good idea and I added my own to Rennie's. Then, I delivered Granny's message, and scuttled back upstairs.

I could hear Vince kind of arguing with someone—almost pleading when I walked past his study again. Wudn't nobody in this ol' house soundin' like themselves today. I made tracks. In a minute, Rennie brung in the tea platter, with Camille's favorite little china cups and saucers, and set it down on the small table between our two chairs and Granny's bed. There was a plate full of golden tea cakes and some small triangles of ham sandwiches Rennie had thrown together. Camille was in no state to pour, so Rennie started to pour.

"No, Rennie," my granny stated quietly. "You go downstairs to the kitchen—Ben'll pour this time. Would you stay behind a little longer tonight if you can?" Granny paused and caught her breath, "And, Rennie, try not to cross paths with Vince," my Granny repeated the same thing she'd told me and then added, "Camille will take you home if she can get away. If not, call Dr. Prescott's sister, Hannah. Tell her I need a favor. She's not a talker and she's known the family a long time. She'll take you home or find a way for you. It'll be too late to walk home," and Granny paused, then added, "Rennie. I want you to stay in the kitchen out of sight. Don't cross Vince. You hear?"

Rennie looked at Miz Eulee Barton Caudell for a moment, and I could see respect and concern mingled there. Then she nodded, turned and walked resolutely down to the kitchen.

I listened for household noises as I poured the tea and offered Granny and Camille sugar and cream. I figured Rennie had made it to the kitchen, when the slamming of what I was sure was the study door, made me almost slosh the tea I poured for myself out. The three of us coconspirators or victims, whichever you choose to think, eyed each other nervously. I tried not to gulp my tea as we waited.

Granny sucked in a breath and started telling us about the time her grandmother had attended a ball as a girl in Savannah and Beulah Chisholm had gotten her hoop skirt slung over her head when she'd missed a step in the waltz and fell. Camille must've heard the story before, but it was new to me, and I almost forgot the tension in the household.

Granny was explaining how Beulah was the biggest snob and took pleasure in embarrassing anybody with less money than her Father— when the door was flung open so hard that it banged into the wall. A livid Vince strode into the room muttering under his breath.

"You're sittin' heah, havin' tea! I've had the worst week of my life, and all you can do is sit around and talk about someone else's heyday and sip tea!"

He sounded incredulous. He reeked of an odor I had hoped never to smell again. It stirred up my memory of horror and death. I didn't have long to suffer the old nightmare, because as I watched, Vince redirected my focus by slamming the whole tea set off the side table.

He turned to Granny and slurred out, "Old woman. I'm going to be taking money out of your account—a lot of it. And you aren't going to say *nuthin'*."

As the next few weeks eked by I would come to realize that, on occasion, when Vince was really mad, he lapsed into improper grammar. I had never heard him do it before, and it made no impression on me amidst everything else. But I'd never heard him speak to my granny like that, and that *did* register. I began to grit my teeth and fist my hands.

He jerked open the night stand drawer and slung the spitting cup and its contents over Granny's bed and against the wall. Then he grabbed the two remaining snuff cans and stomped them on the floor grinding them into Granny's rug. The old lady's face was flushed and she trembled with anger. But the last thing he did reared me up out of my seat.

He turned and slapped Camille full on and screamed at her to quit staring at him like a dang idiot. Only he didn't say "dang". As he grabbed her up, I plowed into him as hard as I could. He must've been pretty drunk because I knocked him off his feet and that sent Camille sprawling, too.

Grandma was hollering, and by this time, Rennie had made it up the stairs, and was saying in tones I'd never heard come out of her mouth, "Heah now. Heah now, Mr. Vincent. I'm on call Axell Arnett if you don't stop!"

I had crawled over to Vincent and was in the middle of bloodying his nose. Rennie managed to grab my collar and I come to my senses enough to obey her.

She was saying, "Hey, now, Ben. He ain't gon' feel that none. He's out cole."

The room kind'a hushed then, 'cept for all of us heavin' air in and out. Sure 'nough. Vince Caudell was stretched out across the very snuff cans he'd stomped and I do mean OUT. Rennie said he'd hit his head against the bed post she thought. She leaned over and felt his pulse.

"He still with us," she reported.

Camille and I were both helping each other up. Rennie had been feeling the back of Vince's head.

"Whew. He gon' have quite a bump an' headache when he come to." She turned to look at the two of us and took her first real look at Camille.

"Law. Chile! You okay?"

I looked then, too, and could see the purpling imprint of Vince's hand on her face and a trickle of blood underneath her swollen bottom lip. Granny's face was an unhealthy looking dark red. I could see she was some stirred up and hoped it didn't hurt her none. Turning to the mirror, Camille got a look at the bruise.

"It's fine," she reassured us dabbing at the blood with a napkin.

She seemed to have regained her senses just as her husband had lost his.

"We should call Dr. Prescott for Vince, right Mama Lee?"

This was directed at Granny, who nodded—disgustedly eyeing the district attorney of Freeman County sprawled out on the floor beside her bed. Then I saw her face sort of crumple and a big tear squeezed out her eye.

"I promised Richard I'd try to help that boy. Lord, how I've failed—Go call Doc Prescott, Rennie. Please."

I don't know how Rennie got that mess off Granny's wall and out'a her rug that night. But she did. And I don't know whether she found time to call Earl, or if he was just worried about her being late and come to check on her. I only know when he showed up I was some relieved.

But before all of that, she'd helped me an' Camille drag ol' Vince to the bedroom he and Camille once shared down the hall. Not long after we got him in his pajamas, Doc Prescott showed up along with his sister, Hannah.

Vince still hadn't "come to", and Doc Prescott quickly shooed us all out the room only allowing Hannah to stay and assist him. Wasn't too long after that, he sent her to Granny and then Camille to make sure they were okay.

I had followed Miz Hannah into Granny's room, and seeing the worry on my face, she told me Camille was okay—

"Jest have to outlast that bruise, is all, and it hasn't affected her eye atall. Lip's okay, too, Ben," and she checked Granny's blood pressure amidst her mumbling assurances to me; and found it "slightly higher, but that's to be expected," she'd said. Then she told me to help Rennie bring up some tea.

So, down I went, and we started the tea party thing all over again only this time with a different tea pot. Because Uncle Vince had smashed the other one.

Granny shouted out behind me to ask Earl and Rennie to stay the night in one of the guest rooms. I was purely thankful to hear Granny's request. I couldn't yet smile after all that had gone on that night, but I felt one gradually comin' on.

Chapter 4

"All my life I wanted time to sit and contemplate what had passed and what was coming up. Now that there's plenty of that, I'm not so enamored with it."
—Constance Eulee Barton Caudell

It was a raw February day—John could feel it even though he couldn't see it from his position in the truck. He had been in some fixes, but never as bad as this one—leg-shackled to a prison truck. The weight of the chains about his arms and legs lay as heavy as his future on his heart. He had just turned twenty-five in February, and he was looking at just that many years of his future invested in the Sayreville State Prison. Twenty-five years—Twenty-five different years of days to spend behind prison walls, while his children were out there in what he knew to be a twisted world without him to protect them. And besides all that, somewhere out there was the person who had ended Raynelle's frenetic life span; and he wasn't sure who or why.

His thoughts only darkened with each mile they put behind them. Every now and again he had to grab at the edge of the truck as they swung sharply around a curve. The two guards sitting a little away from him talking just loud enough for them to hear each other, would hush long enough to hold on to the sides of the truck, too, and watch him carefully. As the curve rounded out and they "came back to center", the men seemed to relax their vigil and turn back to their conversation.

He closed his eyes, remembering how little Bo thought he could hide that way. Oh, how he wished Bo was right. And where were his sweet children now? His lawyer had said their Great Aunt Lydia Fleming had come from Phenix City, Alabama to take the two of them to her house.

He'd only met her twice. Once when she'd come out to keep little Annie while they went on their honeymoon and then again when they'd driven back from Louisiana to Georgia after he'd gotten out of the service. They had stopped by her house just before crossing into what he considered his home state, and been invited to have dinner with her and "stay the night".

He'd been impressed. She was every bit a southern lady, with a gentle heart and a great love for the Lord; and she reminded him much more of little Annie than Raynelle. He knew she lived in a big old two-story house on the outskirts of town, and that she was in the church any time the doors were open—even at her age.

He had been so worried that Annie's real daddy would show up and demand to take her home with him. But no one had been able to find him. He'd never been so thankful. He wanted Annie and Bo to at least be together; and he didn't know a thing about Annie's daddy except what Raynelle had told him. He was pretty sure that he wouldn't be able to untangle the truth from the lies in that tale.

She'd admitted after the first week of their marriage that most of what she'd originally told him was a farce. When he'd first met her, she presented herself as a helpless, young, unwed mother who'd been deserted by her boyfriend. Later, when she'd received mail addressed to Mrs. Jeffrey L. Perkins, she'd adjusted her story, and insisted he was still an abusive, cheating so-and-so, whom she'd had to divorce a few years before, and she didn't want to talk about him ever again.

It had always puzzled him that Jeff Perkins had never sent any amount of money to Raynelle, and that she had never complained about that fact. Money was a defining theme in his wife's life, and her insouciance over his lack of support just didn't fit.

He thought back to his time of military training in Missouri—how hard it had been. The drill sergeant had seemed to take special joy in trying to "bring him to his knees". He always figured it was his size. He'd tightened his gut literally and figuratively to make it through. Back then, it didn't mean a thing to take a fist to a recruit's abdominal muscles.

When he made it through basic, they stationed him in Texas for a few months; then, it was on to Louisiana where he'd met Raynelle the summer of 1958. He was lonely and tired of military bases. Having lost his Uncle Burt not long after he entered the service, there was no family to go home to, so he took his civilian clothes to the Laundromat in the little town just outside of the fort on a beautiful Saturday afternoon in June.

He had a few days of leave coming and he planned to dress in his civies and ride the back roads to see Louisiana. John picked up a paper next door at the drug store and had just settled down in front of the dryers to read, when *she* walked in wearing short shorts and a thin cotton blouse. She had blonde hair all teased up at the back and flipped out at the bottom. She was carrying a basket of dirty laundry and he could see the fingernails of the hands clutching the basket. They were long, perfectly shaped and painted bright red.

A little behind her ambled the prettiest little girl he'd ever seen. She was toddling along with no eye for anything but her surroundings.

"Come on, Annie," the young woman begged irritably without looking back.

But Annie, who looked to be around three years old, was clutching a teddy bear almost as big as she was and studying every inch of the Laundromat with her big violet blue eyes, as she slowly followed her mama. Her mama had reached the washing machines by this time and was busy dumping her loads into the big metal drums.

Annie slowly came to a halt when she caught me watching the two of them. "Hey," she mumbled softly in the dulcet tones of the south.

"I brung my teddy bear," and she held him out for me to see. "Ma Daddy gave him to me for ma birfday."

At this juncture, Raynelle had turned and fixed her little girl with an expression I was hard put to interpret—but it was focused and dead serious. After a bit, she told her to "stop bothering the man, honey" in clipped tones.

Then her eyes turned from Annie to me and seemed to widen and then focus narrowly on my person.

"Hey," she echoed her daughter softly. "My name's Raynelle. This here's Annie." She laughed then, "Never knows a stranger, that one."

If I'd had just a little more savvy, John thought, I'd have sensed that description encapsulated the mother, not the daughter.

She wasn't wearing the ring of the aforementioned Daddy. I smiled back. How could I help it? The little one's mama was as beautiful as she was. What was not to smile at? We had finished the laundry day together. Piling their clothes basket and mine into the trunk of my 1953 Olds 98 convertible, we drove down to a nearby park Raynelle had mentioned. The top was down. It was a warm day all wrapped up in blue skies. The three of us had fun.

Later, we ended up at a local burger drive in. It had been a perfect day. I was thoroughly engaged by these two charming females.

Looking back, I knew there had been signs of warning about Raynelle; but I was lonely, far from home, and I think maybe it was really Annie that actually reeled me into marrying her mother in August of 1958.

I'd never had a real family. My folks were both alcoholics. They'd never held a steady job. Just worked long enough to rent a house and buy the cheapest liquor they could find. Then, of course, they'd eventually lose the jobs and stay in a house as long as they could milk the landlord and the grocer.

Back then you could put things on account even at the grocery store. Of course, it hadn't taken long for them to destroy that venue of provision. Their names became synonymous with poison as far as local credit was concerned.

We kept on the move a lot as a family, but mostly keeping to small towns in Southern Georgia with an occasional foray into Southeastern Alabama and the panhandle of Florida. I think a time or two, we actually lived in an abandoned home out in the country unbeknownst to the owners. They'd buy a paper and read the obits and check out the locations.

I had been too little then, to understand it all. As soon as I got old enough to catch work as a stock boy, busboy, yard boy or "any-odd-job boy" in town, I kept some food on the table. They hadn't been able to abuse me too much, because I'd grown so fast. I towered over my Daddy and Mama. Made me feel like a cuckoo or something, but I'd seen a picture or two of my granddaddy, Herbert Lloyd Melton, my mother's father, and I looked just like him—both in stature and facial features. Only my coloring was different. Like my Dad, I had the dark hair and complexion of his grandfather who was a full-blooded Cherokee Indian; but I had the same color eyes as my Mother.

The last place I'd lived with my parents was Carverville. They moved there mostly to get help from my Uncle Burt who lived in nearby Bennington. We'd been living first one place then another in Freeman County for the better part of two years, when my father was hired as a farm hand by an elderly farmer out in the country. The farmer's name was Gerald Eddington, and he was a good man.

He was a good influence on my Dad, too. He talked a lot while they worked and seems to me he was the reason my dad was sober for the longest stretch of weeks I ever remembered. I don't think my father had had a lot of love or respect growing up; and Mr. Eddington filled some kind of void for him for a time.

While working there my dad noticed some of Mr. Eddington's vehicles needed mechanical work—a couple of them had just been parked, because the old man was tight on money. Now, my father could make anything run if you'd just hand him a wrench and pliers—didn't matter if he was sober or not. He could fix it. So, he'd offered to fix Mr. Eddington's farm equipment and even the old Ford sporting a "FOR SALE" sign on it.

Ended up, he fixed a tractor and a pickup truck for the man, did the harvesting, and got the old Ford running. So, the farmer had paid him extra by signing over the title of the old Ford. It had been sitting in the front yard with that "FOR SALE" sign on it for over six months, he'd said.

My dad was pretty proud that first afternoon. Mr. Eddington had bought him a full tank of gas, and he came driving up a little after five and asked if anybody wanted to ride uptown. That day was one of the good ones I remembered from my childhood. We had had fun *that day*. He took us to a drive-in movie and treated us to hotdogs and drinks. I'd been ten or eleven—I'm not sure.

A few months later, Mr. Eddington had a massive heart attack while weeding the small garden behind his house. His children weren't interested in the farm and so it sold and my Dad's income went with it. A year or so later, my father wrapped Mr. Eddington's old Ford around a tree on their way home from picking up a little more booze one Saturday evening. Looking back, I am amazed it hadn't happened sooner.

He'd picked up too much speed on a curve not a half-mile from the house where we were staying, and when the light rain that had set in helped him skid off the road, he'd hit a tree. My mother, riding beside him in the passenger seat, had been on the side that had full contact with an old live oak.

"She never knew what hit her," I'd heard the coroner tell the undertaker.

I always wondered if he meant she'd been too drunk or if it had happened so quickly. I missed my mother, though. On good days, she had been loving and fun. On bad days, I chose not to remember.

My dad had left town before he'd paid the funeral home or hospital.

He'd had a few bruises and scratches and a broken arm, but that didn't stop him. Nothing stopped Jonathon Walter Abrams, certainly not me.

My mother's brother had come after people realized I was by myself. I was twelve years old when my uncle took me home to live with him, and things were better after that. Herbert Eugene Melton had lived in Bennington, Georgia across the road from the Lindens for forever, and Adam Linden was my best friend.

Nothing could've made me happier than living with my Uncle Burt. I never think of him that it doesn't make me smile. Along with a whole host of other people who knew him, I loved that man. He was what Mr. Eddington called "the salt of the earth"; but he always made sure I knew that anything I admired or loved about him had come from His Lord Who had grace enough for anyone.

Uncle Burt, whose charm didn't lie in his outward appearance, was the closest thing I'd had to a real father and an honorable man. He had never married, so it was "just us two old bachelors" he'd often say.

He told me once, he'd just never found anyone he loved that would love him, too. Then he chuckled, and left me to wonder if someone had given him the "Dear John".

Uncle Burt was a decade, and more, older than my mother who'd been born late in my grandparents' marriage. My grandmother had died not long after my mother had been born. Uncle Burt had told me these things. I'd have had no idea about my mother or father's families if it hadn't been for Uncle Burt and some old pictures in a box Mama usually parked under her bed wherever we settled.

In the weeks that followed, I bought bubblegum trading cards with all my favorite baseball players. I taped them to the wall of my bedroom after asking Uncle Burt if it was okay. It was a big deal to me. I'd never stayed anywhere long enough to "put down roots". Took me awhile before I could bring myself to unpack my duffle bag and put my stuff in the drawers, though. I'd lost some things over the years with Mama and Daddy by unpacking my stuff too quickly.

Uncle Burt, never questioned my hesitancy to settle into his household. He simply waited me out. A few years later, I'd framed a picture of Adam and I that Abby Weston had taken and given me when I was in high school. I kept it on top of my chest of drawers as much for the fact she'd given it to me as Adam being my best friend. She'd gotten a Brownie camera for her birthday. Adam and I had been sophomores and Abby was only in the eighth grade. Abby had taken the pictures after we'd gotten off the bus.

Now, there was something to think about. Abby. When we were all in high school, she didn't get out much. I figured she was kept pretty busy studying and taking care of her daddy and the big house they lived in, alongside of Rennie, who'd only come twice a week by then. I knew the Weston girl was special, but just couldn't work up the nerve to do anything more than speak to her; but I made sure nobody messed with her back then either.

Abby and I had walked a chalk line trying to balance distant friend-ship and a male/female "awareness". At least, I'd hoped she'd been feeling the same as I had. We, neither one, had ever worked up the nerve to ac-tually get to know the other person. I guess that had been my fault. I just couldn't feel like I was good enough to eat lunch with her at school, or have a date, or go to church with her.

I kept remembering who my folks were and how people had talked about them. And I'd always known that Abby was different. I'd never met anyone like her. I could see her now jumping down from the bus and running down the dirt road that led to her house, Archie's bird dog, Blue, running beside her. That dog was always waiting for her at the bus, rain or shine and could've powered one of those Chinook helicopters they used at the Fort now with the wag-action in that tail of his.

Abigail Faith Weston was two years younger than me, so she'd been ten when I'd come to live with my uncle. She was petite with dark brown hair that sparkled red in the sunlight. Her eyes, though; and I didn't even remember the color of most people's eyes; they were a deep blue-green. I could close my own and see them even now. More arresting than the color had been the amount of expression she could show in those eyes without even a word spoken.

I'd overheard Miz Rennie talking to Mr. Archie at Barne's a few months after I'd come to live with Uncle Burt. Mr. Archie had driven the two of them to Barnes' to get their mail and buy a few groceries. They were watching Abby make her selections at the candy counter, and Miz Rennie turned to Mr. Weston and said, "She look just like Elizabeth, Mr. Archie, even down to her 'smiling eyes'." I'd never heard of anyone having smiling eyes, so I'd watched Abby to see what they meant. She had them, alright.

I saw the few friends she'd chosen were nothing to do with wealth or class. And then, I saw how she'd treated people that seemed to have no in-trinsic worth to other folks. Long after my parents had lost any respect in our little community and when Abby was still a child, she greeted each of them with kindness and regard. I'd noticed her feeding all kinds of strays behind Barnes' old store after she started working there. I heard from the local vet that she even took some of them to him for mange or injuries and later, they'd found homes for most of them. Some of them had even found a home with Abby.

It was odd that on this darkest of days, I found myself smiling. But Abby was that way.

The truck took an abrupt left, then and began to wind down what I assumed was a country road. Surely was bumpy. The two guards and I swung toward the front of the vehicle as our driver brought the big truck to a halt and thumped on the division between the cab and us.

"Prison gates, boys," he called to my two guards.

I could hear some talking outside the cab between our driver and what I decided were two more guards at the gate of the prison. In a minute the door at the back of the truck opened and one of the guards peered in at us.

"Everything okay?" he asked the other two.

"Yeah. We fine," the oldest guard replied.

He slammed the door shut then, banged on the side fender, and yelled to the driver to "Take him on in!"

Chaplain James Rogers and his wife, Carolyn, had been living five miles outside of the State Prison for a little over two years. James and Carolyn had been married not much longer than that time, and this year in April, they were expecting their firstborn.

At least they'd hoped it was the first of two or three more. They were still pondering their "druthers" on that one. But they'd laugh and say together, "Whatever, whomever God sends."

Tonight, Carolyn had had a long-distance call from Bennington, a little town a couple of hours drive to the south of them. Carolyn's friend, Abby Weston, lived there. Abby and she had met at a little junior college in the north Georgia Mountains back in the fall of 1958. They had been room-mates and quickly best friends.

Abby had only attended for the first year. In the middle of the spring quarter, a friend from home had written to tell her that Dr. Prescott had diagnosed Archie Weston with cancer. Abby knew that they'd found a tu-mor during her father's checkup, but Archie had told Abby it had been be-nign—holding back for fear she would not finish her freshman year of col-lege. And as soon as she'd read the letter revealing the truth, she'd packed her bags, informed her house mother, hugged Carolyn, tears streaming down both their faces, and headed her little VW for Bennington.

Archie had postponed treatment, in hopes he could take care of it in the summer, when Abby came home. But of course, all that changed as soon as Abby blew in the door, threw her bags on the floor, and ran out the back to find her Daddy walking in the twilight where he'd once pastured cows. He was checking the dewberry bushes growing along the fence line, all drooping with green fruit and delicate white flowers.

They had a long conversation then—way into the night; laced with Archie's coffee, Abby's hot tea, and both their tears.

Dr. Prescott was informed of Archie's change of heart. They booked him at a large hospital in Savannah. The tumor was removed. Lab work informed them that the original diagnosis had been correct. It was cancer-ous. A round of radiation treatment followed. Abby had prayed and driven him back and forth for his appointments in Savannah.

The two friends and former roommates had been writing to each other during the long months of treatment that had followed, as well. Carolyn had called her every few months to pray with and encourage her friend. But in late 1959, Archie was weak and aging. He succumbed to the on-slaught of cancer just after Thanksgiving of that year.

Abby had not been able to return to school, but she and Carolyn had kept close through letters and the odd phone call. Abby had managed to attend James and Carolyn's wedding in the spring of 1960 and acted as Carolyn's maid of honor. She had been thrilled and somewhat fearful upon hearing that James would become the chaplain at the State Prison just a few months after their wedding.

But, she had never been so thankful, in February of 1963, to have a friend who had access to the inmates within the stark blocked walls of the penitentiary.

Chapter 5

"Back when Mama and I lived with the Jensons in Tallahassee, I thought television was as excitin' as life gets. Turns out I ain't always right; sometimes I wish I wuz."
—Richard Benjamin Caudell, at age 10

I t was Saturday, mid-March, and Ben Caudell had watched "Sky King", and "Fury", and "Tarzan" and now there was nuthin' else he'd wanted to see on their big cabinet Zenith television. He had clicked the big chocolate-colored, plastic knob off, watched the picture disappear to center, then headed outside.

Ben had made plans to ride his bike that afternoon, but as was his habit lately, had already cleared this ride with his aunt because Camille and Granny had decided they'd each take a nap after lunch.

Young Ben had had lots more of an idea where John Glenn was on the 20th of the last month, and he'd been orbiting the earth in Friendship 7, than the whereabouts of his Uncle Vince. So, he slapped on his prized Paladin cowboy hat and black jacket and jumped on his bicycle.

He pedaled down to Elizabeth's house, which was less than a half a mile from his Granny Caudell's. Ben let his bike rest on the protruding root and trunk of a Live Oak at the Linden's house. It was a two-car house he knew, but only one was there now. Their blue Chevy was pulled up under the carport.

He was glad their dog wasn't in the yard. Everything seemed pretty quiet outside, but he could hear Del Shannon bemoaning his "Runaway" from within the house. He walked up to the front door, took a deep breath and knocked.

He could hear the clicking steps of high heels in the foyer. So, it would be Mrs. Linden then. One more deep breath, and he summoned up his manners. *Not quite Eddy Haskell now—just go for Wally.* The door opened.

"Ben," said brightly, but real, "come on in."

I noticed she had on her apron and smelled the "come hither" of choc-olate from somewhere within the house. I took off my hat, let it fall to rest by its cording on my back, and stepped over the threshold.

"Hi, Miz Linden," I offered while taking the time to close her front door, "I was just checking to see if Elizabeth was at home."

She turned and clicked her way into the back of the house motioning me to follow. Over her shoulder she said, "Let me just turn down the radio. Janie turned it up too loud before she left."

In a minute, she had wrestled the volume knob down to a level we could talk over, although I could now hear Johnny Preston singing about Running Bear and Little White Dove—the "ooga, ooga's" were making me smile. I think she must've known this because she kind of grinned, too, then said, "Elizabeth is upstairs. You can sit in the den, if you like, while I get her."

"Yes, ma'am," I said and dutifully sat on the couch.

It wasn't a minute before Elizabeth was making her way downstairs with her mother, who headed for the kitchen.

"I just made some chocolate oatmeal cookies. They're cooling on wax paper, but you can both come and get some in a few minutes," floated back to us from her retreating figure.

Elizabeth was wearing her penny loafers, blue jeans, and a white tee shirt. She smiled a little.

"Hey, Ben," and she looked at me questioningly.

I hadn't "run" into her since the Christmas Program.

"Hey," and I got up from my seat in the den. "Look. I didn't want to bother you or nuthin', but I wanted to look at your notebook."

She raised her eyebrows now and looked kind of lost. I saw she thought I meant her school notebook, and I didn't even have any classes with her.

"No, no. Not school—the one you wrote all the stuff in at the Abrams' house."

I could see she was catching on, now.

"Just a minute," and she turned and hurtled back upstairs—I figured she was headed for her room. She came back with not only the notebook, but extra paper and a pencil.

"Here," she said, "only you've got to copy it on this paper if you want to take it home. I'm still thinking on this stuff and I don't want it out of the house, okay?"

I nodded and took the paper and pencil, then carefully took the notebook like it had come from some kind of archaeological dig. She smiled. I think she liked the deference I'd shown her "evidence".

"Come on in the kitchen. You can sit at the table and copy down what you want," and she led the way into that wonderful chocolaty smell I had had faint whiffs of throughout my visit.

Mrs. Linden was putting away a pot when we entered the kitchen, and pointed out the cookies she had left on the table for us along with two glasses of milk.

"Hope you like chocolate," she said, "but I've got some sugar cookies in the cookie jar if you'd rather?"

"This is great," we both said together, then laughed about our answer.

So, I sat. And ate. And copied. Elizabeth's Mama wanted to know what we had there; so Elizabeth told her about it. She smiled and said to be careful in our nosing about; that she didn't think Big John had done it either.

I noticed as she was leaning over Elizabeth's chair inspecting our "document" that she'd ditched the high heels and was wearing slippers. We talked a bit, too, after Mrs. Linden went upstairs. We talked about the stuff we'd found and the names on the list, the address and the key.

Elizabeth said that the address had been for Annie and Bo's Great Aunt.

"Yeah," I agreed, "I heard they were living in Phenix City, Alabama."

"Yeah," and she looked a little sad about Annie and Bo. We were quiet for a minute except for the sound of the chewing of chocolate oatmeal cookies.

'Lizabeth continued, "But they still don't know about that key. Remember it? I wrote the words it had on it in that book, too. And I outlined the key. See?"

Thumbing through the notebook I found it and nodded my head. I read off the words, "Master Lock." I looked at the silhouette of the key, too, and thought I knew what kind of key it was. And then there were some numbers.

"I reckon it's a padlock key," and we nodded together.

"I didn't see anything at the house or hear about anything the sheriff took that would have needed a lock key," and she took another bite of cookie thoughtfully.

"Maybe she hid it real good," I said in between copying and taking another bite of my cookie, too.

Man. That stuff was good. I began to wonder if Rennie or Aunt Camille knew how to make these.

"It would have been too big to put behind the baseboard. Let's go look again," and she jumped up and ran outside the kitchen to the foot of the stairs.

"Mama!" I heard. "Ben and me are going to ride bikes for a little. Is that okay?"

Then, I thought I heard Miz Linden say, "Ben and I, Elizabeth. Ben and I," then a pause before she added, "be careful. Don't be gone long."

Something like that. I folded my copy of 'Lizbeth's "evidence" and stuffed it into my back pocket. I mulled over using that shortened form of her name aloud. I had heard one of her sisters call her that while they'd waited to get on the bus, but I'd, also, noticed she'd grimaced. So. I b'lieved I'd save that one for later. Much later.

Elizabeth came back into the room just as I was finishing up my milk. She'd seen me swallow those cookies whole, so she stepped over to the cookie jar then and got out two more, wrapped them in tin foil, and handed them to me.

"Put 'em in the basket of your bike," she advised. "otherwise they'll melt. I found that out the hard way," she paused to grin before she half commanded, "Come on."

"Thanks."

It was heartfelt. And I was so deeply grateful that I hadn't used the shortened form of her name or complained about when she'd become queen.

Didn't take us long to ride down the highway, then down the dirt road to the Abrams. It was a lot quicker than climbing all them fences. We didn't have the key to the indoors this time, so we just walked 'round the outside of the house looking up and down and under—nuthin' too much different than prob'ly what the Sheriff and his Deputy had done outside four months ago.

I asked her if it would be okay to crawl under the house and take a closer look. She said she didn't see why not. She reckoned Sheriff Arnett and Deputy Starnes hadn't gone that far. They prob'ly thought Raynelle would be too squeamish to crawl under the house.

But we both knew one someone who wouldn't mind hauling it under there for her. Bo was only two, so we eliminated him even though he was a great "crawler". Ended up, we both crawled in together. I'm not sure if I'd a'done it in summertime—snakes and all. But it was still winter and a little cold for things like that, so in we went and made a race of it.

We almost slammed into the underpart of the fireplace because we'd been spotting each other to see who was ahead more than looking where we were going. Anyway, it brought us to a halt, and we carefully crawled around it. Elizabeth went round one way and I went the other.

It was a pretty big fireplace as it serviced two rooms. Halfway around my side, I ran into a black tin box just layin' in a loosely dug hole on the ground. It had a padlock on it, too. And, yes, it was a *Master Lock* brand padlock. I was really excited now.

"Elizabeth!"

She was just crawlin' up to me and her whole body jolted with my sudden yell.

"Man, Ben!" and she looked mad. "You scared the wee-nillies out'a me!"

I grinned unashamedly. Then I remembered something that had been niggling at me for three months.

"Why'd you run out'a that Christmas Program so fast?" I asked.

Yeah. It still bothered me. She stopped looking at the box to stare at me.

"What?"

"You heard me," and then I repeated it. "Why'd you run out'a the Christmas Program so fast? Was it me? I heard you tell Miz Bernie you didn't want to play Mary in the first place. Was it *me*?"

She was still gawking at me like I'd sprouted two heads or something. I gawked back at her feeling a little "out on a limb" and agitated now. We still stared at each other for a minute, unbelievably, with another Abrams' House Discovery within our grasp, and all oblivious to it.

Finally, Elizabeth dropped her eyes and said. "Aw. I just didn't know whether to stand or sit during the last hymn, and I was embarrassed."

I kept on looking at her, a little surprised, and tried to remember the last hymn and what she'd been doing.

I remembered my Granny's old saying, "Everyone is odd, except me and thee. And sometimes I wonder about thee."

I wanted to laugh, but suspected it wouldn't be appreciated. "Oh," I said and left it at that, feeling a good deal better.

Then she told me about running into Jerry Bigham and my uncle when she'd "lit out" of the building and what seemed to be happening between the two of them. I had to ponder that some. I wudn't no ace sleuth, but even I knew a rookie policeman didn't collar the DA in a county without some comeuppance.

I thought about our "find", then. "Let's get this little box out'a here and figure out how to open it.

Camille turned away from the afternoon sun filtering in through the lacy white curtains. She had been studying the wavy glass that had survived generations of Caudells, and then had turned to the dappled sunlight sifting through the curtains to her bed spread. She found herself noticing the shadows more than the light.

It was still a bit cold and blustery, but she'd lit the kindling in the bedroom before she lay down, and the room was beginning to cradle a little warmth. These small things that normally pleased her in the afternoon's last light had not smoothed the tiny frown that gathered her brows over eyes the color of a pale winter sky.

She'd tried to nap with good reason, but only the Lord knew the incessant battering of worry at the peace she longed to have. It filled her heart like the raucous black crows covered the pecan orchards on fall mornings. Of course, and here she managed a smile, the hired man, Curtis Rabun, would slip out and fire off a few shots with Vince's Daddy's shotgun.

She'd watched him slip out quiet as a dandelion seed on the wind, but he never got that gun to his shoulder before the whole mass of them would lift like a dark cloud and scatter to the four winds. Curtis would fire anyway, rarely having anything to show for it; and in a little while she'd hear them filling the skies with the cacophony of their exulting caws.

They would return first to the back of the orchard and later, arrogantly filled the trees closest to the homeplace. It was evident that they considered the whole orchard of pecans their possession. Their behavior was so very much like the anxiety that was even now consuming her thoughts.

She watched the light and darkness play across her covers, mirroring the movement of moss-laden oak limbs in the wind. How had she become this timid person who crept shadow-like through the old Caudell Home seeking to alternately avoid or please Vincent Deland Caudell? It wasn't just that he was older than her, or the public regard that seemed to accompany his very public profession; but it was almost like he had set out from the very first by emotional and physical means to subjugate her in such a way that she was still very much a solitary stranger in a close community where she'd lived for over a decade.

This fact, suddenly realized, astounded her. She was so far from the girl her father had raised that she didn't recognize herself. The closest she'd come to the repossession of her person was the time she'd spent with young Ben over the last three years. She loved Mama Lee, but she had to be so careful not to turn any of her troubles loose in the elderly lady's hearing. Mrs. Eulee Barton Caudell knew enough about Vincent to occupy her thoughts without adding his wife's knowledge to it.

And Rennie was always a blessing with her great faith and the wisdom only God could give, but Ben, now, he made her forget. At first, he had been so troubled that she had feared he'd chosen to walk down the road his uncle had taken. But somewhere across the three years spent together, they had turned a corner and she had begun to see glimpses of the child Ben really was. He made her laugh out loud sometimes—a thing she hadn't done in years. He could spin a story in such a droll fashion that it was impossible not to let loose with a hoot of laughter.

Cammie couldn't remember when she'd had a deep "belly laugh" like that. It seemed to cleanse better than tears, she thought; but maybe that was because she had spilled so many.

As a girl, she had been easy to cry and very tenderhearted. Now, she couldn't recall the last time tears had coursed down her cheeks. She didn't know what that meant but didn't think it was good.

Alice Camille Winslow had met Vincent Deland Caudell at the Bennington Presbyterian Church in late April 1948. She'd lost her mother to cancer when she was a toddler, and the death of her father only the month before she'd met Vince had deprived her of any close family. She had a string of distant cousins that stretched throughout small towns in Georgia and northwestern Florida, but none she was close to. Therefore, it was with some surprise, that she had opened a short note from a cousin on her mother's side of the family reintroducing herself as Clara Bradford Hilton and requesting that she play for their church homecoming in Bennington, Georgia.

Mrs. Clarissa Adelaide Bradford Hilton had further extended an invitation for lodging and supper after the homecoming festivities were over. Cammie had written thanking her cousin for the offer and accepting.

Clara had called after receiving her response and given directions and more details. After replacing the receiver, Camille wondered about her decision. There had been no hint of rancor, more a cloying extension of over-sweetness from her cousin's conversation. Clara had mentioned her employer and indicated that he would meet her at the church in his capacity as deacon. Somehow the whole conversation had been unsettling, but she hadn't been able to put her finger on what had troubled her.

She thought through the almost frenetic activity with which she'd filled her days over the months after her father's death. She'd tramped down her loneliness walking over the vast fields and woods that comprised her father's homeplace.

In between walking she'd played her piano almost obsessively. She had practiced incessantly and at all hours of the night or day. Cammie had filled the sleepless nights and the stillness of her home with music. Technically, she was where she had longed to be as an aspiring student in college and she had begun to accept any decent offer to play a piano anywhere within a three-hour radius of her hometown. She would come for anything from one song to a concert, paid or not.

The driving and piano playing seemed to soothe her loneliness and occupy her hours, as well as taking her away from a poignantly empty house. She was from a small town in South Georgia, and had earned a reputation in the surrounding countryside, as well as Savannah and Macon, as a talented pianist.

Cammie had travelled a good deal since she'd turned twenty playing for both civic and church functions. She'd studied to be a music teacher and was expecting a job opening in Dentin in the fall. She had been hired to teach the fifth grade—the small school couldn't afford a full-time music teacher, but she had been hired knowing that she would add to the music education program for the elementary wherever she could.

Her father, Charles Walker Winslow, had inherited and amassed a great deal of wealth and left it all to Camille. This included thousands of acres of woodland and some city properties which were currently rented and showing a good return. She really didn't have to work, but her mind and heart demanded it.

Vincent had been all charm that first morning and afternoon. He was a deacon and along with the organist had met me and helped to set up my music and make sure the lighting and piano bench suited. He had beautiful brown eyes and thick, wavy blonde hair. He had an olive complexion, with the whitest teeth I'd ever seen. He seemed to like to flash a smile often—at least, that afternoon, he'd worked that perfect grin a lot. He was the proverbial handsome older man, and he had my focused attention.

I have often thought through this time in my life; and wonder how I could've missed the man Vincent really was. I think a part of me was searching for a way to shore up the grief I'd felt at losing my father; and the very fact that Vince Caudell *was* older and very attentive during these first months of becoming acquainted colored my vision of his person.

Vince lost no time in cutting through the little knot of people who'd gathered after the service to express appreciation, and I felt he'd almost rudely whisked me away to meet his parents. He was not a young man, but he certainly acted like one, and I found myself smiling at his impetuosity.

He asked me to share his picnic blanket with him and assured me it was his pleasure to fill a plate for me. After ascertaining an idea of what I liked, he brought me a plate that could've filled the belly of a prize hog. He'd done his best to include a serving of every food on offer. Appetite had not been the foremost of my accomplishments during the past months, but I did my best to taste a bit of everything, and marvel over its delectability.

It had been fun having Vince point out various Freeman County personalities, and he had a host of amusing stories he accompanied them with. If they were tinged with a slight sarcasm and condescension toward their characters, it was muted and had gone unnoticed by a younger me in appreciation of his company and the laughter.

Before the meal ended, he arranged for me to have dinner with him and his parents instead of at Clara's home—all done as smoothly as oil polishing furniture. Clara and Dennis Hilton were sitting close enough to Vince's spread blanket that he easily conversed with them and me. Clara seemed almost honored to trade off her supper guest for his smile.

Between the lawyer and his secretary, it was arranged that I should go to Vince's parents' home after the church celebration was over. This was done almost without consulting me. Lonely as I was, I was actually happy to have someone planning my day for me.

I had loved Richard and Eulee Caudell almost on sight. Vince had introduced me before the meal, but we had not eaten together, as his folks had been seated at a picnic table surrounded by friends. He had quickly escorted me to his car after we'd thrown away our paper plates and folded his blanket; but I insisted on driving my car to save him the inconvenience of driving me back to the church.

Having been born and bred in the south, I was used to lovely old southern mansions. I had nevertheless been amazed as I pulled up beside Vince's convertible. Something about the house just called to my sense of home. With its beautiful old columns and wide wrap-around porch backed by a wealth of floor-length windows, it embraced the light within and seemed to emanate joy.

In the ensuing months, Richard and Eulee Caudell had filled the longing I'd had, not only for the mother I never known, but now a father fervently missed. Richard was twelve years Eulee's senior; but I had seen on that first visit how thoroughly they loved each other; how comfortable they were together; and how uncanny their sense of the other's thought before spoken.

Perhaps, this feeling of warmth I'd so appreciated in them had as much to do with my accepting Vince Caudell's courtship as the charm he exuded. In retrospect, I could see that he had pursued me with just the right amount of attention. He had been almost diligent in his courtship; and yet, with such a light touch, he had managed to entirely fool me. Within a two-month period, Vince had visited me at least once or twice a week and arranged for me to stay the weekend with my cousin Clara and Dennis twice, while tooling about the countryside with him. By July I was making wedding plans for September and accepting his advice on how to administer my father's estate.

He eased me into the idea of having the wedding at his church—better for his parents, he said, and reminded me of his father's precarious health. I had no family in my hometown, just a few people I'd come to cherish throughout the years; and Vince assured me we would invite them and arrange overnight lodging for any who'd come. We would pay for it or put them up in his folk's home.

And, later, he'd intimated, we would visit my friends often. All those years ago, I'd stuffed down the pain of losing my Dad, and replaced it with the excitement of short visits with Vince and his family, and planning a wedding.

September's excitement was replaced by day to day living with Vince. He'd put off our honeymoon, citing work at his law office and his father's health, again. I accepted this and busied myself setting up a household in his bachelor home just a few blocks from his office at the courthouse.

I left many things at my father's home in case we chose to visit it some-time; and, also, Vincent had so many things already settled at his place. There were a few things I brought though, like my mixer, a few family photos and paintings, some special linens my mother had embroidered, two quilts with both my grandmother and mother's hand stitching, a sew-ing machine, and the Steinway grand piano my father had bought for my tenth birthday. The piano had been too difficult to get into Vincent's home; and so, we had agreed to place it in his parent's home and buy me an up-right of my choice. Mama Lee had been pleased to have the grand placed in her large drawing room and I was given a key to the house and told to come over and play whenever I desired. This of course pleased me because I loved visiting either one of his parents and knew this to be a great excuse to do that.

The first week of our marriage had not passed before Vince had me signing papers concerning my father's estate. Vince had let our old family lawyer "go" and proffered his Uncle Julius' services, which he smilingly said would be free and so much more accessible to us.

There were plenty of papers to sign he warned me ruefully, and we rode to Judge Connors' offices to do it. I shyly looked up at my mature, handsome husband and agreed wholeheartedly with everything he said. The Judge met us there in a plush back office and had coffee, tea and small sandwiches on hand for our visit.

He had a deep southern voice and gave me a hearty hug at the front of our visit.

"Sit down! Sit down!" he boomed. And I sat.

"Mel!" he hollered out the open door, "Bring on the tea and coffee!"

Mel came dutifully in after a moment's lull, almost as if she'd been lying in ambush. She smiled and spoke, and after serving us, quickly stepped out. Mel had long, lovely legs, and I noticed both the judge and my husband seem to follow them as they stepped elegantly out the door. Being new to wedded bliss, I experienced a mixture of feelings—amusement and a bit of feminine rankling at Vince's continued focus.

As I was sipping my tea, papers began to be shoveled across the desk at me. Judge Connors had small reading glasses lowered to the end of his nose and began to mumble under them, checking where I should sign. This, he said, would consolidate mine and Vince's holdings, so in the event we had children and something occurred to either of us, a will could easily take care of our prospective progeny. Vince's possessions would become mine, and mine would become his.

I didn't think too much about it because I was twenty-two years old and had the kind of innocent expectations of health and wellness that only a twenty-two year old could have. Besides, what could go wrong with your own built in lawyer-for-a-husband convenience.

Vincent had assured me that having read over all the papers in his office the afternoon before—everything was legitimate. At the end of the visit, we signed wills with Mel and her cohort witnessing, and were urged to "hurry back", while being ushered out of the good judge's office.

Almost immediately, Vince's attentiveness began to waiver. Of course, I knew that a marriage did not go on as a courtship, but this was more than that. It was almost as if another man had taken up residence in his body.

As we approached our first month anniversary, I acknowledged to my-self that I didn't feel quite as ardently toward my husband as I could have wished. He stayed late at his office, frequently coming home after ten and as the year dragged by, it more often became midnight.

I had driven over to the courthouse when this first began occurring. I knew that his offices were on an outside corner with a good view of the main thoroughfare because he had given me the guided tour while we were dating. Although, those first few nights his car was there, every light in the building was off. On succeeding evenings, his car wasn't even there.

I checked this at several different times after hours over the next week, and before I could confront him, he informed me by phone that he'd be out of his office for a few days and was headed to Atlanta for an old friend who was a former client.

He would not confide in me, saying it was a delicate matter and, no, he didn't think I would enjoy going along. His time would be completely monopolized by his old client's affairs. How closely his description represented the truth, I came to realize in the years that followed.

It was more than the issues of trust, though. When Vincent was home, he exhibited a coldness I at first could not understand. What had happened to the man who had so ardently wooed me only this past summer? By the fourth month, we were only occupying the same home. Husband and wife, we were not, and it seemed to bother Vincent not one whit. He came home only to eat and bathe and change his clothes; never sought my company and seemed irritated if I foisted it on him. I quickly learned *not* to foist *anything* on him—not my questions, opinions or presence, and could almost time his "explosions" by a certain nervous tick he exhibited when he became agitated.

He forbade any kind of music when he was in the house, piano, radio, or phonograph. He did watch some boxing on television, though, and would turn it up so loud that I could retire to my room and listen to the radio there, if I was careful.

I began to brood, then, and wonder how long it would be before the neighbors would shun the house because of all of the cats and dogs I would soon be acquiring. I could see myself an eccentric in the future, saved only from insanity by the Winslow/Caudell money.

I wasn't yet ready to throw in the towel, and thought I'd see about teaching school or music again—anything to keep my mind occupied. After filling out applications and being assured of placement, I drove that afternoon over to talk with my mother-in-law about my intentions.

When I arrived, the house was in an uproar. Dr. Prescott was racing upstairs bag in hand, and the then current housemaid, Winnie Gunnels, was wringing her hands, and mumbling under her breath.

After some minutes of tenacious inquiry, I learned that she had discovered Richard lying on the floor beside his bed after lunch; that she could not get him to respond; and that Miz Eulee was out visiting a Sunday School Class member who had recently been released from the local hospital after an operation.

I knew that this was Miss Edna May Barnes who lived in the downtown area of Carverville. I tried calling Miz Edna's, but continued to get a busy signal. Back then everybody was on a partyline and shared phone line access, so I opted to fetch her in my car which had been Vince's old Cadillac.

I ran back and called to Winnie, instructing her to contact Vince's office, and get Miz Clara to find Vince and tell him about his father.

It didn't take longer than twenty minutes to fetch Mama Lee and drive her back home.

When we rolled up in the yard it was to see the big black hearse, which doubled as our ambulance, pulling out, siren on, dust puffing from beneath its tires, and Richard within. We immediately turned around and followed it to the hospital.

Vince's dad opened his eyes while we were in the emergency room and found his wife's fastened on his face longingly. They exchanged a few words. He'd asked her not to give up on Vincent.

"I'm sorry he's been so hard to deal with, Lee—if he'd only given us a chance." Then he'd sighed and pulled in a raspy breath.

Mama Lee had squeezed his hand and said, "Oh, Rich. It'll be okay. We won't give up. He's got some of you in him. He'll make it. You'll see—" and her voice had trailed off.

I could see she was gritting her teeth and trying not to let the moisture in her eyes spill over. Rich had worked up one last smile for her then.

"Honey, I'm so sorry about Connie. I *know* she's alive. I believe she'll find her way home somehow." He drew in another breath his voice weakening as he continued, "It's okay, Lee," he'd assured her. "We'll both be alright. Keep your hand in His. I love you."

I'd thought he was gone then. But she called out his name almost by reflex and he drew in another breath and opened his eyes again. "Hon, tell Vincent—" and that quick he was gone.

She still held his hand, and stood there for some time unbelieving. The doctor had moved to his side with his stethoscope, and employing it quickly while fingering Richard's pulse point, shook his head at Mama Lee sadly.

I saw a tear course down her cheek and she leaned over and brushed the hair from his brow.

"I love you, too," I heard her whisper as she kissed his cheek for the last time.

Vince never made it to his father's bedside. Clara later told me apologetically that she had no idea where he'd been, and had called every possible place she could think of.

I'd told her thank you and left it at that. A small town fairly resonates local news and gossip. Mama Lee often said, if you planned on doing something, especially if it was bizarre or unusual, you only had to think it to find it front page news tomorrow morning in the local paper.

Someone, somewhere, must've found Vince and informed him. He showed up late that evening at his father's home.

I'd driven Mama Lee home and she'd asked me to go into the drawing room and play every hymn that Richard loved. I saw her into the kitchen where Winnie began to make her a cup of tea, then turned and did as I had been bidden.

I loved Constance Eulee Caudell and I'd loved Richard Vincent Caudell as if they'd been my own parents. I appreciated being able to let my feelings flow out into the keys. I don't know how long I was there and wasn't even aware that tears were flowing unchecked down my cheeks. Winnie came in and told me she'd taken tea up to Miz Eulee's bed and that Miz Eulee wanted me to come up and have tea with her.

People began to come to the house about that time, bringing food. I made excuses and asked Winnie to tell them Miz Eulee was resting and that visitation would be tomorrow at 6:00 PM. Most folks were just dropping by food dishes and didn't seem to mind.

After we'd settled and poured our tea at a small table kept in her room for just that purpose, Mama Lee began to talk. She said there were things she wanted to explain that Richard hadn't wanted to talk about—a lot of them I had heard a little about, but she felt I needed to better understand some family matters. She seemed to know that Vincent would never share these things with me.

Eulee Caudell rubbed a finger on the edge of her china saucer and began to talk about how she and Rich had met and how unexpected their love had been for the both of them. How she had tried to be a help to young Vincent, but he had never accepted her. Apparently, Vince had spent several years with his mother's family in Atlanta after her death before coming home to Bennington to be with his dad. The Connors had been proud people, very cognizant of their standing in the community, and expecting deference from servants and friends alike.

Vince had come back to Richard with a liking for that, and Richard's subsequent marriage to a woman who was not "pedigreed" had only stiffened his adherence to what his mother and later her family had tried to instill in him. It was true she'd explained that her Grandmama had come from an old southern family, but she had married a young man from Pennsylvania that she'd met at a cousin's house.

He was apprenticed to a shipbuilder and was purported to be a wonderful mix of diligence, innovation and talent. Mama Lee's Grandfather had managed to cross paths with her Grandmother many times over the ensuing summer, thus revealing a definite flair for innovation. She'd smiled at this juncture of the story before going on.

The young couple had developed a tendre for each other by the end of summer and had eloped before the first frost had hit Savannah. She had been succinctly cut off from her family. Mama Lee's Grandfather, however, had excelled as a ship builder, worked his way up through the ranks, and had brought wealth back to their little family.

Their son James had a flair for business and had owned a chain of grocery stores that still dotted the whole southeastern coast. Constance Eulee Barton's family history did not seem to endear her to Judge Julian Connors or his nephew, her stepson. Much to Mama Lee's chagrin and heartache, she had seen her entrance into the Caudell family drive father and son further apart.

Judge Julian Connors, brother to Vince's mother, was only too willing to take the place of father in Vince's life; and became mentor, friend, and educator.Through the years, she and Richard had tried in many ways to reach Vincent but were never allowed to share his inmost thoughts. It had been one of the two great heartaches in their lives.

She told me, then, of the birth of their daughter, Constance Leigh, in February of 1934; how astounded and overjoyed they had been to find that she was pregnant after ten years of marriage, and then how, conversely, and from the beginning, Vincent had seemed to hate his half-sister. Even when she'd been an infant, he'd never referred to her unless it was to complain.

Finally, Richard had spoken to him and in angry response the young man had moved out that very night to live with his uncle, and gotten a job in Julian's office, as well. Vince had been attending the University of Georgia Law School in those years, but had been home for summer break. Connie Leigh was still a lap baby, and Rich and Lee could not believe the rancor he held against the tiny baby girl.

She was beautiful, too, Lee had mused quietly. "She had soft auburn hair like my mother," she'd said. "And the biggest blue eyes you've ever seen."

She quieted then for a while, thinking about her Richard and the daughter they'd lost. Her past with him seemed to fill up her eyes and Cammie could trace the longing of the elderly woman's heart toward her husband and daughter. They were silent together, but after a few minutes, Miz Eulee resumed her story.

"Rich kept trying to reconcile Vince to our little Connie and himself. I couldn't help but encourage him to keep making overtures. I could see that he was heartbroken at the loss of his son." She paused again and wiped her hand across her forehead and eyes roughly—a thing I had noticed was a habit of Richard's when he was perturbed.

Looking up at me she resumed her tale, "In 1944, this area was so busy. The government had bought up so many people's land just after the announcement in 1940 that a military base was going to be built here. There was an influx of builders and military and the land went from mostly rural farming to a bustling military base. Soldiers had poured in as we became embroiled in World War II. Savannah was the same—so many people everywhere we weren't familiar with; and we were trying to help the war effort and support our soldiers."

"Rich and I thought it would be a good idea to try to get Connie and Vince together away from Bennington--hoping a change of scenery and a trip would help him to see her differently. So, Rich called him and put forth the idea of a trip to Savannah."

"Vince decided to drive up to Savannah with them for the day—in the spring of 1944. It was a big thing for Connie because the country was still gas rationing and we didn't go out of town very often." She paused and looked as if she were back in that time frame for just a few minutes, then "came to herself" and continued, "I would've gone with them but thought they stood a better chance of having a good time if I weren't there to upset Vincent."

"I remember that Rich was really surprised that Vince had accepted his invitation. He usually refused all invitations that involved his sister—even her birthday parties. Oh, how I've wished he'd refused this one. Maybe Rich and Connie wouldn't have gone then. At least, I would've been there, too." She rubbed her forehead again, and sighed, then continued.

"Anyway, they were going to visit Tybee Island, walk on its beach and then have lunch at Mrs. Wilkes Boarding House. Later, they planned to visit Ft. Pulaski. Vincent at 33 was an avid history buff and loved reading about both the revolutionary and civil wars. Then, they were going to shop downtown on Broughton Street for Connie Leigh."

"Everything went well until they stopped impulsively at a truck stop on Highway 17 on the way back home. Vince had heard that the little café had very good food. Rich was trying to appease him, and Connie seemed amenable. The three of them talked it over and decided to try it."

Miz Eulee cleared her throat and took a sip of her tepid tea. I reached over and tried to warm it from the teapot. She took another taste, used the linen napkin in her lap and started back on her story.

"Connie Leigh had never been to a truck stop before. Vince said she seemed eager to try the new diner. She just ordered desert, Rich said, her favorite—pecan pie and a Coke. Rich had left the table after finishing his meal to visit the restroom. Not long after he'd left, Vince followed."

"They had to wait within the restroom because there were a few customers before them—a bus full of high school kids on their way from Waycross to Savannah had just unloaded at the truck stop, and then Vince had detained Rich to talk about several minor cases he was prosecuting."

"In the space of about ten minutes Connie had disappeared. They waited a little bit thinking she'd gone to the lady's room; but as the minutes ticked by they asked their waitress to check for them. She wasn't there."

Mama Lee's whole frame shook with a dry sob. It took her several minutes and she apologized as she regained control.

"They paid the bill," she continued haltingly, "and searched the parking lot—even the big tractor/trailers that were parked in a line at the back. No one had seen anyone approaching Connie, and most had not even noticed *her*. The restaurant had been very busy with that bus load of high school students and Vince had asked the waitress for a corner booth tucked behind a divider at the entrance."

"No one had even seen her leave the restaurant. The police had to wait for 24 hours to act on a missing person's report, they informed Richard."

"He called me to see if I'd heard from Connie or if she'd gotten a ride home with someone else. Rich waited at the restaurant in case she came back, while Vince retraced the steps they'd taken in Savannah, asking if any of the park workers or store clerks had noticed anyone following Connie—grasping at any hope that she might be found. Vince came back from a fruitless search and convinced Richard that he needed to get home to take care of me. They left our phone numbers and addresses in case anything was heard about Connie. Vince drove Richard back home, then returned to the truck stop to wait in case she showed up there."

"We were distraught. That night no one slept. We walked the floors and called everyone we could think of that might have some knowledge of Connie's whereabouts or any plans we hadn't been aware of. Vince had assured us that no one had been following their car and the last stop had been an impulse stop; so that Connie could not have planned any trips with anyone else and no one we'd known could've planned a meeting—only a chance encounter might have occurred."

"We thought that she must've known whoever had talked her into leaving the restaurant; and she had still been sipping on her coke and reading a library book she'd brought along when they'd left her at the table. We called girlfriends and asked if there were any boyfriends or anyone, old or young, who'd been pressuring her or acting in any unusual way. Connie was only ten years old; we came up with a no to every question."

"Connie didn't have a special beau, she had just been friends at that age. There were no new friends, or strange confrontations, or anything to cause suspicion."

"In the weeks that followed the house was somber and almost eerie. It was as if there had never been our little girl. Just her room and a book or barrette left by a chair attested to the fact that she had been there—that and the aching in our hearts."

"Richard hired a private investigator, Ed Norris—Julian had recommended him. Mr. Norris reported back to us over the next few years monthly. Once, in 1947, we thought we heard of her in a coastal town in Alabama. Apparently, a responsible citizen, and a former landlord, had found the library book she'd had with her on the day she'd been kidnapped. He'd sent it back to the school, and the librarian there, familiar with our family and Connie's abduction, recognized it as the overdue book that she'd had from past records."

"She immediately got in touch with Rich and gave him the book, knowing it would mean something to us. He brought it home and we cried over it and prayed. It was Carol Ryrie Brink's 'Caddie Woodlawn', a book Connie had read more than once. I began to read back through it that night myself."

"It's a wonderful book. At the end of the third chapter where Caddie's Uncle Edmond comes to visit, I found a message penciled in what I was sure was Connie's handwriting."

Mama Lee paused in her story and had me open her little desk then and fetch the worn beige library book. I turned to the page she'd indicated and she quoted it by heart while I read the words written at the bottom of the page. The penmanship was obviously a child's, and the cursive ran together in places as if it were hurriedly jotted down.

"Daddy and Mama, I am okay. I miss you so much. I don't have long. We are moving tonight. I don't know where to. I love you. Pray for m..."

"Richard took the train out of Savannah over to Mobile the next day, and searched the area himself for over a week. We had no way of knowing who the landlord was that mailed in her library book. There was not even a note with the book or return address—just a postmark. There was not a sign of her. No one recognized her picture or name."

"She was ten years old when we lost her." She drew in a convulsive breath. "She'd be sixteen now. She would be so heartbroken about Rich. Oh, how she loved her Papa."

Her shoulders began to shake, and I heard deep wracking sobs as she hunched over the table, once again distraught with the losses of her life.

I got up out of my chair and knelt before her, wrapping my arms around her small form, I hugged her to me. There wasn't anything I knew to say, so I just held on tightly and prayed.

Somewhere in the middle of all these memories I'd fallen asleep, only to dream crazy snatches of nightmarish dark rooms, chasing and running, and falling dreams where your whole frame jerked with imagined gravity.

Reaching up gratefully out of this confused slumber, I heard Rennie's step on the stair, and a light knocking followed.

"Miz Cammie?" she spoke softly outside the door, "You awake?"

I lifted up on my elbows and swiped the hair from my face.

"Yes, Rennie. Come on in."

The door opened, and she peeped through.

"It's young Ben, Miz Camille. He ain't in yet and it's nigh time fo' sup-puh. He usually heah by now."

I swung my legs over the bed and tried to get my thinking in order.

"Let's see. He was going on a bike ride and I'm pretty sure he'd end up at Elizabeth Linden's."

We smiled at each other here. Rennie and I both listened and watched our boy.

"Sho' right, Miz Cammie. I bet he thayuh," and she turned to leave.

"I'll call and see. And, thanks, Rennie. You're a Godsend."

She smiled at me as she left. I went downstairs to phone but was prevented by the rascal sauntering through the door. He was grinning like the cat who'd swallowed the canary and whistling the "Theme from Andy Griffith". He looked like he'd been crawling on all fours through Curtis Rayburn's chicken yard, too.

"Boy," I said, borrowing a page from Mama Lee, "where've you been?"

He stopped "mid-saunter" and only relaxed after spotting my smile. "Oh, Cammie! You won't believe it. Well, I can't tell you yet, but me and Elizabeth got a secret! Man, what a secret!"

I held eye contact with him still smiling, "*When can* you tell me, then?"

He looked back unblinkingly, "I think tomorrow," he said.

Chapter 6

"Ain't nobody know the heart of a man 'cept the Lawd; and how He stan' it I ain't know."
—Rennie Esther Jones Baker

J udge Julian Parker Connors stretched his long, lean limbs out from the swivel chair in front of his sprawling desk. It was a rounded semi-circular piece of furniture made from rosewood. He liked the unusual.

Turning, the judge peered out the window onto the street that passed his office. He had a corner office at the front, because he liked looking out at the personalities of this little town—*his* little town. He was the big fish, here, and soon they'd *all* know it.

He liked thinking of himself as "the judge". He smiled and chuckled, causing his slight paunch to shake. He had left Atlanta with such mixed feelings in his late twenties. He'd loved the idea of an inheritance and old money in Carverville, but dreaded leaving his home city. Even now it beckoned to him.

But he'd never have had the head start he'd had here. His Great Uncle Edward Parker Connors had left his great nephew, then a young lawyer, a huge estate on the outskirts of Carverville. Widowed and childless, Uncle Edward had amassed most of his land during The Reconstruction. Upon his death most of the cash Uncle Edward had saved, and it had been a lot, had been given to a worthy university in the northern states where he had been raised. A portion of the money had been set aside for his great nephew, Julian, to help maintain the estate until the young man had more understanding of the land's usage and, also, to allow time for him to build up his law practice.

Julian, however, had never allowed his great uncle free access to his thinking. Maintaining a light pleasantness with the old man, and presenting an expression of deep respect on all occasions, he had soothed Edward's fears for his legacy's future. Once possessions had changed hands, however, Julian lost no time in spending his inheritance to buy an office, refurbish his great uncle's old mansion, and hire the best employees away from his old firm in Atlanta.

He travelled to Europe and bought expensive furnishings for his study and bedroom and parlor. He bought the best wines, and liquors, hired the best tailors for a completely new wardrobe. He quietly made arrangements for the old servants to leave and brought in a chef, butler, housekeeper, maids and gardeners as befitted his station and breeding.

He sold off as much of his uncle's old furnishings as he could to out-of-town buyers. The young lawyer had then sold a great deal of the land holdings, purporting to have no interest in agriculture or lumber. Early on, he found himself short of cash, and easily slid into back door deals with certain unsavory characters in the community.

The years rolled by, and although he no longer needed the cash, he had become enmeshed in the sense of power that money and connections bought. He was an elected superior court judge, and on occasion lightly worked at twisting outcomes on some of the cases that came before him. Take that John Abrams Case about Raynelle, he mused. He'd hastened that one along as much as he could; fostered Vince's side of things. They both needed the Raynelle affair to die quickly. Future favors and money were assured "under the table" for most of the trials he "influenced".

He continued his felonious dealings and even was a sleeping partner to several establishments skirting the edge of the law, and one entirely over the line. This latter business had come into being around the time of the opening of the big base. He and his partners had bought an old hotel/ diner at the edge of Freeman County. It had changed hands many times over the years, and was in a dilapidated state.

He put up a great percentage of the money to refurbish the property by establishing out of town bank accounts and giving his partners access by having their names as the owners. He never dealt with anyone that he *didn't* own in some manner—either by blackmail or monetary enslavement, and usually both.

The "establishment" had flourished through the years of World War II and even later when the base had shrunk in population to dwindling numbers compared to its heyday, Julian's little venture had continued to prosper. With the reawakening of the military base, his business was booming.

He smiled to himself thinking about his partners. Yes, it was sometimes an uneasy sleep with his business bedfellows; but he had always enjoyed maneuvering people and situations, and he craved the excitement of breaking the rules while maintaining a spotless reputation.

At thirty years of age, he had cut quite a figure in the small town of Carverville. He'd enjoyed his position in the community, in law, business and amongst the female population. He'd finally married a young woman from an old Carverville family, Charlotte Anne Hilton, in 1929, and after a few years she had had one child—a son named after his father.

Julian Parker Connors, Jr. had followed in his father's footsteps precisely—except in one area. He knew how to cause moneys to dissipate, but not how to amass them. Parker had had no inclination for law, business or work; but had known to a "T" how to party. He went through a fortune before he'd finished high school, some said. And the year before he was old enough to drive he'd slipped a set of his father's keys, and taken their brand new 1947 Cadillac convertible out for a drive with friends.

One of the older boys had gotten them drinks and after a night of deep drinking, he'd wanted to drive them all to Savannah—out from under his father's eyes, young Connors had said, while elbowing a best buddy. He'd filled up his father's car with as many friends as he could and on their trip out of town, he'd wiped out part of a restaurant on the Bennington curve and taken several cars with him.

All of the boys had been killed. Out of the family of four in the first car he hit, all four had been killed. The first hit had caused a tractor trailer to jackknife and cross the other lane taking out another car and killing a young family man. Subsequently, several cars rounding the curve on their way to Savannah had crashed into those strewn across the road. The deaths had not only stunned the Connors family and community alike, but ensuing court cases had caused financial burdens that had tied the judge deeper into the mire of illegalities.

The loss of their son had almost destroyed his wife; but he was a proud man cut out of the same cloth as his father before him. He mourned the passing of his son, and then turned his hopes to his nephew. As his childless uncle had poured his riches into Julian's pockets, just so, he would groom young Vince for the reins of the Connors' fortune.

He set about refilling his coffers and preparing Vince for a partnership. Well, *maybe,* on that last thought. There was no hurry on making up his mind about Vincent. He had toyed with *many* ideas about Vincent for some years now and was not altogether satisfied that Vincent's hold on his temper was strong enough to take the reins of the Connors' fortune.

Perhaps if he waited and manipulated a few events he would have ownership of the Caudell Estate, as well. There was no hurry to groom anyone to replace him. He was in the prime of his life! He stretched his arms above and behind his large frame, bringing them down to cradle his head, elbows thrust out on either side, and reared back in his swivel chair.

Someone had slotted a quarter in the big, turquoise juke box that sat to the right of the Blue Heron's bar. The man sitting alone at one of the tables that filled the room could hear the sweet guitar work at the front of Marty Robbins' "El Paso". He cradled his head between his two hands and groaned.

Vincent DeLand Caudell eased his aching skull deeper into those well-manicured fingers while resting his elbows on the shining turquoise of the Formica table edged at the back of the restaurant. It was eight A.M. and another night that he hadn't made it home.

Everything seemed to be closing in on him at one point in time. *Why didn't trouble spread out some so you could handle it*, he wondered. One of the girls passing through in her negligee banged a glass on the bar and asked if he'd like to join her.

He could still feel the echo of her shrill voice pounding back and forth between his ears. He made the mistake of moving his head a little and whatever anvil that was caught at the front of his forehead found a way of rolling back to the base of his skull, picking up momentum and pain like a timpani's rolling crescendo in an orchestra.

"No. No," he whispered his reply.

The redhead widened her eyes at him and then relaxed them knowingly. She quietly took her drink to the back where the cook would be coming in for lunch preparation, unplugging the juke box as she went. Vince was left to ponder his troubles and nurse his hangover alone and grateful.

He'd be 52 years old this year, if he could make it through June. At one time he'd thought he had life by the tail shaking it at will. Then, he'd thought, *at least*, his uncle still grasped it. Now, he wasn't so sure. This mess with Raynelle had really shaken him.

He still hadn't found where that woman had put those papers. The only comfort in the "lost" papers was that he was pretty sure no one else knew either. Of a surety, Big John was ignorant of Raynelle's blackmail, and was safely out of the way for at least twenty-five years—with no chance of parole.

Early on in his career, this injustice would have niggled at him, but not today. He was deeply involved in saving his own hide—forget anybody else. He went over the details of John Abrams' trial again. Vince had been so afraid that he might slip by some expression or word in pursuing this case. He had almost asked the Judge to relieve him. Intuitively, he knew it wouldn't do to show that sign of weakness before Judge Julian Parker Connors. So, he'd rejected that and gutted it out.

He didn't think, in perusing the events of the trial, that he'd allowed any facial expression or terminology to reveal in any way that he had a much more personal knowledge of Raynelle Anne Abrams than the public or Big John was aware. But it woke him at nights whenever he *could* sleep.

He'd jerk up in a cold sweat seeing the courthouse full of people look-ing at him in disbelief. He'd slipped up! And then it would come to him that it was just another nightmare. He'd taken to drinking heavier than ever just after the trial.

He'd come home one night and cornered Camille in her room. He re-membered a scuffle, but nothing after that. He didn't know what he or she had done or even if he'd hurt her. He'd awakened in her bed the following morning and she was nowhere to be found. Rennie was cooking breakfast and all seemed normal.

He'd promised himself after his Atlanta visit when Dr. Prescott had informed him that he'd struck his wife, and in front of his family, that he was going to control his temper and cut back on his drinking. Vince could see that after all his careful planning, he might just lose it all by his abuse becoming common knowledge. As it was, he'd had to fob off the doctor's insistence that he might like to try AA or seek out some kind of counseling in Savannah privately.

He couldn't afford to let his stepmother know how often he had in-dulged his temper at someone else's expense—mostly it had been Camille. The last incident he remembered had been that night in her bedroom.

When he'd finally seen her that afternoon on her way upstairs, he'd breathed a sigh of relief. Nothing seemed amiss about her and when no one had mentioned any damage to her person, he had finally dismissed it when she, too, had said nothing. He hadn't been able to speak with her privately or even get a close look at her, but he was sure Eulee or the boy would've taken him on if they'd spotted anything wrong with his *dear* wife.

Still, the thought that she was avoiding his person disturbed him. Sometimes, he'd had a sense that she'd been there in a room only moments before he'd entered, because a hint of the perfume she wore lingered there. But he never heard her leaving.

He'd gone back to spending most of his nights at the Blue Heron at the edge of town. He never went into the dining room during open hours, but he had hand-picked a little room at the back of the court where he kept extra clothes and toiletries. It had a back entrance, unlike any of the other rooms.

He kept his car parked away from the business, too—just off a two rut, dirt road that ran along a fence line of pine woods. He always pulled in behind a small copse of huge old magnolia trees that were surrounded by palmettos at the road front but just outside of the fenced pines. He'd had the Blue Heron handyman put in a gate right behind the magnolias whose leaves and branches spread all along the ground blocking any view from the road. The little gate kept him from tearing his suit pants as he stretched over the wire.

He had a bit longer walk to gain entrance to the property, but it was worth it for his peace of mind. Staying at the Heron had him arriving at work a little later, but he made up for lost time by staying later, also, and then heading back to his and the Judge's little sideline. He smiled.

He might just stop by old man Linden's and see if he could borrow the key to Raynelle's house. He'd say there were things that troubled him about the trial and he wanted to look around a little more to see if he couldn't find something that would help Big John out. There. That sounded good. Folks in Freeman County thought a lot of John; he'd impress the Lindens that way, while checking on those lost papers. That's what he'd do. Yes, look for the papers at their empty house one more time with no one looking over his shoulder.

And he might just skip over to Harve's hardware store and have a copy made of that key, too.

Then there was that other thing he'd heard in Atlanta There was some talk coming down from the capitol about sending in the GBI to investigate allegations of illegal gambling, illegal liquor sales, and possible prostitution. That all just screamed The Blue Heron. The governor's office was questioning why local authorities never seemed to get in a clean raid on the Heron.

He figured Axel must be responsible for asking for their assistance. He and the Judge should've caught that angle. By the time the police had waltzed in, half the customers usually there, it was contended, had waltzed out.

The hotel rooms were stretched along a little court reminiscent of the auto courts of the thirties and forties. Those, too, were found by the police to be only occupied by families or empty and clean.

He thought back to the night of the Christmas program. That sorry-tailed Jerry Bigham had collared Vince outside of church and told him he'd heard they were going to investigate soon, if local police couldn't come up with an answer about The Blue Heron. And he wanted out! As if Bigham could get out.

Still, he was a loose end and had been involved in the beating of a soldier after the gambling hadn't played out the young man's way. That last thing alone had almost ruined their set up. It had taken the judge a lot of payoffs and favors to squeak their "establishment" out of that one. So, the Judge had said not to worry his head over Jerry.

"I'll take care of Mr. Bigham," and Julian's lips had curled slightly in an unpleasant way.

He had patted Vince on the shoulder and assured him there was nothing to worry about. Vince began to smile at this point in his thinking. He and the Judge had long term plans that did not include Jerry Bigham. He let the incident go and got up wincing.

Making his way over to the bar, Vince leaned in behind the counter. Ed, the bartender, always kept a bottle of aspirin there. The lawyer uncapped the bottle, poured out three, and walked as softly as he could over to the small fridge under the side counter. Opening the door, he pulled out one of Ed's personal six and a half ounce cokes and popped the top off in the opener screwed to the side of the bar.

He stood stock still and drank down the pills with half the coke. Necessarily, he waited for the pain surging through his head to ease off a little, then, gingerly made his way back to the table. He set his bottle down without making a sound, then sat and leaned his head over the back of the chair, his hands resting on his thighs. He closed his eyes and rubbed his temples, remembering how early in their marriage, Camille had done that for him. He sighed and tried to dismiss *that* debacle, too.

Clara, his secretary, had first told him about her when Camille's father had died. Along with a picture she had from a family reunion the year before, she'd shared about Charles Winslow's holdings and wealth. Although, he had found Cammie very attractive when he'd first met her, it was her wealth that brought out his all-out pursuit.

It hadn't taken long for him to see her youth and idealism as a hindrance to any real sharing of himself. There had been no understanding between them, no common ground to meet. She could not appreciate the sharp sarcasm of his wit, the pride he took in possessions, or the hypocrisy of his real feelings towards the people of Freeman County. He often laughed at what he considered their backwardness and dealt condescendingly where he would not experience retribution.

No, he thought, his marriage was a farce. Clearly, he had benefitted from the wealth he had gleaned from her father's estate, but in the process, he had definitely lost her and most probably himself.

He sighed and thought back to the Heron and how they'd devised ways to hide its real livelihood. He still smiled at the plan they'd implemented to warn of an impending raid. He thought it was pretty ingenious. The judge had suggested that he use Curtis Rabun, his hired man, because he knew nothing about the Heron and he was diligent and punctual to a fault. In fact, the Judge had sent Curtis over originally, when Vince had asked around after someone to fill that job. Curtis was a hard worker, too. The Judge was good at figuring people.

Julian would have his secretary trot some legal papers over to Vince's office by hand. He would always instruct her to hand deliver *only* to Vince and to advise him personally of the success or failure of her delivery right away. He would always pack the papers in a manila envelope and color the inside flap with a red dot if the raid was scheduled for evening and a green dot if it was imminent.

Upon receiving the Judge's signal of an impending raid, Vince would drive home to retrieve papers, or eat an early lunch or some trumped up excuse and on his way in manage to talk to Curtis. He'd ask him to go over to the hardware store and pay Harve Whitcomb for a portion of his bill. Harve always carried a charge for Vince, so this would work.

If Curtis paid a twenty-dollar bill on Vince's charge account, then Harve knew that the raid would be that evening. If Curtis carried a ten to to pay the bill, then Harve knew the raid was imminent. Of course, Curtis never knew the significance of the payments. He just had done what he'd been ordered to do.

Whitcomb would then send a bag to Dale Barnes, the front man for the supposed motel/restaurant. He sent nails for "imminent" and plumbing supplies for "evening raid". Either way, Dale would instigate an immediate cleanup and "cover job". It had worked like a charm for over thirteen years because the judge would always delay the imminent, and most raids occurred at night because the law thought those were the prime hours for their "business" to operate.

When a night raid was impending, they had several signals to warn off return customers. They'd put a job opening sign in the office window; unscrew six of the white lights that blinked around the neon BLUE HERON; crank Dale's old Caddy up on a jack as if the tire were flat; or have a couple of the girls dress as maids, wash the office windows, and then mop the office floors. This last signal was the least popular among their girls.

It had only been those incidents where Jerry had gotten rough with some of their customers that had brought down the attention of GBI and other state officials. In spite of all his and the Judge's duplicitous practices, they had managed to skirt the attention of the local law and the county's voters.

Through the years, the people of Freeman County had seemed to consider Vince an intelligent and honorable man. He'd figured his father's reputation had something to do with that. He'd been careful not to show his antipathy for his stepmother or disrespect of his father in public.

He knew himself to be intelligent and quick-witted in the courtroom; but he'd never seen anyone sharper than his uncle, The Judge. Sometimes, it frightened Vince that he couldn't follow Julian's thinking. But he felt sure since Parker's death that he had replaced his uncle's son's position as heir in Julian's eyes as well as on paper.

He was pretty sure that Julian would take care of him if their plans went awry. Just in case, though, he figured he'd better start spending his nights at home until the rumors of an investigation had settled down. If they weren't rumors, things might get a little hot for anyone too involved with The Blue Heron.

Elizabeth and Ben met on the first open afternoon at her Granddaddy's carpentry shop. Elizabeth had piano lessons on Monday afternoon; and on Tuesday after school, she and her sisters and Mama had driven up to Savannah and parked at the Park and Shop—and did just that.

They hadn't gotten home until after 9:00 PM. They'd eaten at Morrison's Cafeteria after shopping Levy's, J. C. Penney's, Asher's, and Punch & Judy on Broughton Street. Mama had even bought a bag of boiled peanuts from the sweet-faced "peanut lady" who always sat just under the Avon movie marquee. They had made a real evening of it.

So, it was Wednesday afternoon before the two could meet to open the metal box. Elizabeth and Ben had hidden it within the tool shop, which her Granddaddy kept unlocked. She'd put it under a pile of old tee shirts they kept for paint cloths in a lower cabinet he seldom used.

She retrieved it now, and Ben reached for the hack saw. She plunked the box down on the work counter and looked out the window to see if either one of her grandparents had come outside. They must be working on supper, she s'posed. She'd seen their car in the driveway when she and Ben had ridden up on their bikes. They'd parked them down the fence line and just beyond the grape arbor to keep the "unveiling" private. Ben wielded the hacksaw across the padlock's U-shaped shackle while she'd been checking the yard.

He let out an exasperated "Dag nabbit!" then explained, "I'm having a little trouble starting the cut. It keeps slipping on me."

I noticed he clamped the tip of his tongue between his teeth and pulled the blade slowly and determinedly across the original cut on the exposed prong of the U. Two more back cuts and he'd started the regular back and forth rhythm of sawing without it slipping.

Finally, I prompted, "Can I have a turn, Ben?"

"Oh," and Ben looked up apologetically. "Well, sure. I didn't think, you know. It is your Granddaddy's hacksaw," and he shot a crooked grin at 'Lizabeth. "Here," He said handing it over.

I took it, returned his smile, and began my own back and forth happily. I liked lots of "girl stuff", but there were things my Daddy and Granddaddy did that I liked, too. This was one of them that Claire and Janie thought was crazy.

About half way through the lock, I handed it back to Ben knowing how he was probably feeling. He grinned and thanked me and went to work. After a while, just a thin wire of metal was left holding the lock in place.

"Let's do the last stroke together," he said, making room for my hands on the hack saw handle.

It took two more strokes and it broke through. We were both so excited we fumbled with the lock, and made it take twice as long pulling it out of the box latch. Under the shade of the house, what we'd perceived as a "black box" was really a military green color and we both recognized it as an old, World War II Ammo box. It measured almost six inches by eleven by seven.

We opened it together. At the front of its contents, rested a gray book with fancy corners and the word "Ledger" written across it. Under that was a large manila folder of papers kind of curled over on itself because of the box being too little. In one corner, there was a stainless-steel cigarette lighter.

"Wow," Ben breathed picking up the lighter and turning it in his hands.

I just stared as he opened the lighter and closed it pressing buttons as he held it to his face. He made me nervous.

"You're gonna burn your nose," I complained.

He put it down and helped me pull the box closer to the edge so we could examine the stuff we found better. We decided to put it on the floor and sit down beside it.

Once we'd situated, he picked up the lighter, handed it to me, and said, "Take a closer look at this." I began to turn it over just as Ben had.

"It's a camera," he said. "I saw one just like it at the Drive In with my Mama and Miz Jensen back in Tallahassee. We used to go see older movies on 'Rerun Night'. They were cheaper," he laughed.

"It was a Gregory Peck/Audrey Hepburn movie—somethin' about a princess. Anyway, they had this lighter that was a secret camera and the guy snuck pictures with it!"

He paused to see if I was duly impressed. I was. We talked about that a bit, and wondered what Raynelle was doing with one of those. Ben thought it might have film in it still; and I said we'd take it to a friend of my sisters who was in the Camera Club at school.

"He can develop his own pictures!" I added.

Then we turned to the ledger. It had lots of numbers and some familiar names. Ben thought he'd seen Judge Connors' last name, but jerked up tightly when he recognized the Caudell surname amongst them. It looked like payment records. On the inside flap there was a pretty little blue stamp that looked like a heron in the water.

We closed that and went on to the papers. It seemed to be a letter, a business letter from its format. Ben looked puzzled when he read the address. It was a lawyer in Tallahassee and it was addressed to *Richard* Vincent Caudell—*his* Granddaddy. We wanted to read it right then, but we heard some commotion outside, and had to hide the box back in the cabinet.

We just had time to cover it with the cloths, and slip out a window at the back wall before my Granddaddy opened the front door to his work shop. I eased the window back in place, promising myself to come back and lock it later, just as my granddaddy strode in with a piece of wood in tow. We squatted quietly beside the back wall waiting for something to cover the sound of crunching leaves when we left.

Finally, I heard my Granddaddy start up his circular saw, and grinned at Ben. He wouldn't hear a thing now. We bent over and ran down the fence line that bordered the fields behind my Grandparents' house toward the grape arbor.

Chapter 7

"I have faith that each person's journey to know our God is significant and unique. No cookie-cutters. I have seen that nothing is ever wasted in His Hand; and what seems to us a horrible waste of choices and months and years, yet to Him can be all a part of the journey."
—James Thomas Rogers

I faced the entrance to one of Sayreville Prison's cell blocks. A big burly guard addressed me as he held the metal, barred door open.

"Chaplain Rogers, you can pass through."

This guard was new to me and we stood eye-to-eye as I noted his name tag and tried to memorize Keith's name and his face.

It had been necessary to me, especially at the beginning, for my own safety, to know people—especially staff, although there was no way I could know all of the prisoners. There were well over two thousand inmates, but I had learned a lot of them as the months had passed. I tried hard to connect names with faces, as well as learn my way around the prison. But it had always been important to me to remember the people God placed in my path.

Keith looked to be about my age, but the guard that was escorting me inside was familiar to me and about twenty years older than I was. An inmate was busy mopping the floor in front of us and the smell of cleaner assaulted my nose as we walked down the corridor. I was getting used to it though.

We headed down a long row of cells. I counted ten of them before Ted stopped and put the keys into the door. I peered between the bars and watched as the biggest guy I'd ever seen unfolded from the small prison cot and stood questioningly at the back of the cell.

I'd noticed before that prisoners often took this stance when guards opened doors. They stood awaiting the guard's instruction before approaching the door.

"You've got a visitor, Abrams," Ted told him.

I watched as the big man looked at me inquiringly.

"John? I'm James Rogers—chaplain here for anyone who needs one, or just a friend if you'd rather."

The door was pushed open then and the guard motioned for me to enter. I walked in and extended my hand to this big, silent man, smiling as evenly as I could. Inside, I was praying this was the right John Abrams and that Carolyn had gotten the facts straight from Abby—I wasn't a small man, but John Abrams made me feel like one.

He seemed to hesitate a minute and then leaned forward meeting my hand with his. While I wouldn't describe it as a hearty handshake, I did notice it was firm and sure. Only his eyes looked unsure.

"Abrams doesn't have a cellmate right now," the me, "so the warden decided you could meet him in here. But he says if you'd like, you can come back tomorrow and we'll put the two of you in the office room designated for meetings between prisoners and staff."

"Let us talk awhile and we'll decide, if that's okay?"

"Sure," Ted returned.

I heard the sharp clunk of metal on metal as the door closed. This sound always heightened my perception and caused a slight unease to my person. The guard withdrew to the end of the row of cells, and I willed my thoughts back to the plight of the big man at hand.

"John, my wife got a call from an old friend last night; well, her best friend from college—Abby Weston."

I watched his face lighten as he heard her name. His head came up from where he had been surveying his shoes.

"Abby?" he asked hopefully.

It was the first thing he'd said to me, and the first bit of light I'd seen in his eyes.

"Would you like to sit down, Chaplain?" and he motioned to the bunk across the cell from his.

We both sat. I took a deep breath.

"Carolyn, my wife, and Abby went to school together in 1958." He smiled. "Abby wanted me to come by and check on you—see if you were okay, and tell you she was praying for you."

I focused on John Colton Abrams' eyes while I talked. I watched them shadow and sadden as he listened. I knew it wasn't possible for one person to know another person's heart. Only God could know that, but I was about as sure as another person could be that this man had not hurt anyone.

"She wants to visit you, John," I said.

His eyes flared with hope and then as quickly as it had come, the light flattened to a deep sorrow. He was quiet. But then I thought this man carried a kind of quietness with him anyway.

His gaze had fallen to the floor again, and he just sat there on the bed across from the one I was sitting on for a long time. I waited him out.

Finally, he raised his eyes to mine and said, "She can't do that. You probably know, but I've got twenty-five years in this place. No chance of parole. I won't have her coming here. You tell her 'no', Chaplain."

He clamped his mouth together and seemed determined to say nothing more. I wriggled on the little cot uncomfortably, but all the while asking God for wisdom. What did I know about John Abrams and the years that most probably stretched before him here. And then there was Abby Weston.

There was a time in my life, when I would've jumped right in there and filled this deep silence with a lot of words. I was still young—I knew it. But I had learned some things—and a lot of them right here. There were times when words didn't help or cover anything. So, I just sat there for all of that extended silence and prayed for the man before me.

I prayed for the young woman who, Carolyn had assured me intuitively, loved him. I prayed for the two children I knew were somewhere in Alabama, who no doubt ached for their father. And I prayed that out there somewhere, God would change the heart of the person who had killed Raynelle Abrams.

Our visit was to last fifteen minutes—the warden had dictated the time; and at the end of a quarter of an hour, Ted came over and said our time was up. He began to unlock the door. So, I stood and told John that I held services on Sunday morning and I'd like him to come.

He looked steadily at me, and for just a moment I could see whether he'd come or not hung in the balance. He sighed and put his hands on his knees as he rose and extended his hand to shake mine.

"I'll be there if the warden will let me come," he said.

I turned and walked out of his cell, watching while the guard closed and relocked the door.

"I'd like to meet with you next week in the conference room, if I can okay that with the warden; and if you want to come?"

I paused and he nodded in the affirmative.

"And John, I haven't known Abby as long as you, or even as long as my wife has known her; and I'm going to tell her what you said. **But**. I'm pretty sure she's coming anyway whether you'll see her or not. Probably wait outside the gates and holler over if she's as stubborn as my wife is."

I smiled at him then and turned to follow Ted past the long row of cells. It was late in the afternoon. John had been the last of my visits for the day and I looked forward to seeing what light there was left of the afternoon outside this place.

Abby Weston's Home

I had just hung up the phone and still sat, pensively, while Persimmon curled in and out my legs. The little cat turned her piquantly expressive face upward to mine and then rose on hind legs, pushing with her front paws against my knee, to rub her head beneath my lowering hand.

Studying the little splotch of orange on her face that was typical of the tortoiseshell coloring, I informed her that that had been Carolyn. Sitting back on her haunches she returned my study with a now inscrutably calm expression; but I thought despite her impassive demeanor that she awaited further confidences.

Carolyn had called me just after dark—not too long after I'd gotten home from Barnes'. I had just finished up a little vegetable soup and a half a grilled cheese sandwich. It was one of my favorite meals for cold weather, but tonight it hadn't interested me at all.

I hurried to the kitchen counter at the br-r-ring of the old black phone's bells and gave my best hello in spite of the dreariness of my thoughts. The familiar voice on the other line was a relief. I knew I could relax and let my heart soreness out if I needed to.

My friend told me of her James' visit to John. I heard a smile in her voice as she told me how James had come home telling her that was the biggest man he'd ever shaken hands with. She told me he was healthy and currently had a cell by himself. That he had been cordial to James, though very sad—

"and Abby," she paused deliberating how to say it, "he was firm about you not visiting."

I hadn't counted on that and it hurt down to the depths of me. I wrapped my free arm over my stomach and bent quietly over it, laying my head on the cold counter beside the housing of the phone.

"Abby?" I heard the line crackle a little after my name. "Abby? Are you still there?"

Every now and again, you got cut off when using "long distance", and I knew I needed to reassure her, but I couldn't talk right then.

"If you can hear me, I'll call you back in a minute," I heard her say.

I waited until she hung up before I let my emotions "take voice". She rang back in about ten minutes just like she'd said, and I was ready with my apology. I managed to keep my emotions down enough to finish our call. She told me that Visitation for family and friends was on the second and fourth Sundays of the month normally.

"But," she'd added, "You have to be on the approved list of visitors, and that has to get both the prisoner and the warden's approval—unless the warden overrides it."

We were both quiet for few minutes.

"If I were you, Abby, I'd write to him. Give him a little time at that and then, we'll ask again. James says prisoners who aren't 'reprobate' often go through a deep depression and don't want to see anyone."

She paused again, and said softly, "James was very impressed with your Big John. He says he agrees with you, that John is innocent. But, Abby, if he is innocent, that means a murderer is on the loose in Freeman County, maybe. You be careful, Honey. Promise me."

And I did.

Then I asked her for the prison's address and details about how to address a letter to John. After we'd "three-partied" that through James, and I'd copied it down, I asked her how the baby was. I could hear the smile in her voice as she told me about the gymnast she'd been hosting for the past eight months. She laughed in that musical lilting way she had that always made me feel better.

I had to smile, too. Carolyn could make even Elise Parrish smile, I'd thought while still conversing with my old friend. Elise must've been about Cammie Caudell's age, and was a newcomer to Bennington. She'd been living in Freeman County for about a year and only came in to get her infrequent piece of mail or a forgotten item from her grocery needs.

But, she'd come in this afternoon just before I'd locked up for Mr. Barnes and had leaned over the counter as if to confide in me when I'd handed her a letter. Unfortunately, or fortunately, I couldn't decide, Harve Whitcomb had come in about that time, too, and wanted his mail as well as some items his wife had forgotten to pick up in Carverville.

Miz Parish had seemed peeved and turned on her heel and walked out without another word. I'd puzzled about that for some time, and here I was talking to Carolyn long distance and wondering about that strange woman again.

I was glad to let those thoughts go as I heard Carolyn tell me the doctor had told her she might need some help right after the birth. She said her Mother and brother's wife were coming for the first week, but wanted to know if I might come on the first weekend after they were gone.

"Maybe after that time, John won't be able to hold out against a visit," she put forth. "And you could stay with us over the next few days, if you can get off. Do-o-o, Abby," she wheedled in her most winsome voice.

I agreed readily to try to work that out with Mr. Barnes on a "when-the-baby-comes" basis. I smiled, then, and assured her I was praying for their little one and both she and James. She said, she had been praying for me and John and little Annie and Bo, too.

I heard James holler in the background, "Keep looking up, Abby!"

We hung up then, me feeling a little better, and at the other end, Carolyn pausing to pray for me as she put the phone back in its cradle.

Chapter 8

*"It's a whole lot more fun to read about mysteries than to live through
one with people you care about."*
—Elizabeth Ann Linden, age 10 years

The mantel clock chimed the hour. Four "bongs" broke up the silence of the room. The woman with the graying red hair had marked
off another Thursday from her calendar and now sat fidgeting at a
small card table on a folding chair eyeing Carverville's small-town newspaper. An article caught her eye and she pulled the sheet away from the
rest and began to cut out a small neat rectangle, the "swick-swick" of a
long wicked-looking pair of scissors the only sound, now that the clock
had hushed.

She had rented the small garage apartment to the side of Dennis and
Clara Hilton's home completely furnished almost a year ago. That was one
of the major reasons she had rented from Dennis Hilton the first week
she'd arrived in Bennington. All of her furnishings were in her family's
old home place in Pineville, Louisiana. Although, she had plenty of money from her father's estate she didn't have full access to the estate or
her funds, and she had no inclination to live in what she considered this
God-forsaken little county. So, she had been glad not to invest anything
in her surroundings. She was just here for a season. Long enough to take
care of three things—one of which she'd already "seen to". She slashed a
little too expressively with her scissors and cut across a headline. Grimac-
ing, Elise cleaned up the missing piece and placed it over its partner. She'd
fix that later, and pursing her lips she thought again of her first arrival in
Bennington.

When she had inspected the Hilton's apartment, Dennis had assured
her that she would only have to pay her rent, electricity and gas. Situated just inside of the Bennington city limits, she'd get her mail at Barnes'
"just down the road a mile or two". He was retired he'd confided, stayed at
home most of the time and would be ready to repair at a minute's notice,
should that unforeseen circumstance arise. His wife Clara worked; therefore, Elise hadn't met her until the day after she'd moved in. Interestingly
enough, she worked for the DA, Vince Caudell. Now there were two characters, Elise had thought. She continued cutting articles from the Carverville

Clarion and pasting them in a large, brown scrapbook. She hummed an unrecognizable melody, not seeming to realize it was off key.

That was probably the only mistake she'd made since coming to Freeman County, and she paused, the long black and silver scissors suspended above her clippings—well, of course, there was one more, but she'd find it yet. Living next door to Clara Hilton had been her first false step, but it did keep you on your toes, she had to admit. The doorbell startled her musing.

Elise placed the unfinished cut and the scissors between the pages of the scrapbook and carefully closed the cover over it. She put the book on top of the pile of newspapers she'd collected and walked to the door.

It took the woman a moment to pull back the bolt and turn the knob lock, she jerked the door open a little impatiently, and chided herself mentally—*careful now, Elise. Now's not the time to act out.* The odd thing was it sounded like her mother's voice instead of her thoughts.

She was brought back to the visitor at the door by a childish voice saying, "Hey, Miz Parrish. Miz Hilton thought you might not mind me coming by to see if—"

The child was interrupted with a snapped off "Well, I do mind! I'm busy right now."

Then the woman stopped in the middle of closing the door.

"Wait," she said emphatically. "Wait. What did you say now?"

The red-haired girl in a girl scout's uniform twisted the deep green sash decorated with badges between the fingers of her left hand and plunged in again with a bemused look on her face.

"Umm. I came to see if you'd like to buy Girl Scout Cookies. Miz Clara said she didn't think you'd mind."

Elizabeth Linden didn't add that Miz Clara's exact words had been, "Elise Parrish never has company and she's probably lonelier than old 'Lije Jones living back in the swamps. Go on up, girl. She'll thank you, I know."

Elizabeth thought this wasn't *her* idea of thanks, but she put forth the paper with the list of names of those who'd ordered cookies and handed over her mother's fountain pen, anyway.

Elise took the paper, and while studying it asked, "And your name is?"

"Oh," and the Girl Scout seemed a little embarrassed that she had belied their motto so miserably. "Well, uh, I'm sorry," and she smiled and started over, "My name's Elizabeth Linden."

"Well, then. Nice to meet you, Elizabeth Linden. My name is Elise Parrish."

Then she wrote something on the list of names and seemed to indicate a box of cookies. As she handed back the paper, she commented on Elizabeth's silver chain and ring.

"What a lovely ring," she cooed.

"Thank you, I found it at one of my Grandfather's rental houses," Elizabeth replied. "Mama said if I wore it, the one who lost it might see it, and I could find its owner that way. But my grandma says it looks old and has probably been lost a long time. She thinks all of the rains a few weeks ago unearthed it."

"Oh," she confided, "my initial's in it, too," and Elizabeth pointed at the cursive "**E**" engraved on the inside of the silver ring. "See. It says, 'To E from Papa'."

Then she admitted that she really loved the ring, even though it was obviously a man's by its size, and wasn't looking forward to losing it. Elizabeth was busy looking at the unusual silver signet ring and didn't notice the odd look that crossed Elise Lee Perkins Parrish's face.

The silver ring had an amethyst that covered almost the whole face of it, and had been carved into a heraldic lion. 'Lizbeth had talked to the town jeweler about it only last week, because he attended their church and was also a history buff and a great lover of antique jewelry. He had informed her that it was a "passant lion". The lion had its right paw in the air with the other three on the ground in a walking stance. The lion itself was looking forward in the direction it was going—and the jeweler had given it a profile pose.

The early English had called it a leopard because of its profile walking stance although they actually recognized it as a lion. The name referred to the walking attitude of the lion. Also, he had told her that it was only about two hundred years old and not the medieval find she'd hoped it had been. He had shown her the markings on the inside of the ring embedded in silver by the craftsman who had made it.

Mr. Miller had looked up the Felton name in a book of heraldry he owned and found that their family crest did indeed feature a passant lion. And Elizabeth had hugged that fact to herself, knowing that no one had heard of the Felton family in many, many years. Then he'd assured her that it was a beautiful work of artistry and probably worth a good deal of money.

Elizabeth reluctantly turned from inspecting the ring and took the Cookie Brochure from Elise.

While looking over Mrs. Parrish's entry, she added, "I'll bring the cookies by in a couple of weeks. You don't have to pay until delivery. Oh, and I'll call before I come to make sure you're here," then she paused and noted, "Oh. Your first name starts with an E, too! It's not yours, is it?" and she extended the necklace out from her neck so that the ring dangled before them as she laughed.

She was greeted by silence and a suspicious look. The longer she stayed at Miz Parrish's door the more uneasy she felt.

"Oh. I didn't mean anything by that, Miz Parrish. You okay?"

The chilly winter wind circled between them pouring in through the open door. Miz Parrish seemed to "come to herself" then, and shaking the short curls of carrot red hair infused with gray, she looked out beyond Elizabeth, and noted the girl's mother waiting in the car below.

Miz Parrish offered by way of explanation, "Nothing's wrong. I just have other things to do."

There was an icy pause before she continued. "Be sure you call before you come."

She seemed to have missed Elizabeth's promise of a phone call before delivery, and she shut the door quite firmly. Elizabeth wondered about that visit all the way downstairs and to her mother's car. She related what had occurred as they sat in the car outside Clara Hilton's home.

Finishing up with a "She was kind'a weird, Mama," she turned to look once again at the garage apartment as they pulled off, and saw the window curtains move back into place just as she turned her head.

It wasn't just the strangeness of her customer that disturbed Elizabeth. There was a worrisome feeling that she'd seen Miz Parrish's face before, and she couldn't remember where.

The Caudell House was silent except for the echoing of Aunt Cammie's footsteps, which only served to punctuate the quiet of a peaceful Saturday morning in a house that was young before the War between the States. Still, I could tell she was trying to hold the staccato tapping of her high heels to a quiet cadence.

This particular Saturday found me finally admitting I'd like to ride my bike over to Elizabeth Linden's. We had wanted to read some articles and ride by a friend of her sisters, I'd told them. Of course, by "them" I meant my Granny and Aunt; certainly not my Uncle Vince who was still asleep upstairs.

My uncle had spent the night at home for a change, but had come in stone sober, if a little grumpy. He never acted crazy when he was sober, so I decided it would be okay to go on over to 'Lizabeth's. Especially since he was still asleep, and Granny and Aunt Camille were making a point of being real, real quiet—I'd noticed.

Elizabeth had a tree house her Daddy had made with Adam when he was little, and 'Lizabeth had inherited it. It had a rope and pulley system to raise up anything too bulky to carry up. It had walls, too, and windows. We were climbing it now and had gotten the tin box from her Grandpa's work shop and placed it in the milk crate that was attached to her pulley system.

After we got up, we easily rolled it on up to the railed deck of the treehouse. This was great, I thought. I wished for the hundredth time that Uncle Vince were a different sort of man. I didn't have too much time to feel sorry for myself, though. We hauled in the crate, pulled the tin box out of it, and took it inside her hideaway. We sat down at an old Formica table with two spindly metal chairs and vinyl seats looking a little the worse for wear. Then we began to study the contents of the tin more thoroughly.

It didn't take too many minutes before we both had our mouths agape. I had grabbed the letter when I saw it was about my Mama oblivious to Elizabeth's "supposed ownership". It was only a couple of sheets and intimated at things the lawyer wanted to say in person about my mother's whereabouts for the last fifteen years—who had been involved in her kidnapping, and why she hadn't made her way back home—stuff like that. I think I must've been in some kind of shock. I'd never even *known* she'd been *kidnapped.*

It was some time before I began to wonder how Raynelle Abrams had possession of my Grandpa's letter, and if he had ever even received it or not. And then I wondered, who could've kept him from getting it?

Abby leaned over the bed to the far side where a black phone sat on her night table. Her hands shook a little as she replaced the heavy receiver in its cradle. She registered the fluttering in the pit of her stomach and wasn't too surprised to find her legs weren't the reliable limbs she thought them as she stumbled across the rug to her closet.

She pulled out a small stool from behind the hanging dresses, stepped on it, and reached for the white marbled Samsonite suitcase resting on the shelf. Banging it around between the door frame and shelf, she finally extricated the thing from her closet and set it on her bed; then began to pilfer her chest of drawers for clothing.

Despite her emotions, she tried to stack her things neatly and quickly. She turned from the drawers to her closet and began to pull out dresses and fling them over the suitcase her mind busily reviewing the phone call.

It had been the wee hours of the morning and Abby had wakened from a deep slumber. She felt befuddled and fearful at hearing Carolyn's husband's voice. He had told her Carolyn's sister-in-law had had appendicitis and had her appendix out yesterday. Carolyn's Mother was keeping their toddler and five-year-old for her son and daughter-in-law and could not come for the birth of their grandchild.

Then he'd said excitedly, "I'm at the hospital, Abby. The doctor thinks by dawn I might be holding our baby!"

She'd had to smile. This otherwise calm young preacher was short of breath as his words tumbled out one upon another. When she'd hung up she'd prayed for Carolyn, the baby, and James. Then she'd had to pray for herself. She felt shakier than James had sounded and not only for her friend, but the thought of one large man had given her the jitters.

Midway to the finish of her packing, she had calmed and begun to "streamline" her efforts. This was more like it, and she heaved a big sigh letting out the last of her tremors. Tying the silken sashes over her clothes, she mentally ticked off the things she needed to do before locking her house and heading out to Sayreville.

A full moon poured light through her windows. She walked over and paused before pulling the curtains back to center. Earlier that night, she had opened them as she stood musing at the wide-open sky filtered only by the familiar silhouette of the old live oak that cradled her side of the house. Abby smiled wryly at herself.

She had been considering the letter she'd mailed at Barnes' four days ago. She had firmly refrained from scenting it, and had poured more effort into its composition than anything she'd ever written. Painstakingly, she had printed John C. Abrams name and number across the front and the address of the prison below. Would he notice the neat flare of her handwriting or recognize it as hers? Would he even read it for that matter?

Things seemed to fall so easily into place for so many folks. But there had never been anything easy about her feelings for John Colton Abrams. Not from the first moment she'd seen him as she'd stepped off her bus to head to her third-grade classroom.

Across the school grounds, she had seen three older boys surrounding another one. Every now and again one would take a shot at him from his back; and kids came running from all over with shouts of "A fight! A fight!"

She'd jerked her satchel a little higher as she'd resumed her walk to her class. She could see her path led right by the four boys. The closer she got, the more it raised her temper. Never one to tolerate injustice even at this young age, each step brought with it a searing anger. It was Harve Whitcomb, the biggest coward and bully in the school, and with him his buddies, Will Hilton and Bruce Lyle.

She could hear Harve razzing the new boy about how sorry his parents were and how they'd cheated his Dad. He didn't get much further with his shoving and taunting, because that last one must've been too much for the new boy. The tall, gangly boy with shaggy dark hair drew back and laid a right cross on Harve's nose, who stumbled back in the dust yowling and holding his bloody proboscis.

Meantime, Will had tripped the newcomer from behind, and Bruce, who was quite a bit overweight, plopped down on their victim's stomach and began to pommel his face. She watched as Harve stomped at the boy's hand and missed. Harve had wiped his nose on his shirt, and upon seeing his "victim" in the dirt, continued to hold his nose with his left hand and rejoined the fray.

Will was helping Bruce hold the tall kid down and Harve went around kicking their victim wherever he could find a place to kick. Nobody said anything much about their ganging up on the boy, because nobody wanted to have to deal with the three of them about it.

Abby had always been shy and preferred the background to the forefront of any situation, but her temper had taken over and she pushed in between the crowd and shoved Harve Whitcomb back in the dirt as hard as she could. He hadn't expected a spectator to take up the fight and the hard clip she gave the bully sent him sprawling in the dirt.

The sideways flight of his friend caught Bruce's attention for a minute and allowed the new boy to buck him off into the dirt beside Harve.

"Oof!" was all she heard out of Bruce.

Then their "victim" made good use of their surprise and jumped up from the dirt to knock Will Hilton right down beside the other two. Bruce just lay there gasping like he'd had the breath knocked out of him.

Harve and Will were acting like they were trying to get up and rejoin the fight, but didn't seem too eager. In the end, Mr. Hansen, our principal, saved them the effort. He dispersed the crowd and quietly told the four to come with him. Somehow, he'd missed my participation in the event, and I looked the new boy over good as they all turned to go. He trailed last and turned to me.

"Girls ain't s'posed to fight, you know. I'd a'got 'em in the end," he whispered firmly and *I* thought, *ungratefully.*

His brows were down low over his gray eyes, and I couldn't believe it! He seemed mad with *me!* Later, I learned that this was John Abrams, the boy Mr. Burt Melton and my Dad had unknowingly inspired me to pray for all those years ago.

A hoot owl's call off in the deep woods brought my musing to a close. The urgency of the trip and the piles of things I had to do before I left were once again uppermost in my thinking. I closed the curtains and picked up the notes—one to Mr. Barnes and one to Earl and Rennie. They were just reminders of the circumstances and thanks for all they were allowing me to do by their understanding and help.

Earl and Rennie had promised to feed Blue, Deacon and Persimmon. I'd already talked over everything with each of them and knew that as far as I could plan, things would be okay at home and work. I planned to drop both letters off at Rennie's, entrusting my employer's letter to their delivery as soon as the store had opened.

I had been reminded many times to call Rennie once I'd arrived in the little town where James and Carolyn Rogers lived.

I lugged the old suitcase and the letters downstairs and left them beside the door under the portico which was the kitchen entrance. I took the time to make three roast beef sandwiches, one for the trip, and the other two for James and me while we waited at the hospital—I figured he'd be hungry, too. Then, I poured a steaming cup of tea with lots of milk before leaving.

Tucking two slices of Rennie's Graham Cracker Crumb Cake in a piece of tin foil, and, yes, the extra was for James, I shoved it and the sandwich in a brown paper bag. As an afterthought, I added a package of Teaberry Gum and some peppermint sticks to help keep me awake. Driving at night always worked like a lullabye for me, and that would never do.

I checked all the locks, then paused at the door to rub Deacon and Blue behind their ears. Deacon rolled over and insisted on a belly rub while Blue ambled back to his space by the gas heater. I picked up my little tortoiseshell and scratched underneath her chin and placing her on the floor gave her the full length rub up to the tip of her tail. She of course was purring full strength by this time and I gave them the prerequisite speech about being good.

Turning to the door I spied Daddy's old woolen coat. I smiled at it and gave it a pat before gathering up my little load for the car. I managed to get the whole armload of letters, purse, bag, Bible and a magazine out to the Bug while dragging the suitcase along beside me.

Having stuffed everything except my purse and the paper bag in the back seat, I ran back to get the tea and lock the door. The little car burbled to life and I couldn't help, but smile.

"Now, Carolyn," I said aloud, "hang on just a few more hours. I'm coming." And then, "Look out, Big John."

John's precious daughter and son had been living for the last three months in Phenix City, Alabama with their beloved "Lyddie" who was really Raynelle's aunt. It was just a bit past their bedtime, and they had been asleep for about thirty minutes when Lydia heard the little noise.

She turned on the hall light and opened their door quietly. John's little Annie was sitting up in bed staring at the door as it opened. Her Aunt approached quietly to avoid waking Bo.

When she got close enough she could see traces of tears down the little girl's cheeks, and Annie in her turn, looked up into her Great Aunt Lydia's deep blue eyes, and whispered, "Lyddie, I can't sleep."

Lyddie's eyes crinkled, adding to the wrinkles that etched her face, as she smiled at this sweet baby.

"Oh, Honey. I'm sorry. Did you have a bad dream?" and she sat down on the side of Annie's bed to Annie's right—between her and the window.

"Well, yes," and Annie looked down at the big Teddy Bear she was rubbing and clutched him a little tighter. "I have it a lot. It's about my Daddy."

Here she looked back up at her Lyddie and asked, "If I tell you, will you promise never to tell? 'Cause I promised Mama I would never tell. She said if I did that we would all have to go to *prison*. But now I don't know what to do. Daddy, my second Daddy, is already there, you know? Maybe it wouldn't be so bad if we could stay with him in the prison place."

Great Aunt Lydia looked befuddled, but tried to project calm and security for her little niece. Bo was asleep in a trundle bed just beside Annie's twin one, so she had to keep her "projecting" on the quiet side.

"I tell you, Annie. Why don't we get up and have a cup of tea and a cookie? And we'll talk about it at the kitchen table. Don't wake Bo though, or we'll just be listening to him."

And here the old lady chuckled in spite of herself. She had come to love these children more than she could've imagined in the three and a half months she'd had custody. Their mother was her little sister's daughter.

Lyddie's sister, Nell Ann had gotten pregnant late in life. Raynelle was born when Nell Ann was in her early forties. Both Nell Ann and her husband Ray were gone now. Lydia's own husband, Frank, had died about ten years ago with emphysema. He'd loved to smoke and his hands shook if he didn't have one between his fingers.

Lydia was the only one left of the family. She and her husband had never been able to have any children and now even Nell Ann's beautiful and wild daughter was gone. But she had these two, and she had come to cherish them.

She helped Annie up and smiled as the seven-year-old gathered her teddy bear to her like he was an only child. They tiptoed out of the room with Bo never having heard a thing. He was smiling peacefully as they eased the door to.

Downstairs, each behind a cookie and a cup of tea with lots of milk and sugar, Annie's Lyddie smiled and asked her what was troubling her so. Annie's lips thinned and she pulled the bottom one under the top one as she thought.

She had placed her teddy bear in the chair beside her and he had a cup and saucer, too. She fastened her big blue eyes on her Aunt Lyddie seriously, then hesitantly she began.

"My Daddy come to see me," she said.

Lyddie stilled and waited out the words the little girl needed to say without interrupting—a very common failing in adults she thought—*interrupting.* Annie continued.

"I mean my first Daddy, Lyddie," she specified. "He came to see me when we lived in Louisiana. Before Big John. Before Bo," and her niece stopped again—Lyddie guessed to let that sink in.

It's a bad thing when even the babies know you're getting old, the old lady mused. She squelched the urge to smile, and returned the little girl's questioning look with an "I-understand" one and a slight affirmative nod.

"Mama and him—they argued. Well, I seem to 'member they did that a lot when he came. Daddy had brung me a teddy bear for my birthday. This'n," and she pointed at Coop beside her, then continued, "He said he was goin' to move into a house real close to me, so's he could see me any time he wanted. Then ma' Mama told me to take Coop up to my room so's she could talk to ma' Daddy; but on the way there, I could hear 'em fussin'. So, I turned 'round to see what they wuz fussin' about this time, and I heard her say, 'You cain't have 'er. Not now! Not ever!'"

"He got up from the chair so sudden then it crashed over. I still 'member, Lyddie. I don't think I'll ever forget. He made for her then like he could kill 'er, and she hit him with a cast iron pot she'd grabbed off the stove. But when he fell, his head hit this big metal thing—I think it was a radio-ater."

A tear slipped down Annie's cheek and made its way to her collarbone. Lyddie sat stock still, torn between going to her niece and letting her finish her story. She got up and tottered over, squatting down by Annie's chair and hugging her. Then she interrupted—there were sometimes adults just couldn't help themselves, "Oh, baby. I'm so sorry."

"Lyddie. I was little then, and I guess I'm still little, but I don't think either one of them meant to do that. They just couldn't ever seem to get along for long at the time."

Annie said it in a monotone, more tears spilling down her face and onto her pajamas. Little Annie waited a bit before she continued, "She saw me then. She turned and saw me and kind'a screeched-like. Then she ran to me and told me that about the prison and how we'd have to keep it a secret just between us two. Never tell nobody, she said. And I agreed. But I couldn't stop crying. He was my *Daddy*, Lyddie. He was *good* to me. He *never* fussed at *me*."

She heaved a deep breath for a little girl and continued, "Mama waited till really late and then drug him to his car. She laid him in the front seat kind of crumpled between the floor and the door. She told me to ride in the back seat. Took us a long time. I don't know where we went. I cried myself to sleep, I guess, 'cause when I woke the car was stopped and Mama was puttin' Daddy behind the wheel."

"She told me to get out then. We wuz out in the swamps somewhere, the bayou maybe. I don't know. She had brung that pan with her and took a few swings at his headlight—which she'd left on. She threw that big iron pan as far as she could out in the water. Then I heard her say, 'Hellman's Creek. That's a good restin' place for you.' I don't know if she was talkin' 'bout the pan or my Daddy. I never knowed."

"She rolled down the windows—every one of 'em, and made me get way back away from the car. I think she might have done something to the gears. I know she cranked it up, 'cause I could hear the motor start again. It was rolling a little bit and she ran around to the back of his car and kind'a sat on the bumper. Then she started to shove with her back and it started to roll faster. It rolled down the incline and right on down into the water. We waited until it had sunk the whole way down. And then she suddenly screamed a word I ain't supposed to say, so I won't."

Annie paused for a breath here. "Anyway, she said she'd left her purse in that blasted car, and why didn't I remind her to get it. She yelled the last part, and I kind of backed up. But she said to come back, she was okay now."

"I was glad I hadn't brought Coop with me." Lydia knew that Annie meant the teddy bear her Daddy had given her.

"He was almost all I had left of my Daddy, and I'm pretty sure he would've gone down, too."

Annie looked up at Lyddie.

"We walked a long ways after that. I don't know how far. Mama carried me some, but then she said I'd have to walk for myself after awhile. We come to a farm house and she made me hide in the woods with her beside the road until mornin'. When we saw the lights come on, we walked up to that farmhouse, and she asked the man there could she use his phone. 'No use to do that,' he'd said, and told my Mama he'd be glad to take us back to town if that's where we needed to go."

"She bummed a cigarette off'a him and after she'd smoked a bit, agreed to it. She made him take her to a hotel on the other side of town. She said we were from Mississippi and had hitchhiked all the way to wherever that place was; that when the last ride let us out, they'd taken our stuff and shoved us out. Then she told him we'd gotten lost."

"After he drove up to the hotel, she got rid of him pretty quick. Mama was good at stuff like that. She made like we was going in the hotel and call her brother—and the man got mad an' left. An' after that, she borrowed a dime from the desk clerk and called Miz Betty Sue—Mama worked with her at the café. They wuz friends."

"Anyway, Miz Betty Sue, she picked us up not too long after and drove us home."

"Mama began to get calls from my Aunt Elise, then. Aunt Elise was my Daddy's sister, you remember don't you, Lyddie?" And she paused for another nod from the old lady.

"I know because she complained to me about her. Pretty soon after, we moved. Not too long after that, Mama met Big John at the Laundromat."

It was quiet in the big yellow kitchen then. Surrounded by sunny colors and gleaming appliances and counters, the old lady and the little girl sat curled in each other's arms and wept together.

Chapter 9

"No matter the uncountable number of times it has happened before, the birth of a baby is always such a miracle, such a hope and wonder."
—Abigail Faith Weston

Ben and Elizabeth had agreed to hold off on turning over the papers to the sheriff until they'd found what the little camera contained. They replaced the papers and the ledger, but kept the lighter/camera out when they'd hidden the box in the tree house. Ben pocketed the little camera and they rode bikes over to Gordon Clarke's house.

Gordon came outside and sat on the porch with them, because his little sister was practicing the French Horn.

"It's awful," he'd complained as he sat down on the stoop—and they could still hear the proof of his complaint sliding off notes loudly through their firmly shut front door.

"Now, show me this camera Claire was telling me about."

Ben pulled it out and handed it to the older boy. Gordon turned it over and over and made a little whistling noise of amazement.

"I've never seen anything like it."

He kept marveling at it and seemed honored we'd brought it over to him to see if it had film.

"I tell you," he'd finally volunteered, "I'll take it in my dark room and see if I can open it. If I can and there's film there, I'll develop it for free."

Gordon's father was a camera freak, too, and so they had worked together to set up a dark room for film development; and thoroughly enjoyed their hobby together. I don't need to tell you we were some pleased. But Ben and I took the time to tell him about the need for secrecy for a little while and how important the film might be to John Abrams' future.

I knew Gordon was a "good guy" from my sisters and felt pretty secure in trusting him.

"It could be dangerous," I added, "that you know whatever this film contains. So. Don't. Tell. *Anyone*. Not even the police."

I think he got it. He nodded and said, "I'll call you if I have anything when I finish."

We gave him both our numbers, then pedaled away for lunch.

Abby had arrived with the dawn. Carolyn was still in delivery, and when Abby entered the waiting room beside the nursery section of the hospital, the first thing she saw was the broad back of Carolyn's James, hunched over, one hand in the pocket of his dress pants, and the other rumpling his brown hair into wild disarray.

He was stationed by the windows and seemed to be staring fixedly through the glass. It was silvered around the edges since they had had an unseasonably heavy frost the night before.

He abruptly walked away from the window and plopped down in a chair that was one of those unyielding mostly metal and vinyl varieties sported by hospitals of that time. He leaned way over, and propping his elbows on his knees, he cupped his hands into a single fist. Then he pushed his forehead onto his interlocking fingers.

Abby could see his brow wrinkled in deep concentration and noted that he'd closed his eyes. She knew he was praying for all he was worth. Her heart dropped as she rushed toward him.

He opened his eyes again as Abby drew up in front of him.

"Abby."

"Is she alright?"

I couldn't keep the worry out of my voice.

"Yeah, I think she's alright. They let me come in for a minute to see her about an hour ago. They were going to give her twilight sleep."

"Oh. I guess that's good, huh?"

I really didn't know too much about hospital procedures in the delivery room, but I could hear strange sounds emanating from its general vicinity, and I wondered. I had been praying all the way there, and in between James and my talking, I kept right at it.

Were there any other women in there?" I asked.

"Oh. Hmmm?"

He had been either in deep thought or prayer and hadn't heard me. I repeated the question, and he answered, "Two, I think. But neither one of them are as far along as Carolyn. The doctor thinks she might deliver fast," and he looked over at me worriedly.

I tried to smile reassuringly, however you do that. He seemed unfazed and propping his head in his hands, began to rub his temples as he returned to staring mode with the object of his focus seeming to center on his shoes. I followed his gaze and realized he had on one blue sock and one black one. I had to smile at that, but said nothing to him about it.

It seemed like we sat there forever. Once, I was sure I had heard Carolyn cry out. This was nerve wracking stuff. James and I had short bursts of conversation and long stretches of silence. I could sense that he was still praying and I helped him silently.

On our first trip to the coffee area, I had remembered the roast beef sandwiches and took them out to offer James one. He looked like a starving man eyeing a steak. We ate almost in silence except for the occasional "mmm-ing" noises James seemed unaware he was making.

We headed back for the "waiting room", only to put in more of that. We kept visiting the coffee area, and pacing to the window, and every so often, James would go to the window and ask the lady stationed there if she would mind checking to see how Carolyn Rogers was doing. After a while they were on a first name basis.

There was the obligatory clock on the wall to watch, of course, and its hands seemed to be moving through sludge. So, we talked a bit more, and wondered whether their baby was a girl or boy. Then, we talked about

Carolyn. Mostly, we shared funny stories from the past, and even managed a good laugh or two between us. We prayed together a few times, and a nurse came out once and told us that Mrs. Rogers was doing well. And, no, she didn't think it would be long now.

"That's good, then," we both mumbled in our own variations.

I fumbled through my purse and found what was left of my Teaberry gum from the trip. I took the one spindly flat stick of freshness and offered him half, as I tore it. He smiled slightly, said thanks, devested it of its wrapper and slid it between his teeth.

Finally, I thanked him for going to see John, and asked if he'd talked to him recently.

"Oh," and James lightly smacked his head. "I meant to tell you. He came to the Sunday Services, and I really think he's doing better. We had a long talk the other afternoon. He got your letter. I think, Abby, that letter meant a lot to him." He paused here and made sure I was returning his focus, "He says, he'd like to see you once. Just one time though. He has some things he'd like to say to you. They have visitation on the second and fourth Sunday of the month. That fourth one of course will be this Sunday. If you can be there in the afternoon, he's put your name on his list."

I pulled in a breath then, as quietly as I could, realizing I hadn't been breathing, but listening so intently I'd forgotten to. It felt like my heart had been let loose from some kind of vise, and I knew that I couldn't keep the joy from spreading all over my face.

"James. *Thank* you. *So* much," I managed somewhat breathlessly.

And right at this juncture the doctor pushed the double doors to the delivery open and came striding out. He was pulling off a white mask, and used it to wipe his forehead.

"Well, James, you've got twins," and he grinned broadly, as James and I gasped together.

"Your little boy was born first and then a little girl. Congratulations!" and he shook James' hand vigorously in spite of the doctor's obvious exhaustion.

"I've got to go back now. The nurse will come after you in a minute so you can see them. Mama and babies are doing fine!" and he turned and disappeared into the inner recesses of the Maternity Ward.

James had his hand rubbing at the back of his head now and a wide silly grin pasted across his face.

"Well, can you believe it!! Two! Hey! I've got to call my folks and Carolyn's. They're coming next week."

He purely strutted to the payphone near the snack area and began pulling change from his pockets. I rummaged through my purse to help him. You could get carried away talking about such an extraordinary event as the birth of your first baby, but twins! I hoped between the two of us that we'd have enough money for his calls.

Vince had been sleeping in the old Caudell mansion nights and leaving off visits to the Heron. He'd heard from Dale that a certain long-legged blonde had been missing him. His brow puckered with irritation. Word had come down through some of Julian's contacts that the GBI were definitely sending a few men down in the coming weeks. With the knowledge that GBI involvement was a fact, fear had been growing to an all-pervasive presence in the DA's mind. Nothing that had mattered to him in the past was of any consequence—there was only this controlling, debilitating fear. He wished they had that ledger and the letters that infernal Raynelle had stolen the night he'd taken her to the Judge's house.

It had happened last summer, about three and a half months before she was killed. Uncle Julian's wife, Charlotte, had gone to her sister's in Augusta for the week. Julian dismissed all his normal staff and had the house to himself that Friday night. Vince brought Raynelle over and another girl from the Heron for the evening. The Judge had arranged for their cook to leave supper in the kitchen for him before she'd left; and after they had eaten, Raynelle asked where the "little girl's room" was. She'd grinned then, and the judge explained she'd have to walk down the hall past his study to the last room on the right.

She'd jerked up her big purse and smiled about as sweetly as Raynelle could.

"I'll be right back," she had assured them.

Only somewhere along the way, Julian and Vince had figured she made a little side trip to his uncle's study—whether by accident or with purpose, they never knew; but she found the ledger and letter that the Judge had left in an open security box on top of his desk. Julian had pulled out the box from his safe earlier with the intention of destroying that old letter addressed to Richard Caudell from the lawyer in Tallahassee about Vince's half-sister, Connie.

However, in his wife's absence, the judge had already been drinking and became careless when the doorbell signaled Vince's arrival. Julian had acquired the lawyer's letter by warning Vince to watch for an envelope addressed to Richard from a lawyer in Tallahassee.

Their felonious obstruction of the delivery of the US Mail had occurred almost three years ago. Richard had been dead then, but Vincent, who shared his father's first name, and was by this time living with his step-mother, checked the mail diligently at Barne's until he'd spotted it and took it to his uncle's to peruse at the judge's home office.

Julian's source, surprisingly was Ed Norris, Rich and Lee's own hired detective. Back when their ten-year-old daughter, Connie, had first disappeared, the Judge had advised Richard to find a good detective to search for her. He'd then recommended Ed Norris, saying the law offices often hired him when cases required it.

Julian had let Richard pay Ed and he'd topped off the payment generously for hiding Connie's whereabouts from the Caudells with promises of further rewards at the end of the ordeal. The PI had kept a close watch on the girl and successfully preempted any communication she had tried except this one letter which led to her demise.

Chapter 10

"To paraphrase Burns' poem, 'The plans of a man are prefaced by a huge IF.' And I thank God it is so."
—Richard Vincent Caudell, Sr.

E d Norris had only had to intercept two attempts to contact Richard and Eulee Caudell since Connie Caudell had achieved adulthood.

From the first moment in that Savannah truck stop, when her half-brother, Vince had asked her to take the keys, go out to their Dad's car, and retrieve his wallet from the glove compartment; a steady diet of misinformation had been fed to the young girl.

Once she had left the café, in the Jensens' terms—she had been easy pickin's. Connie, at ten years old, posed no obstacle to her hired kidnappers. A middle-aged couple, also hired by the Judge, simply played on her sense of respect for her elders, and her natural empathy toward someone in need to assist them in a flawless kidnapping.

As planned they had placed the keys Vincent had given them, to Richard's car, under the driver's seat then left quickly with a blanketed Connie sprawled unconscious on their back seat. The next six years had been spent mostly in a series of basements and back rooms at their mercy—or lack of it.

Between the Jensens and Ed Norris, Connie had been thoroughly subjugated. No one in the places they had chosen to live during the first few years of her confinement had any idea that the "sweet" middle-aged couple had anyone besides themselves within their home.

Later, Norris had so bullied and overpowered the girl, that she had been afraid to acknowledge anyone even when in public. She kept her head down at all times and learned to get from one destination to another while looking at her feet.

Of course, she never left the house without Norris' or either the Jensens' escort even at the end of six years in what amounted to solitary confinement. After noting a decline in their captive's health, the older couple began to make noises about a healthier environment for the girl. The Jensens maintained if she could spend time "above ground" and amongst other people –of course, never unaccompanied by one of them, that she would begin to put on weight and look healthier, too.

Mrs. Jensen particularly had been worried about her physical health and insisted that she did not want to face that horrible Georgia Judge if Connie went into a worse decline or perhaps died. And Norris, not knowing Julian's ultimate intentions for Connie's life, thought on this and felt there was some merit to her argument. But mostly he began to like the idea of accompanying the young Caudell girl on her outings.

With the Judge's approval, they rented a house near the gulf in Alabama and out in the country. There were no near neighbors and they had Ed install an industrial height cyclone fence with barbed wire at the top in the back yard with a padlocked gate. Norris and the Jensens allowed her access to the outdoors in that location so that she could regain a healthy tan and pick up some weight. She was almost wraith-like and beyond willowy in those days. Mr. Jensen brought home a puppy to occupy Connie and for a period of about four months she was almost happy.

Unfortunately, with the regaining of her health and her quickly approaching seventeenth birthday; she also began to "fill out", and with a lightly curled mass of auburn hair that was only overshadowed by huge deep blue eyes she had become a beautiful young woman.

This necessarily caught Ed Norris' eye. Over the past years, he had made her believe that her parents and anyone else she contacted would not live to act on it. His "attentions" became more pronounced especially when the Jensens were absent. His presence so disturbed her that she had tried to lose Norris on a city street en route to a dental appointment. He caught her before she'd made a city block, an alley providing a convenient solitary place for correction.

The next day, Ed had brought in two of his buddies—they were big guys and they looked not only tough, but their eyes had a cold "absence" about them; she couldn't have described it, but it was chilling. J.C. and Della had been sitting at the kitchen table with Connie, just finishing up lunch. The entrance of the three had brought their meal to an abrupt end. The two men even made the Jensens nervous when Norris had introduced them; and the couple had quickly claimed business in town. After their departure, the room remained still with three pairs of eyes focusing on her.

Norris cleared his throat and told her icily that these gentlemen had

been hired by her parents in Bennington as grounds keepers and handy-
men, but were, in actuality, watching the Caudell's every move. He assured her blandly that her folks were alive and well, but wouldn't be if they
heard anything from her.

She had believed him, after one of them had let her see a series of pictures of her parents walking in their garden. The pictures had been taken
two years ago, just before Richard died, but Connie was unaware of any of
these details. She'd gasped and sprung from the table, sending her chair
backward to the floor.

Connie made a grab at the pictures, shocked at seeing them, and over-
whelmed by her desire to just look at them. *Her parents looked so much
older.* The younger man who'd been holding out the pictures, snatched
them back from her, glancing at Ed, who'd nodded at him. He held them
above his head while his partner grabbed her from behind.

She watched helplessly as he crumpled the pictures in his hand, threw
them on the stove's gas burner and lit it. He released her then and she
covered her face and turned away from them, unwilling for the three to see
her inner depths on display. She heard them leave, her shoulders shaking
with the great heaving gulps of air she'd drawn.

Before she regained her composure, Norris grabbed at her arms and
shoved her out to the patio in the back yard. Stubby, the mixed breed
Della Jensen had brought home to Connie, came dancing up to her, but
cowered as soon as he caught Ed's presence.

"Sit!" he bellowed at her.

They both did—she in an aluminum lawn chair and little Stubby on
the concrete just to her side.

Connie knew that Norris always carried his gun in a black leather
shoulder holster, but she was totally blind-sided when he stepped around
her, and without any hesitation drew it from his side and shot the dog
she'd taken such comfort in having. Sheathing the weapon, he turned to
lay the retribution at her door.

Since the first twenty-four hours of her captivity, Connie had been
docile and easily intimidated; but the death of the little dog birthed a sudden warrior. She plowed into the big man before her, nails and teeth doing
as much damage as she could manage; at the same time, she kicked and
pounded anywhere she could land a blow.

At first stunned by her aggression, he quickly came to his senses and hastened to overcome her. Although, he hadn't just talked aggression in the past, but had exercised it over the petite auburn-haired girl—it had never been enough to send her to the hospital. In the fight that followed, Norris cast off any restraint he'd ever had.

He could feel a burning dribble of blood at the side of his face where she'd inflicted her own retribution. The Jensens weren't there to curb his anger or the extent of the form of his punishment of the girl; and Ed Norris had a gut desire to crush that stupid kid. She'd almost blown the whole set up he'd had with the judge.

When all her fight was gone, he locked her in a walk-in closet off the hall of their rental. Norris felt shaken enough to have been battling a man, and the girl had slumped to the floor as soon as the door shut. He experienced a sense of foreboding at what he'd done. But he knew he'd crushed any idea she'd had of rebellion.

He laughed. It hadn't just been her rebellion, he'd crushed *her*.

In about three months' time, Mrs. Jensen discovered Connie's pregnancy. When the woman had shared that fact with her husband, he had stepped in and gotten in touch with Julian, advising him on her "condition" and worrying that a hospital delivery might land them all in jail.

The judge had arranged for a retired doctor who was a friend of his to check on the girl and eventually deliver her baby boy. He'd flown down to Tallahassee after the old man's phone call, ostensibly to visit a sister, and met with Norris while there.

They'd come to a better understanding about Connie, and Norris, somewhat hampered in his abuse by the judge's instructions, had turned his attentions to another woman. But between the Jensens, and Ed Norris, Connie Caudell had entered early womanhood thoroughly intimidated, and prone to believe any suggestion aggressively put forth by her captors. Julian's henchman had been very good at what they did.

As the years passed and their captive showed no signs of escaping or trying to contact the law, Norris had grown a little lax. She named her baby Ben, and the Jensens found that after all, the little boy made a great way to control Connie's behavior.

Connie had felt tainted after her experience with Norris; but somehow, she had separated her baby from his conception, and the young woman loved that boy from the first she'd known he was a part of her. Mrs. Jensen had asserted that Connie was a better mother to him than many an older woman she had observed; and they had taken advantage of that by assuring her that the less Ben knew as he got older, the safer and more normal his life would be.

After Ben was almost four, Connie was allowed to take a job at a local bar. She had taken piano lessons since she was very young and had a great memory. She could play most anything from the forties, had picked up some current tunes "by ear", and the small bar wasn't picky about the year of the hit.

She played a few nights a week and was always accompanied by either J.C. or Della, so that one was with her and one was with Ben. Whatever money the owner gave her or patrons tipped her, J.C. and Della spent except for a small clothing allowance for the boy and his mother.

There was no record of her even working there as the owner paid her cash. She'd hated the bar she'd played in, but had loved the opportunity to play a piano. She had precious little reading material, just Ben's school books and an occasional magazine. They tried to keep these, as well as newspapers away from her. It was a way of keeping her under their authority—taking away her autonomy.

One afternoon, a few hours before Connie's stint at the bar, Della had severe stomach pains and told the girl to walk down to the drug store for some Pepto Bismol or Milk of Magnesia. Della was doubled over on the couch where she'd been sitting before the attack, but lifted her head as Connie stepped to the door.

"Walk down to Woolworth's and get J.C. after you get the medicine. Their line is busy. Hurry, Connie."

J.C. had worked part time at their local Woolworth's for several years. Connie headed out to do Delia's bidding, but on the way, she had spotted a lawyer's office. With mixed feelings she turned aside from her errand. Walking into his office she experienced a surge of courage and a feeling of rightness about her decision to seek help.

He was a young man, just starting out in practice, and his secretary had hurried her in to him. Connie took up twenty minutes of her precious time trying to summarize her history and current predicament for him, and then took his advice. She left the office and almost ran to her destination; but was advised at the department store that Mr. Jensen had left to attend his sick wife.

Returning to their apartment, she discovered an angry Ed Norris awaiting her and no elderly couple to buffer his visit. Ben was not quite seven and attending school. He still had no idea of his origins or his mother's kidnapping. When Ed finished with her she'd crawled to her bedroom and hadn't awakened until the next morning.

Ben stayed home from school and was trying to put a cold washrag on her eye and forehead when she finally woke up. They kind of whimpered together over it. Ben asked why she didn't quit that job—assuming a drunk had hurt her there. She promised him that she would, thus keeping another secret from the boy; but it was his very ignorance which helped to keep him safe. In any case, she didn't think the evidence of Ed's beating would allow her to go back to work before she and Ben made their escape.

For the first time in many, many years her heart lifted with the hope she felt.

Norris had emptied her purse when she'd come home and had found the lawyer's card. It was after he stuffed it in his own wallet, that he came after her for defying him. He got in touch with Julian Connors and had been instructed to fly to Savannah during the short call to the angry judge.

Norris met with Connors' nephew, Vince, in the parking lot of a small drug store not far from Tybee Island, and talked over Connie's plans with young Harrington. It hadn't taken long to agree to break into Chase Harrington's office, subsequently burn any Caudell papers he might find, and take care of the lawyer, too.

Julian hadn't delayed any further in sentencing his step-niece to a terrible death; and sent word through Vincent Caudell to finish off Connie Caudell and the Jensens, too. The night after Ed arrived home, he broke into the young lawyer's office; searching the files until he came across Connie's.

There he discovered carefully written notes about her history, including parentage, hometown, former addresses and details of her kidnapping—*naming names*. On the last sheet, he noted the lawyer had made a plane reservation for Connie Caudell and the boy to Savannah—just two weeks away. The lawyer, Chason Harrington, was to accompany her.

He let fly an explicative and growled, *"Not while I'm in charge."*

Norris smiled and pocketed the incriminating notes. He carefully replaced the empty file folder in the proper drawer and took out a whole set of files below it. Scattering several on the floor, he later dumped the rest in a drive-in's trash receptacle.

Before he left, Ed Norris rifled through all the drawers of both desks taking any cash he could find. The man then waited until the evening she and the boy were to leave before taking any other action.

Connie hadn't packed anything as she and Chase had agreed that would have alerted the Jensens. She'd been confined to the house since the discovery of her visit to the Harrington Office, but she was sure that the young lawyer would find a way to free both Ben and her from the Jensons and Ed.

Norris had shown up right before her planned escape, put Ben in the older couple's hands, and said he would only stop to drop off his girlfriend. Young Ben had smelled the heavy odor of alcohol on Norris and the girl with him, but there was nothing he could do. When he'd protested loudly about his mother leaving, Ed Norris had back-handed the boy, and sent him sprawling across the checkered linoleum.

Della had rushed to see if he was okay; while his mother had to be restrained and eventually he'd turned his fists on her until she was completely compliant. Norris had thrown the unconscious woman on the floor at the back of his car, her midsection sprawled across the hump that ran through the length of his car; and rethinking the instructions his employer had given him, he stopped at a payphone down the street to check once more with the judge.

After the call, he turned back to the car looking grim and determined.It had been raining almost non-stop for three days. The complete cloud coverage over Tallahassee didn't bode well for the evening's task, Ed thought, but you never knew. Things could clear off quickly if the wind would pick up.

He was tired of the rain, and more than tired of Valery. He glanced at the girl sitting beside him. She was sliding a tube of lipstick across her mouth using a compact in between primping and whining about being late home. He grimaced and toyed with the idea of placing two bodies at the site he'd chosen. It would make things easier for him to do it all at once.

They had been driving towards his girlfriend's apartment after the call he'd made, when he decided to make a u-turn and take the girl with him. He was running out of time to catch the lawyer and he really felt Valery had run out of time, too. She had become too nosy over the Caudell business and was beginning to make noises about needing a new car, a better apartment, and more jewelry.

Connie was still unconscious, and he'd used this as an excuse to keep Valery in the car. He'd instructed Val to keep an eye on her while he took care of the lawyer. Ed had swung by Harrington's office and waited a little way down the street. He knew the man's habits by now, as well as those of his secretary's.

Mrs. Trent, the secretary, walked out at precisely closing time, flicked open a yellow umbrella and turned toward her Ford Fairlane. It was parked on the other side of the street and she held back while a passing truck swished up water that had collected at the bottom of the hill. She turned and looked carefully up and down the road, causing Ed to feel a moment of vulnerability.

He turned off his wipers and stilled at the wheel appearing to look at the gages on his car, yet he surveyed her from under his lashes. The woman at his side kept talking; whining a bit about his not dropping her at her apartment.

"She's out cold, Edward. Anybody can see that!" and she'd paused to toss a Chiclet in her mouth.

The nervous energy in the pit of his stomach reared up into anger as he followed the secretary's progress across the street.

"Shuddup!" he hissed without taking his eyes off the Trent woman.

A few minutes after the Fairlane had pulled into traffic and disappeared over the hill behind them, Chason Harrington had stepped out to the new Mercury parked in front of his office. The driver side of his car was adjacent to oncoming traffic; and it didn't take Ed a minute to gun his engine as the lawyer opened his door. Chase Harrington never stepped into his car. The woman sitting beside Ed Norris gasped and screamed as she watched the young lawyer and his door torn from the car.

Ed barreled on through the red light at the top of the hill, leaving behind a cacophony of horns and screeching brakes and a young man lying in the street.

He headed for the country. There were a lot of wooded areas on the outskirts of Tallahassee, and some months back, he had found a deserted area easily. Ed took Mahan Drive, Highway 90, towards Monticello, but by the time he found the road he wanted, Connie was awake and "coming to her senses". She could hear two people talking up front. Recognizing Norris' voice, she pondered who the female might be beside him.

They were arguing and she heard weeping in the woman's angry voice. She surmised that the woman had wanted to go home and that she was shocked at something Norris had done.

"...and what are you going to do with *her*?" the girl demanded, then clamped her lips together as a strained silence ensued.

Connie was pretty sure that Norris was going to kill her this time. So, she bided her time as the quiet erupted into more bickering, and waited for the vehicle to slow enough for her escape. She felt Ed hit the brakes and heard the blinker begin to click. *He was turning!* Connie was glad to be lying on the floor as the turn slung her to the right. She scrambled toward the right rider's side door, jerked the chrome handle upward, and pushed with all the strength she had—out and away from the door. She tumbled and her momentum carried her over the embankment down the incline of a deep ditch.

It took Ed a few valuable seconds as he was speeding up to realize he'd lost a victim.

The last three days of rain seemed to have collected all at the bottom of the ditch, but it had, also, made the road ahead of Norris' vehicle a treacherous mess. Ed Norris had chosen a site to dump Connie's body before the tropical depression had hovered over their area. The road he'd picked was a single lane dirt road and almost impossible to turn about with all of the muck.

It took up enough time getting the car stopped and turned around to give Connie a decent start. By the time he was racing back toward her, she'd managed to climb out of the swirling waters and up the sides of the ditch in spite of her dousing. Her intention was to run across Mahan Drive for the woods beyond.

Her wet skirt clung to her legs. She had kicked off her shoes heedless of their loss or the burning in her throat. She ran faster than she ever remembered running, sucking in the misty, damp air by the gulps. She hadn't paused to look for traffic when she had bolted onto the highway in an all-out run.

Her pursuer gunned the engine to cross the road behind her and was caught by an oncoming tractor trailer. Connie watched in horror as both vehicles slid on the slickened roadway, the tractor trailer shoving the rumpled car in front of it. Despite the rain, the car burst into flames and the tanker at the back of the truck quickly followed.

The turmoil of the last twenty-four hours and the shock of the horrendous accident she'd just witnessed left her numb. She had just enough alertness to edge back into the woods away from the highway. She only hoped she'd not been seen.

It was twilight, the rain had stopped, and the sky was finally beginning to clear. Connie could see the moon low in the sky with scudding clouds hurrying across its face. There was just a chance that no one had seen or noticed her. She waited in her hiding place on the other side of the road from the wreck. She had to make sure that Ed Norris would not walk away from this accident. Connie puffed out a gusty breath. She didn't see how anyone could walk away from that flaming car.

She shivered, although the night was quite warm. Dark was closing in and who knew what might be slithering around her. She'd seen the trucker climb from his cab before it was completely engulfed in flames and exploded. Apparently, his load was combustible.

He'd limped some, but looked to be okay.

It had taken the firemen a long time to get the fire under control and finally out. She had watched, then, as policemen and rescue workers had examined the accident and cleaned away the wreck. She stilled as they shoved two covered gurneys up into the ambulance.

She only knew the woman as Val, but it hit her hard, and she felt her stomach churn. She watched the emergency vehicle leave and stepped behind the pine tree she'd been leaning on to allow her stomach to empty itself. Connie plucked the dampened leaves from a nearby sweet gum to wipe her mouth with and suffered a barrage of water down her back.

That snapped her out of it. She edged back to watch the scene before her. Several police cars were on either side of the accident siphoning off traffic.

Pondering her options, she remembered Chase Harrington telling her if there was any problem in their plan to get her and Ben out of the Jensens' apartment, she was to contact his brother and he would meet her there. If only she had Ben with her. She knew the Jensens wouldn't hurt him, and Ed could no longer get at him. But that still left the Judge and her half-brother. She could not afford to involve the police at this point. It was too much of a risk for her father and mother and Ben.

She waited until the ambulance and tow trucks were gone. It took quite some time, but finally the lanes cleared and traffic resumed. When the final police car left, she stepped out and crossed the street for her shoes. It took her about thirty minutes to retrieve them in the dark, but they were still usable though battered. She shoved them on and started walking.

It wasn't too long before an elderly couple pulled up beside her and offered her a ride. She'd hopped right in. With no purse and no money, this was probably her only chance to put some highway between her and the Jensen's. She'd looked pretty bedraggled, but explained her car had broken down on a side road and she'd fallen down getting out.

Her mind was churning through her options throughout this first ride. Ed was no longer a factor, but her half -brother and his uncle loomed before her mind as malignant and threatening figures. She thought through her decision to leave Ben where he was for the night. Connie was still sure the Jensens would take care of Ben, in her absence until she could get Chase Harrington to pick him up.

So, she was headed for Blountstown, a small town not too far from the state's capital. It was where Chase Harrington's older brother lived. She pushed aside her desire to go after Ben once more, feeling that it would mean a death sentence for him. His only safety was in making sure that Chase had gotten to the Jensens. She'd get his brother to call Chase from Blountstown. She was sure he'd pick him up right away.

Chase Harrington's older brother had received word the evening of his brother's death, that the young lawyer had been a victim of a hit and run accident. Dr. Alex Harrington was still in shock the next morning, when a bedraggled looking female had knocked loudly at his front door.

Chase had called him and sent several letters about the young woman who stood before him. Of course, he'd never expected to really meet her. When she'd stepped in and introduced herself, he'd been speechless. Her face was bruised and there were cuts over her forehead and chin. Every-where else was devoid of any color—she looked almost bloodless.

For just a moment, he had stood frozen at the entrance of his home— the two looking hollowly at each other. Somehow, he knew it was Connie Caudell, but he'd read about her death in the paper and couldn't believe the young woman was tottering at his door. This caused him to grab her arm and urge her inside where she confirmed his assumption by her in-troduction.

He was still unable to believe his brother was gone and now the ap-pearance of a woman he'd thought dead but a few minutes before stole his speech. The letters and phone calls from Chase filtered through his thinking and he found himself wondering what he should do now about her situation. His brother had seemed so taken with her and her case. He had Chase's instructions in a letter in his study, but he pretty much knew them by heart.

During their exchange, her eyes traveled to a copy of the Tallahassee Democrat Newspaper lying across the coffee table in his living room. The headline had caught her attention—

CHASON FLANDERS HARRINGTON VICTIM OF HIT AND RUN

She tried to hold off the darkness that was claiming her, but without success. She folded in on herself like the rumpling of a sheet dropped from a clothesline.

Alex had called in as soon as he'd heard about his brother and secured time away from his practice. He was in the process of packing his bags for Tallahassee when Miz Caudell had knocked on his door. He was stunned by the rapid fire of events that had crowded into the last twenty-four hours, but he immediately jumped to Connie's aid as she hit the floor.

It had taken quite a bit to rouse the young woman, but Alex hadn't attended medical school for nothing. When she came to, he'd made sure she'd eaten and drunk something; kept her resting for awhile, and then allowed her to tell him what she knew of the evening's events. Her biggest worry, she'd kept repeating, was her son, Ben.

After retrieving Chase's letter and a lot more discussion, Alex had showed her an article a little further back in the paper. A Mr. Edward Platt Norris had cut across the path of a tractor trailer the evening before on Mahan Road. Both he and his passenger, Constance Caudell, had been killed. Connie had looked shocked and then relieved. Seeing it in print was disconcerting. But in one stroke it provided them with another plan.

Alex drove to a small town on the gulf where he and Chase had shared ownership in a cottage on the bay in Santa Rosa. He set her up there with supplies and money, gave her a key and left his auto with her, cautioning her to stay put until she'd heard from him again. He took the bus to Tallahassee; alerted an old friend in the police department about the need to place Ben in protective custody until his grandparents picked him up; and after making plans for his brother's funeral, he, also, called the Caudells in Bennington, Georgia.

With Mrs. Trent's help, he called from his brother's office. He said that he was Chase Harrington, and delivered the terrible news of their daughter's death in an auto accident. Then he told them that they had a grandchild named Ben. He hated the deception, but when she'd told him of her step uncle's involvement and her half-brother's collusion, as well, it only remained for her to reveal their professional titles to seal Alex and Connie's desperate plan.

For Connie, her anguish had been in letting her son go and allowing him to believe a lie. They both believed that his only safety lay in his very ignorance of all that had transpired. This had been three years ago, and it had taken that long to ensure Ben's safety and the gradual closing of their trap over both Julian and Vince.

Now, they had information on the Jensen's, who'd disappeared the next evening after Connie's supposed death leaving young Ben at the apartment, as well as Ed Norris' involvement, which connected the three of them to Connie's step uncle and half-brother. In addition, he'd tied Ed's car to his brother's death.

They had made a contact they could trust with the Georgia Bureau of Investigation and found that they were only a part of the net that was swiftly closing around Judge Julian Parker Connors and Vincent Deland Caudell.

Connie was 29 years old on the day she and Alex set out for Freeman County. It was not the apprehension and punishment of those who had wronged her nineteen years ago that was uppermost in her mind. It was her boy's face she carried in her heart.

Chapter 11

"The Bible say, they's a time for weepin' and a time fo' joy and some-times, seem to me; they come in on de same wind. But it also say, weeping last fo' a night, but joy cum in de mawnin'. He don't evuh leave us wit'out hope. No nevuh."
—Rennie Esther Jones Baker

A bby had filled out a long form asking everything about her life history except whether her folks had come in on the Mayflower or not. She had turned over her purse and coat, submitted to a "pat down" by a female guard, and now she waited with a large group of men and women who were mostly family members of inmates within the walls of Sayreville State Prison. There was some talking and a laugh here and there, but mostly the group looked serious and pensive. Finally, a group of guards came to escort them into a meeting room. It was filled with tables and folding chairs. Guards were stationed at opposing walls every ten feet for the length of the room. John had apparently earned the right to have visitors along with the less threatening inmates. She would be free to sit at a table within this bare walled room and visit the man she'd never been able to get out of her head, much less her heart. They were instructed to choose a seat and told to wait.

Minutes passed. Abby looked down at her hands and was glad she'd found time to do her nails this morning. She resisted the nerves that would have found release in drumming the table with them and brushed at her new woolen navy blue dress instead. She'd taken great care in choosing an outfit, wanting John to—to like what he saw. Her dress was topped with a three-quarter sleeve, short-waisted jacket, set off with oversize black buttons, and its very newness was a comfort. She had begun to study her shiny black patent leather pumps, still wondering if they added anything, when a door at the end of the room was opened and the first prisoner walked in, searching the room for his people.

Abby had the strangest feeling in the core of her being. She was filled with excitement and a great longing to just get to look at John; but at the same time, she longed to run from the room. Her stomach had not allowed her to eat the lunch she'd made for Carolyn and James just before coming here. And now, she thanked God she'd listened to it.

At last, toward the end of the line standing head and shoulders above the other men that had kept filing in, there was John. *Oh, Lord. Help me.*

This was the first visitation John had been to. It was the first real visitor he had had, other than the chaplain and his one visit with the warden. He hadn't felt like this since he was a child. And it felt so much worse than attending a new school in a new town where he had been dreadfully behind his classmates because of his parents' nomadic lifestyle. He had to smile as he shuffled along. If it hadn't been for his uncle he would probably still have been in grade school. He never thought he would've felt this way, but he wished he was back there now. *Buck up, man. She said she wanted to see you.* He straightened his shoulders and felt his chin jutting out. It was the same stance he'd taken on every first-day-at-a-new school a hundred years ago. *Oh, Abby.*

Abby. She would be out there now. Waiting. He couldn't believe it. He couldn't believe he'd allowed it; but beyond that, he couldn't believe she really had wanted to come. Not until he'd gotten her letter, at least. It was the first bit of hope he'd had in forever. The only other light that had pierced the darkened "sameness" of his life after Raynelle, had been the birth of Bo and his legal adoption of little Annie. Raynelle had not been a part of that joy. The first morning after their marriage had been a revelation to him—an unwelcome one. They'd driven down to New Orleans for their honeymoon, leaving Annie with her Great Aunt Lyddie. Raynelle's aunt, Lydia Mae Dell Fleming, had taken the bus over for their wedding and planned to stay at Raynelle's old apartment with Annie until we got back.

He had booked a motel for three days and a weekend, but they'd come back on the Friday before the weekend and he'd moved them onto base housing. He knew it had been the biggest mistake of his life—marrying Raynelle Anne Griffon. He couldn't regret Annie and Bo though, nor had he wished such a terrible end to the woman he'd endured.

"Move forward!" a guard spat at him bringing him to an awareness that his memories were clogging not only his life, but keeping these fellows away from their families. He picked up his pace and began to think about the woman who awaited him. She was as different from his wife as the warm sun was to the chill of winter. He'd wavered back and forth last night as he lay in his bunk after lights out. He couldn't let her waste her life waiting for him. There was no hope his time would be shortened. The judge had said without parole. He had just turned 25 years old. She was 23. By the time he got out, he'd be 50 and she'd be 48. He *couldn't*. He just couldn't let her do that.

And yet, somewhere in the depths of him a hope had sprung up. It had come from his conversations with James and attending chapel on Sundays. And it had come from her letter. He'd begun to talk to the Lord again. It had come from the Lord. Somehow, he had had an urgency to allow Abby to come. And it seemed he was not supposed to discourage her. How easily that could just be his desires, he thought. He could be putting his feelings in the place of God's enlightenment. In the midst of all his double thinking, the line of men arrived at the visitor's room. He felt his heart beat pick up. The door was opened. He began to stretch like every other man, trying to see his Abby. *Oh, Lord. Did he hear himself? He was GONE. He was. HIS Abby. God forgive me, but it's what I want.*

He had every line of her letter memorized. He'd read it over every time he had a free minute. No one had been assigned as his cellmate yet, and he hadn't had to worry about protecting his letter, but still he kept it safely beneath his bedding. Nothing should happen to it.

The first line had brought forth a rueful grin. "DEAR JOHN"—of course it had started out that way. But more than the proverbial *Dear John* thing, it had been such a joy to read that in her fine flowing handwriting. He'd read that line alone numerous times and caught himself imagining she'd actually said it. He smiled ruefully. As he thought about it, this was the first personal letter he'd ever received. His Uncle Burt had died the first day he arrived in Louisiana, otherwise, he'd have received a letter while he was stationed there or in Missouri.

And the things she'd *said*. He'd soaked the words up like a dry, dry sponge would good, clean water.

Finally, the line of men had poured through the door until it was his turn to step in and scan the faces. *There.* There she was. *"Abby,"* and her name was whispered on an exhaled breath of relief. He'd stalked over and they'd acted like persons who'd never heard of rules. She'd flown into his open arms and he'd cuddled her as close as if she'd been Annie or Bo. Closer. Only the guard stepping forward had made them sit quickly with flushed faces and eyes that never left each other, even while apologizing to authority.

The morning had passed quickly in John's company. After he'd come in, the other families and inmates had faded away. It was almost as if the two of them were alone with the distant drone of other voices a backdrop blanked out. Initially, a little awkward after that first embrace, they had eventually begun to relax in the warmth of each other's company. They talked of many things—their childhoods, Burt Melton, Archie Weston, his folks, Annie and Bo and his heartache over losing them. They held hands during the better part of her visit, the guards allowed for that. She couldn't look away from the depths of his hungry gray eyes. She had a feeling her green ones held the same expression. They couldn't get enough of each other. He had agreed to let her come the next time they had visitation, but he'd apologized for his weakness. They'd tussled some verbally over that decision, until she'd told him that there would never be anyone else but him, whether he allowed her to visit him or not. He drank that in, too, and savored it in the weeks between visits. Abby would take her few hours a month of happiness in his presence. She'd acknowledged that her heart had been his long before he'd gone into the military, and although she had tried dating, had ended up feeling that it wasn't fair to any young man. Her heart had a fixed object and couldn't be turned aside. He'd thought of the long years with Raynelle redeemed only by his two babies. He'd turned his eyes to her and mouthed, "I'm so sorry, Abby." He cleared his throat. "I was so stupid. I made so many mistakes."

"Hush," she'd squeezed his hands between her small ones and a small tear broke the confines of her lid and rolled down her cheek. He took the pad of his thumb and wiped it. "I love you, you know," his deep, gentle voice sent the words down to the deep hurt that had been such a constant companion for so long. It washed away a world of heartache and restored her hope and joy. Her head had been bowed to hide the tears, but slowly he pulled it up with his index finger, lifting her chin, his thumb resting on the slight cleft he adored. Her eyes were full of tears now, but also there was light shining from within. She was more like the little girl he remembered—full of joy at reaching home and father and Rennie; jumping off the bus, books in tow, and running for home. He told her, then, what he remembered of her making for home. How she had that same look about her just a minute ago. And before she could speak, he urged her to get James to drop her by next time and to pick her up after. Never come by yourself he'd said.

She'd interrupted him then, as the guards indicated to inmates and visitors alike that their time was up, "John, it is exactly the way I feel," she'd spoken to him with music in her voice; and he loved that about her. "I feel as if I'd been away for so long, and I've just come home."

On a Monday afternoon, just after arriving home from school, Gordon Clarke stepped into his darkroom to see about the little camera Ben and Elizabeth had brought him. His Dad was still at work, so it was an optimum time to secretly process anything he might find in the lighter/camera. It didn't take him long to get trays and developer set up and the process running smoothly. Even extricating the film from the tiny camera hadn't been too difficult. Gordon almost swallowed his tongue when the pictures from the little camera began take shape before him. He'd kept it quiet, just like he'd promised Elizabeth and Ben, but it had been hard. The only one he'd spoken to about the camera and his part in developing the pictures had been Elizabeth's sister. They'd spoken at school, she asking him if he'd finished, and when he thought no one was around he'd replied, "I'm going to do it this afternoon."

His dad loved photography just as much as he did, and he'd had to hide that cool little camera from him. He hoped he'd be able to share it with him before giving it back. So far, he'd pulled four pictures from the wash and hung them on a line they'd strung across their dark room. He had just two more "materializing" now. He whistled at the fourth one. Plain as day, you could see Judge Parker, and their district attorney, Ben's uncle, taking money from Dale Barnes the owner of "The Blue Heron" out by the county line. There were several pictures. All of them were taken outside—he thought it might be the back of "The Blue Heron". One of the pictures, showed the Judge and the DA entering one of the rented rooms with a blonde and Raynelle Abrams. Another one, showed Jerry Bigham, Judge Parker and Vince Caudell heatedly discussing something before getting in a big black Cadillac. The driver was packing a pistol and looked like he could do the job of that pistol with his fists. The picture taken just after that showed surprise on all of the men's faces. The anger and shock that registered on each man's face seemed to be focused on the camera, and their expressions indicated that the one taking the pictures had been spotted. The big chauffer was pointing a finger in line with the lens of the camera, and in this picture, he could see the edge of the car door. Apparently, the photographer had been sitting in his or her car. "This is a mess," he muttered; and he whistled again. "I can sure see why they wanted me to keep it quiet." As soon as he'd finished processing them he would hide the camera and pictures, and call both Ben and Elizabeth. They'd arranged a coded signal for anything incriminating that might help Big John. He couldn't wait to give the signal and share the pictures.

Gordon waited until Tuesday afternoon, because his homework and developing the pictures had taken up all of the preceding afternoon. He caught Claire in the hallway, and urged her to let Elizabeth know. That afternoon he'd called Elizabeth. He'd asked for Claire, so that Miz Ella wouldn't be suspicious of a high school boy asking for Elizabeth. Then Claire had slipped into Elizabeth's room and told her that he was on the phone. She wanted to run down the hall and slide down the banister, but knew it would garner her too much attention. So, she walked sedately down to the foyer and seeing no one about picked up the phone. It didn't take five minutes to decide that the day to see Gordon's "new puppies" was Thursday. She wished she could see them earlier, but there wasn't any time with school and church activities. He'd said fine and that he'd call Ben. They'd chosen the puppies as the signal because Gordon's old hound had actually had four. It was probably her last litter he'd said. Ben really wanted one of the puppies, but didn't ever see his uncle allowing it. Gordon had said that it would be at least another four or five weeks before they were old enough to leave their mama, and maybe he could change his Uncle Vince's mind.

Two afternoons later, Gordon, Ben and Elizabeth were pouring over all six pictures and wondering who to consult about their evidence. They ruled out the city police easily, since Jerry Bigham was big stuff there. Gordon said they should take it to Sheriff Arnette, but Ben and Elizabeth remembered the last time their evidence had been turned "backwards" they thought. It hadn't ended up helping Big John at all. In fact, it seemed to convince the sheriff of John's guilt.

"I think we should talk to your Granddaddy and Daddy," Ben muttered to Elizabeth. "I'd say, talk to Granny or Cammie, but I don't want to show them until I'm sure this really means something, you know?"

"Yeah," Gordon and Elizabeth answered in sync.

In the end, that's just what we did. We took it to my Daddy and Granddaddy. After all, we'd found it at Granddaddy's house. It made since to 'fess up and get their advice. Gordon came with us on his bike. We were halfway there before Ben realized that we'd forgotten to see the puppies.

Ben and Elizabeth and Gordon pulled onto the drive that led up to her Granddaddy's house. On one side was a peach orchard, barren at this time of year, and on the other a small wooded area of sweet gum, red maples and black cherry trees. There were some cedar trees on the edge of the little wood and clumps of palmetto here and there. They passed between all of it, barely noting it, eyes on the house.

"Stop!" commanded Ben stridently. "Pull over here. Roll your bikes behind the Palmetto Bushes."

They'd noticed the big Cadillac sitting at the corner of the house, too, and supposed it had something to do with Ben's odd behavior. The three had pushed back on their pedals and then assisted the stop with their feet, stirring up the dust. After hiding their bikes, they followed Ben into the dense covering of the woods. He whispered that the big El Dorado was his Uncle Vince's car and motioned for them to follow him.

The three of them crept single file down a small trail Elizabeth and her siblings had kept trampled down, and past the small fort that Adam and Big John had begun years ago. Each succeeding child along with friends had kept it usable. Elizabeth stepped closer to Ben and grabbed his shirt tail. He turned and she motioned him back to the fort. Once inside, she showed them a square-shaped cubby hole in the wood. She'd said it would make a good hiding place for the manila envelope in which Gordon had placed all the pictures. She returned the framed picture over the hole, so that no one should notice their evidence.

"We'd better see what's up without that on us," she advised. "Good thinking," nodded Gordon. "Probably best you wait here, Gordon," Elizabeth added. "We'll have to explain what we're all doing together, otherwise. Ben and I have been riding bikes every now and then, so Mr. Caudell won't notice that," and she flushed a little after her statement.

Ben turned back from the door then and asked Gordon was he sure he hadn't talked to anyone about the pictures. "Well," he said, "I did mention that I was developing them for you to your sister, Claire. We were in the hallway between classes and she asked me quiet-like about it. I looked around before I answered. I didn't see anyone, so I told her that yea, I was." Ben and Elizabeth exchanged glances doubtfully. "I don't know how he'd get anything out'a that," Ben reassured Gordon, "but I guess we'll see though." He and 'Lizbeth made for the door, walked up the trail and retrieved their bikes. They finished the ride up to her Granddaddy's house in silence. Before they got off the bikes, they realized the district attorney was on 'Lizabeth's grandparents' front porch taking his leave. His voice carried over to where they were now dismounting their bicycles.

"Thank you, Carl. I'll bring this key back in about an hour or so. I appreciate your letting me look over the place again. I just am not quite settled about Big John's conviction—even though I was the prosecutor. I'd like to go over things and make sure that I got the right man."

He turned at the screen door and shook Elizabeth's Granddaddy's hand. "Thanks, again, Carl."

Then Carl Adam Linden murmured his "you're welcome" in return and turned back to reenter his house. He was interrupted by my uncle spotting both me and 'Lizabeth. His polite demeanor escaped him for a minute. "Boy. What are you doin' here?" he demanded under a heavily furrowed brow.

I looked him straight in the eye, something I hadn't done much since he'd hurt my Aunt Cammie and been disrespectful to my Granny. "Just out riding bikes with 'Lizabeth." I answered him as toneless as I could. He scowled, "Git home! NOW." Lizabeth's granddaddy was watching the whole time. When Vince turned to let the screen door shut quietly, their eyes met—the younger man's startled; the older, discerning and evincing disapproval. Vince turned on his heel and muttered, "Mind what I told you, Ben." Then he left. Ben began to pick up his bicycle like he was going, but delayed it until the last sign of Vince's El Dorado disappeared. Then he turned back to the elderly man to explain. "Mr. Linden. I would go on home now, like my uncle told me, but we got somethin' real important to talk to you about. Me an' 'Lizabeth think it's a matter of life and death and it concerns my uncle. I'd like to ask you to overlook my seeming disrespect for just a few minutes." He'd maintained steady eye contact with Mr. Carl the whole time he'd made his request.

"Alright, son. I guess I'll hear you out."

"Granddaddy, it's terrible important!" 'Lizbeth spoke up breathlessly. Then she turned and ran down the path leading into the woods at the side of her Granddaddy's house. Mr. Carl turned and looked at me enquiringly. "We got a friend down there," I said. "It won't take a minute." Sure enough, before Mr. Carl could get the door open good, here came 'Lizabeth and Gordon with the manila envelope.

"Hi, Mr. Carl," Gordon greeted him properly.

In between huffing and puffing, Elizabeth managed to get out, "Granddaddy, we need my Daddy here, too. Do you mind if I go and get him?"

Her Granddaddy was looking steadily more puzzled. "No, child. Go on and get him."

We all waited then. Mr. Carl was one of the calmest, kindest men I'd ever known, and I studied him some as we waited for 'Lizbeth to get back with her Daddy. Gordon stood quietly beside me.

In a minute, 'Lizbeth's Daddy came hustling down the two-rut road to his Daddy's house preceded by his daughter who was in an all-out run again. Her Granddaddy smiled at her single-mindedness.

"Hey, Son," he spoke first.

"Afternoon, Pa," returned Art.

"That was fast work, Elizabeth," her Granddaddy patted her on the shoulders as she'd come to a stop beside him and leaned over with her hands on her knees, breathing pretty heavily. "I think we'd better go inside to listen to these young'uns, Art."

They all filed in then, much to 'Lizbeth's little granny's surprise. She stood at the open door and looked us up and down amusedly whilst we all marched in.

We had a pretty serious talk, along with a studious session of picture gazing. The six pictures passed through six sets of hands. There were some gasps, not only about the pictures and what they showed, but especially about the incriminating letter that detailed Judge Connors and my Uncle Vince's involvement in my mother's kidnapping. 'Lizbeth's Granny had a lot to say about that matter. It took us a long time to decide what to do with the evidence. The people involved made you nervous about trusting the authorities in Carverville. Finally, it was decided to call Axel Arnette. 'Lizbeth's father and her grandpa both assured us he was as honest as the day was long. By the time the grownups had decided what to do, we heard the deep hum of my uncle's El Dorado pulling up in the yard. Elizabeth's granny was in the process of calling Axel and asking him to come over. Apparently, she had to hold the phone while Vern went for him. She continued to hold the phone as we began to dart first one way and then another.

What a lot of scurrying! I thought we looked a little bit like that time last summer when Pepper Dunn and I chunked a rock at a five-gallon bucket turned upside down on Ol' Bill Goodson's fence post. Wasps had come pouring out from under that bucket like nobody's business—but that's another story. They told me to go through the dining room to the side porch and slip out if my uncle came in and wait until he left. Then they'd use the farm truck to take me and my bike home. I headed for said porch, watching as Miz Lelah held the phone between shoulder and chin and stretched the line from the dining room into the kitchen. She was stuffing the pictures, ledger and letter into the envelope. I could just make out her sliding it behind her flour and sugar canister on her lower shelf as I closed the door and made myself scarce. After I exited, Gordon and 'Lizbeth had been instructed to follow me out the door, and I was surprised when the door opened behind me and the two of them squirted out. "Shhh!" Elizabeth reminded us. "Grandma said she'd skin me alive if Mr. Vince heard anything at all out of us." Then we squatted down on the side porch behind the Linden's old humming freezer—being very careful not to lean against it, because 'Lizbeth had told us on occasion it shocked her. We listened silently as the music and motor from Vince's convertible shut off. We heard his door open and shut solidly and in the next minute his knocking at the front porch made us all three jerk unintentionally.

Sure enough, my uncle did go inside the Linden household. Me an' Gordon an' 'Lizbeth slipped on out the side door and down the stoop. Gordon eased the screen door silently closed. We bent double then so's he wouldn't spot us out the window, and slipped real quiet-like over to the little garage apartment that lay not twenty feet away from Mr. Carl and Miz Lelah's house. We held a quick palaver there. We decided it would be good for Gordon to slip on back to the fort by way of the path that also came out near the garage. 'Lizbeth and I felt that if Vincent saw Gordon, a high school boy who happened to help out at the local newspaper office, it would make things unpleasant for Gordon and his family—especially if they held a prolonged investigation over the stuff we'd found. Also, Gordon could listen out and decide if he needed to call in the sheriff if Miz Linden didn't get through to him first. Reluctantly, Gordon agreed to leave, and we slipped into the apartment and locked the door. Nobody had lived there in a long time, and there was a dusty, old sofa shoved back against the window facing the house. Elizabeth and I immediately trotted over to the couch, and stood up on our knees on its worn cushions, peeping out the window behind it. Seemed like my uncle was stayin' in there an awful long time.

Camille had to talk to somebody. Vince was gone. In a normal marriage he'd be her first choice as confidant—the first to hear any good news. But this was no normal marriage—never had been, whatever normal was. She sighed heavily and used the banister to make her way upstairs. She was thirty-six years old. The secret she carried should have been cause for celebration; not a time where she had to use the balustrade to bolster her spirits while she walked upstairs. She sighed again. She hoped Mama Lee was awake. She had to talk to somebody. And if anybody's good straight common sense could help, it would be Ben's Granny.

She'd made it up to the door now which was wide open. Mama Lee liked it that way most days. Eulee Caudell was just putting her little spittle cup back in her side drawer. Cammie knocked on the door frame. "Mama Lee," she paused as their eyes met. "You feel up to talkin' a bit?"

"Sure, Honey," she extended a thin hand. "Come on in and sit. Don't mind the herd a'people in here takin' up all my time with their nonsense." And the two of them smiled at her small joke. She extended a finger to point at the arm chair that perpetually stayed close to one side of her bed. "Sit," she said simply.

Cammie did. She took her time. The subject she'd come to discuss was a volatile one for her. She didn't know if it would bring joy or sadness to the old lady, but she hoped Mama Lee might be happy. It certainly hadn't happened happily, but somewhere inside her she felt the seed of joy opening slowly. She hadn't had any real close blood family in *so-o-o* long.

"Mama Lee," she said. "Come the first week in November we're going to have a new Caudell in the family." Mama Lee dropped her chin and then had to drag the lacy kerchief from within her long sleeve and wipe a bit of dribble from under her lip.

She sat there for a pure minute taking it in. Then slowly she closed her mouth and curled it in a big smile. "Child!" she exclaimed. "You sure know how to put life in a body!"

Right at that moment someone began to hammer on their front door.

Axel Arnette had had a call on his private line from the GBI. He had mixed feelings. He liked keeping his own county clean without any outside help, but so much was going on now, he could hardly keep it straight. And so much of it seemed to boil right down to old Judge Connors and their fine upstanding DA, Vince Caudell. He frowned. *Never had liked that guy. Either one of 'em.* They, neither one of 'em, had come up to Richard Vincent Caudell's ankle bones. Rich had been a long-time friend, and had been a person you could depend on. How he'd fathered that excuse for a man, Vince Caudell, he'd never know. But the sheriff did know this—the next week was going to be hoppin'. He had a big case of nerves about it, but most of it was just eagerness to set a long record of wrongs right. It galled a body to work a lifetime in law enforcement and see dirty politics cinch that blinder too tight over the eyes of justice. It had become a blinder to recognizing the criminal rather than impartiality to race or creed or wealth. *Yes.* He was definitely getting more excited by the minute.

He'd just hung up from a conversation with a longtime friend, Charlie Gault, who'd been an agent with the GBI for over twenty years. Gault had begun working for that department just after they'd changed the name from the Division of Identification, Detection, Prevention and Investigation to the Georgia Bureau of Investigation in 1940. They'd met in Atlanta at a law enforcement conference in the early fifties, and shared a mutual love of hunting, fishing, and "policing". They'd meet every other year in North Carolina with their families, and would hunt or fish early mornings while their families slept late, played cards, shopped and generally "lollygagged around". He laughed at the memories now. Charlie was about as good a lawman as you could get. He'd trust him with his life. He'd trust him with his family's lives, and that was saying something. He thought about the information Charlie had given him. Normally, in light of the odd things going on in Freeman County, he wouldn't have known a thing about the intended investigation and imminent visit by the GBI; but Charlie had vouched for him, and his record and reputation were spotless in the thirty years he'd been a lawman in the Carverville/Bennington area. On top of that, the sheriff had made the original request for the GBI's help. So, he'd been made privy to a lot of their plans. They would be coming Wednesday of the next week. Charlie would come to his office and apprise him of their plans.

While he was pondering the information he'd received, his phone rang again. He could hear Vern answering it in the other room. *He must think I'm still on the line*, and he reared back in his swivel chair waiting for Vern to take care of it or call him. He heard him tell the party to hold a minute, then heard him walk out the door. In a minute he was back.

Vern poked his head in the door of Axel's office and apologized. "I didn't know you were in here. I thought I heard you go out." He smiled ruefully and then relayed his information, "Miz Lelah is on the phone. Wants to talk to you—nobody else'd do, she said."

Axel brought his chair down, and picked up the phone. He could hear Vern walking back to his office to hang up the phone, and then heard the other phone being returned to its cradle; but he could hardly understand the lady, and she had to repeat her sentence.

"Sheriff Arnette, this is Lelah Linden," she hissed. "You need to get over here now..." and then there was a definitive click and a dial tone hummed in his ear. He sat unable to do anything for just a minute, then jumped to his feet and sang out his usual "call to arms" at Vern. "Come on, boy. We got doin's!"

Vince pranced back and forth before the elderly couple and their son. He held a small handgun and was waving it around enough to make all four of them nervous.

He stopped abruptly in front of Elizabeth's grandmother. "Why'd you make that call Miz Linden? Who'd you try to call?" He obviously hadn't heard her whispered conversation and felt he'd kept her from reaching anyone. He'd been looking fixedly and with great displeasure at Lelah Linden who sat beside her husband on the couch in the den. "I really don't want to shoot all of you," He jerked his eyes over the three of them now determinedly, "but I will if I have to. And either way, I can sure make it hard on you if you don't give me what I want. There are lots of ways."

He was talking quietly, as if to himself now, but had resumed his marching back and forth eyeing the three of them. "I know you've got those papers. I know the Gordon kid was talking to one of your daughters, Art," and here he'd focused on Elizabeth's father with a surly narrowing of his eyes, "about the pictures Raynelle had. And she had other things, too, didn't she? And you three know where they are." And here he raised his voice to shout as loud as he could.

"And I want it back! TO! DAY!" The lawyer's face had turned an unhealthy dark red. The group that sat before him could see the jugular veins on his neck standing out. The more he paced the madder he got. "And where are those kids, anyway?" He stopped to face Arthur.

"I know Ben's bike, and it's still out there!" He waved the gun in its general direction. "That other one was a girl's—had to be your girl's bike.

So, *spit it out*. Where are they, huh?" Now, he waved the gun under Art's nose.

He hurled out a couple of expletives, as if they would act as a catalyst to get him what he wanted. The Lindens just sat quietly watching him, but there was a mess of prayer going on inside. "Is there not but *one* phone in this *house*?" He took his eyes off them for a second, casting about for that object. He kicked a side table and sent a lamp flying to the floor. Vince spat out a few other things nobody in the room wanted to hear, but that was the least of their worries. "Get up, then, *Mama Bear*! And you come, too, Papa and Baby!" And waving the gun from them to the dining room, he indicated their destination, "We're going in there." He moved to the arch of the dining room/kitchen entrance and leaned against the opening while he marched them into the next room. "Sit at the table!" he clipped. "And keep your hands on top of it! MOVE!"

He herded them over to the table like they were unruly cattle, then waited for them to sit like he'd told them. After three pairs of hands lay still on the table top, Vince edged over to the phone just outside the arched entrance of the dining room. He picked up the whole phone by the hollow under the receiver and stretched it to the table. Lifting the receiver to his ear, he kept shifting his eyes back and forth between them and the numbers on the phone as he began to dial. The familiar ticking of the clock on their Frigidaire oven and the shuttle of the telephone dial's steady clicking noises was all that filled the room for a short time.

Art shifted his eyes away from Caudell and quickly at his father and mother. They seemed to be holding up alright. Vince had burst into their house about twenty minutes ago demanding the pictures and "the rest of the papers".

Apparently, the DA had driven straight to the hardware store in Carverville, not the Abrams' House as he'd told Carl about an hour ago. He'd gone to town to have a key made—they'd surmised that it was a copy of the Abrams' House key that Grandpa Linden lent to him. There, he'd run into Harve Whitcomb, who'd inherited Whitcomb's Hardware from his Dad some five years back. Vince had told them that Harve had given him a "head's up" on the pictures and papers that belonged to the Judge and DA—that the Lindens had them. How Harve knew about it, none of them knew.

Vince was a "southpaw" and had held the receiver in his left hand and dialed the phone with it at the same time all the while holding the gun in his right. Now he brought the receiver flush to his right ear and switched the gun to his left hand still managing to train it on all three of the Lindens. Speaking into the phone, he spat out in acidic tones, "I need to speak to the judge." He paused. "*Yes. Now,*" disgust lacing his voice. He kept scanning the room as if expecting to find what he was looking for any minute, and cutting his eyes between each of the Lindens at the same time. "Idiot housekeeper," he muttered.

Some minutes passed in which he shifted the phone from his right ear to the left one and squeezed the phone between his head and left shoulder and paced as far as the curled cord would let him, turning over every piece of paper or letter within his reach with his right hand—which wasn't too much because Lelah Benning Linden ran a taut ship. Nothing but the most pressing papers rested on her desk or table top. He slipped on a pair of leather gloves, then opened the china cabinet. Jerking his gaze between the three Lindens and his search, he turned over each displayed plate. He took his right hand and felt all around the mahogany wood that covered its top. "Not even dust, Mama Bear." He said nastily. The Judge must have picked up his phone because at just that instant Vince belted out, "Julian!" Then he paused as he listened to his uncle. "I'm at the *Lindens*. They *know*." Then there was another pause where the Lindens could just make out the timbre of an angry voice over the line, but not its actual words. "JU—," he paused, then tried again, "*Julian!*" They could still hear the judge pouring out things over the line that back then came with a misdemeanor charge. Anybody who could read the small print on the back cover of a phone book, knew it was against the law to use "foul language" over the phone. Finally, he seemed to wind down, or his nephew successfully cut in, "Julian, they've got the ledger, the letter and the camera. Only, they got a high school kid to develop them. It itn't good, Julian. It itn't good." The judge must've asked if he had the papers in his hands, because he hesitated and then put forth a little sheepishly, "Well, *no*. No, I don't. But I will have soon. They're here, I know it!" Then Julian must've asked where he got his information, because Vince answered with, "Harve Whitcomb told me." There was another burst of fireworks over the phone. Miz Lelah felt like covering her ears, but she didn't want to miss anything incriminating. She hadn't had a chance to tell Carl and Art that she'd called the sheriff. They'd been talking in the front room with Vince when he'd started waving his gun and ordered them to sit. Then he'd burst in on her using the phone. She was sure counting on Axel making a quick appearance. *Please God.*

Vince eventually hung up the phone. "Okay," he said as he walked over to Lelah Benning Linden, and slowly raised his gun to her forehead. "The Judge will be here in thirty minutes. I need those papers before he gets here. So. I'm not going to count, but I'm going to fire straight at you ol' lady, if you don't give me those papers *now*. I know you've got 'em. If you want to see your grandchildren grow up, you better tell me where they are."

"Get 'em, Lelah," commanded Carl Adam Linden.

Gordon sat in the Linden fort alone. He had begun to chafe at just sitting with nothing to do. He hadn't any idea what was going on at the Linden's house because it was hidden from his view by the small wood. *How would he know to go for the sheriff or not—all tucked up in these woods like he was?* Finally, he could stand it no longer. He peered out all of the windows, and saw that he *was* alone. He couldn't take another minute hiding out here while "who-knows-what" was happening at the Linden house. He stepped out and stealthily approached the house by way of the trail. At the opening, he hung back in the wooded area and once again took a careful look at the surrounding area. Just at that moment, the screen door on the side porch popped open and the three adults the children had just met with marched down the porch steps to the ground below. Vince leaned down from the threshold of the porch and jerked old Mrs. Linden closer to the steps. He looked some kind'a mad, Gordon could see. He yelled out in stentorian tones. "*Okay. Ben.* You and the girl come on out. Don't waste my time. I've got the papers now—everything I need. You two come out or I'll shoot Grandma here first. I'm not gonna' count. LET ME SEE SOME MOVEMENT—*NOW.*" Here he leaned down and put the handgun at the back of Miz Lelah's head and lowered himself to the first step. The door burst open from the garage apartment, as Ben and Elizabeth stumbled out in their hurry to get to the three adult Lindens. Vincent let out a belt of laughter as he watched them. It didn't have much mirth in it though.

Gordon turned on his heel and ran silently up the path. He cut to his right at the fort and headed toward the Linden driveway. *Oh, God, let that crazy Caudell man need to talk a LONG time.* He jerked up his bike from behind the palmetto and wheeled it toward the road stirring up puffs of dust. He'd hit the highway full out and swung in a wide circle just managing to stay on the road. *Thank God nobody was on the road at that minute.* Up ahead flying over the only hill in Bennington, Axel Arnette's car swooped toward him. He swung his bike around in the middle of the road and screeched to a stop. The sheriff's car's brakes squealed a little bit, and Gordon winced hoping Vince Caudell wouldn't notice. This road led to the back gate of the military base and there was often a lot of traffic this time of day. Maybe the DA would chalk those brake complaints to that and not get spooked into firing that gun.

The sheriff watched exasperated as the Clarke kid threw down his bike and ran to his passenger-side window. "Sheriff, it's Vince Caudell. He's got the Lindens held up at gunpoint at the back porch of Mr. Carl Linden's house. He's fixin' to shoot 'em!"

Axel Arnette had left incredulity behind a long time ago. Law enforcement had a way of kicking it out of you sometimes. But this did give him just a millisecond of pause. Then he belted out, **"*Floor it, Vern!*"** and turned to Gordon with a peremptory "Git out the way, boy!" The car took off, leaving Gordon to retrieve his bike and head back down the driveway to the path he'd come from.

Julian hung up the phone and frowned—so much for familial loyalty and honoring the head of the family's request. He had specifically warned Vince to refrain from any violence. He'd never realized how easily Vincent could fly off the handle. He'd vacillated about getting rid of his nephew— blood ties had to mean something, after all; but now it was obvious he was a "loose end"; a match waiting to ignite. He'd ignite him alright; and this was the optimal moment in time. The good people of Freeman County would be so shocked to hear that Vincent DeLand Caudell had killed not only Carl and Lelah Linden and their son, but his step grandmother and his wife, as well; and then the judge thought, if I get lucky, that'll include young Ben, too. Julian had intended to do that not long after Vince named his uncle as third in line to inherit the estate and monies. He had known that if he got rid of Vince, he'd have to do it all in chronological order, so that the will would flow through to Vincent and then to him. The time had never been just right; but here it was, and had practically fallen in his lap. He'd take care of whoever was in the Caudell Mansion right now, and then go over and take care of Vince at the Linden's. The Judge had warned him not to hurt the Lindens; but he knew from what he'd heard over the phone that Vince would have already shot that family by then. His lips curled as he thought of the perfection of the timing. He'd get that ledger and doctor the figures and names. And, he had one of Vince's hand guns. Had borrowed it about a year ago and held onto it for just such a time as this. He smiled as he unlocked his lower desk drawer. There was the gun Vince had loaned him, lying pristinely lethal. He pulled on the pair of gloves that lay beside the gun; then picked it up. Julian smiled and grunted as he lifted off of the swivel chair in front of his desk, then walked slowly toward the French doors that connected his study with the outdoors. He smiled, thinking how nice it was that his wife was at choir practice and his house-keeper had left for the day after announcing his nephew's phone call. No one need know he was even gone. He got in a secondary car he kept for his housekeeper's use when she was there and took the back roads to the Caudell Home.

Cammie walked carefully downstairs to answer the door. Rennie had headed home earlier this afternoon, as Earl had come home sick from the mill. It was Curtis Rabin's day off so it couldn't be him. Whoever was at the door must've been impatient, because if possible he or she had just pounded again, faster and louder this time. She opened the door before she thought to peek out. The two people standing across the threshold from her fairly jumped inside and closed the door behind them, locking it. The man took off his hat and took his arm from the figure huddling beside him, giving Cammie a better look at his companion. It was a woman, she'd realized, but when the lady took off her scarf and sunglasses, Camille recognized what must be a "dead ringer" for Connie Caudell from the family pictures. *Poor choice of words.* Taking a second look at the lady who was now hungrily taking in the old home visually, Cammie's whole frame jolted. This had to be Connie Caudell. The covert way they'd entered and the commandeering way in which the big man had handled the door only ratcheted up the culmination of shock at Connie's miraculous appearance. Cammie froze in the hallway gaping at the pair before her. *"It had to be Connie,"* she told herself. True she had a woman's form now, but it was the same beautiful face of the ten-year-old girl whose picture had once hung in Richard Vincent Caudell's study. It was in Mama Lee's bedroom now, because Vincent had wanted it out of the study when he had moved his books and papers in after Rich's death. *She did look like Mama Lee's mother.* Cammie was floored. Her mouth opened, but nothing came out.

The man turned to look back out the door a little nervously. There had been no cars in the driveway. Cammie began to wonder how they'd gotten here. The girl spoke first. "I'm Connie," she said simply. Gathering her wits about her, Cammie said, "I recognized you. It's just such a shock. Mama Lee and I went to your funeral, and got Ben—" she stopped in mid-sentence. *"What happened?"* and then, "Oh, I'm so sorry. I'm Camille, Vince's wife. You must have come a long way. Do you need something to eat or to rest?"

The gentleman interrupted. "Listen, Miz Caudell, I know you don't know me, but in a roundabout way I know you. I'm Alex Harrington, brother to the lawyer you thought called you back in 1959 about Connie's supposed death. I can explain, but we need to get out of this doorway and away from the windows. Connie is still in danger. You may be, too.

From upstairs, Miz Eulee Caudell's voice called out. "Cammie? Who is it, honey?"

Cammie was still shocked. She turned and said, your Mama has had a few strokes over the last two years. She's going to be overjoyed to see you; I just want to take it slowly—you know, to protect her. I don't quite know how to tell her."

Eulee's daughter's face exuded a kind of longing excitement. It had been so many years since she'd seen her mother or gotten a hug. They'd all left so casually that spring morning so long ago. She couldn't even remember if she'd hugged her mother or not. But her boy was on her mind. Was he alright? And how was she to tell him why she'd allowed him to believe such a lie? "Where's Ben?" Connie looked at Cammie somewhat desperately. It had been one of the hardest things she'd ever done—to let her boy go with him believing she was dead and for such a long time. It had broken her heart. She had to see him. She had to make things as right as she could, as soon as she could. It had been three years since she'd seen him and Connie didn't think she could wait a minute longer.

Cammie told her that he was out riding bikes with the youngest Linden girl, that he'd be back soon. Connie remembered the family and had smiled a little wistfully. By this time, they were edging up the stairs and practically whispering to keep Connie's Mama from knowing yet. The man asked pointedly, "Where is your husband?"

Cammie paused in her progress upstairs and looked at him blankly. "I—I don't really know," she responded truthfully.

Alex's chin jutted forward, "He mustn't know we're here— "

Chapter 12

*"See, the thing about reading mysteries is, if I was ever to get on a
boat and saw Hercule Peroit or Miz Marpole or Sherlock Holmes hop on,
why, I'd hop right off, wouldn't you? But in this mess, Ben, there's too
many 'possibles' and even the police are suspects."*
—Elizabeth Ann Linden, age 10 years

Judge Julian Parker Connors pulled quietly down a dirt road that lay
just beyond the Caudell Mansion. He'd traipsed these woods with
Rich often when they were both younger, even though he had no
taste for hunting, or hiking, or Rich's company, for that matter. His attention to the small details of finessing a relationship had served him well
through the years. He knew just how he would approach this house un-
seen, pick up the key from the hiding place Rich used to leave it in, and
enter the house by a side door in order to have surprise give him the upper
hand. He smiled to himself just as if he were performing some pleasant
chore. There would be no long discourse. He would necessarily have to
march Vince's wife up to the stepmother's room, to prevent the old lady
from calling the police when she heard the first gunshot.

He'd decided that he would shoot both of them in Eulee's bedroom and
only hoped that Rennie would not be there. If she were there, he would just
stop by the kitchen and bring her up with Cammie. Julian smiled almost
benevolently and fingered the gun in his pocket. It was a small handgun,
but it would do the trick. He knew just where to aim it. It would be quick.
Merciful, he thought. He was really doing them all a favor. He wondered if
they'd understand.

His had been a long journey of deception, and he could now almost see
the culmination of years of subterfuge. He had been born a younger son,
almost eclipsed by the perfection of the Connors' firstborn son. His elder
brother had excelled at everything and inherited the lion's share of their
father's estate. Russell Deland Connors had been the most handsome of
the Connors children. He'd been a natural athlete excelling at any sport
he'd happened to favor. Julian had been forever walking in the shadow of
his older brother's successes. As a young man, he had been consigned by
his father to develop a relationship with his great uncle in the hopes he'd
inherit from this source. So, he'd been left, and somewhat precariously, he

thought, to pander to an avuncular old man whom he found tedious and boring; and had in the end successfully inherited his uncle's properties, in a small town well and truly removed from the Atlanta area. He still resented his being shelved in what he considered a backwoods area of the deep south.

Yet he'd enjoyed being the "big fish" in a little pond even while missing his beloved Atlanta. And he had found the art of deceit to be exciting. He had been at it so long, he had begun to study and savor it. It was exhilarating to so finely thread the line between the honorable public servant and the cold-hearted mercenary taker he'd hidden from even those who thought they were his closest friends—and he'd done it for decades. He had no loyalties, save to self, and any trace of conscience had long ago become reprobate. The only difference today made in the pattern of his life was that, today, he would not *delegate* someone else's destruction. Today, he would do his own dirty work. *Today*, he thought with some relish, he would become not just the "sentencer" but the hangman. He much preferred that term to murderer.

Coming upon his destination suddenly in the form of a two-story antebellum mansion, he pulled up short and brought his mind back to his current problem. He was a little winded from his quick walk through the woods and took a moment to catch his breath. He spotted the steps leading up to the side door of a porch that extended the length and breadth of the old home. He made a quick survey of the surrounding land and buildings; and after ascertaining that it was devoid of anyone but him, he stepped out into the open and walked up to the balustrade. He quickly removed the finial that decorated the top of the left railing. There was no key. He let fly a word that he regretted, but only because he thought it might warn someone within of his coming. He hadn't visited the old Caudell home since Richard's death. He'd really counted on his presence being a surprise. So much easier to maneuver a person who was busy with the why's and wherefore's of a visit than someone who expected and was prepared to greet a visitor.

He frowned and once again took in the land surrounding the house. Then he quickly inspected the windows for any sign of Camille or Rennie. *No one about.*

Julian was a brilliant man. He retained information effortlessly—never forgot anything, and could "think on his feet". If his heart hadn't been so stunted, there would have been no limit to his abilities to rise politically or indeed in any profession he had chosen. As it was, he had centered his life on the acquisition of money, fine things, and to some degree power and dissimulation. He quickly rethought his plans for entering the house and gaining the upstairs room without incidence. He believed he could do that without revealing his hand even. Oh, he did love poker, he thought randomly. He would have to do more of that after he'd wound up all this messy business.

He'd walk up to the front door. No one, but Camille and Eulee, seemed to be there. Even their gardener/handyman, Curtis Rabin, had left. He'd knock on the door and get Cammie up there by telling her that he needed to talk to both her and Eulee about some papers Vince had wanted them to sign. Yes, that would do it. He'd just have to intimate that it was about the estate. Once upstairs, he would take care of both of them. Then he'd be on his way to take care of Vincent. The gun he held in his pocket would implicate Vincent. No one but Vince knew that he had it; and the judge was pretty sure that some of Vincent's fingerprints remained on the hand gun he'd borrowed—he had been very careful in handling it when it was given to him. Further, Vince had told him that he'd bought it at Whitcomb's Hardware Store, so that Harve would remember his buying it. The judge paused before taking the steps to the entrance, allowing his breathing to ease. He hadn't been used to exercise lately and it took a minute for his chest to stop heaving in and out. After he'd calmed, Julian faced the home once more, crimped his thinning lips into a smile and took the stairs of the front porch entrance. He approached the door and was preparing to knock when the door was snatched open and a tall stranger appeared, his right hand controlling the door the other extended behind his back.

The judge clamped his mouth tight and looked beyond him to see the face of Camille and *God help him—Connie Caudell.* He had eased his hand into his coat pocket as the door had opened. He fired the gun he clutched at the stranger's gut while the gun was still in his pocket. The judge coldly began to step around the man now clutching an area just below his chest and stumbling backwards. Julian slowly pulled the gun out of his pocket and extended it toward Connie and Camille. The man reeling backwards, single-mindedly brought around his left hand and fired almost point blank at Judge Julian Parker Connors' head. Connors went down like a kite that had lost the wind. He was lifeless before he hit the threshold of the door.

Alex Harrington kept himself from falling by clutching at the open door. He turned an ashen face to the women whose own countenances just about mirrored his coloring. "I should've expected that," he apologized. His words sent them scurrying into action. "Sit." Cammie clipped, pointing toward the deacon's bench that was set against the wall and stepping to the small table beside it that held their foyer phone. She began to dial Doctor Prescott. Connie put her arm about Alex's waist and helped him to the bench. He sat obediently and when Cammie hung up, she ran to retrieve some towels from the kitchen. Returning quickly, she handed them to Connie, who quickly folded one and pressed it to the wound. Over her shoulder, she urged Camille to see about her Mama. Feeling the effects of early pregnancy, Cammie gritted her teeth and turned from the bloody doorway. She took the stairs as fast as she could. For once, Miz Eulee quietly awaited the outcome of the events downstairs. When Camille rushed in the room, the old lady let go a long breath, and withdrew her hand from her covers. A small handgun was clutched in her trembling hands. "What happened?" she rasped, then cleared her throat. Camille related the judge's attack and how Alex's quick response had saved them all. She had had no doubt as to the judge's intention from just the look on his face because this time Julian hadn't masked his emotions from his victims.

Mrs. Ella Therese St. Claire Linden was busily preparing supper. She had a ham in the oven and now stood at the counter dicing celery for her potato salad. If Claire or Janie had been there, she'd have had them helping, too, but they were both spending the night at a friend's. Ella had had the house to herself since Elizabeth had come bursting in with her request for her Dad's presence at his folk's house.

They'd been gone almost half an hour. She suddenly experienced a feeling of deep dread within that brought her chopping motions to a halt. She stood for a minute completely stilled, then bowed her head and began to intercede for her family. The feeling and the prayer were more intense than anything she'd ever experienced in that manner. At the end of her prayer, tears coursing down her cheeks, she jerked her head up and ignoring the apron tied tightly around her waist set off for her in-law's home "just down the way", knife still in hand. She ruefully placed it in one of her deep apron pockets and continued her determined walk.

As she glanced at Mom and Pop Linden's, Axel Arnette's police car swooped up the driveway and pulled beside the front porch, sending a cloud of enveloping dust over its the black and white Galaxy and the front porch of the Linden home. She picked up her pace without being aware she'd done so. She watched as Axel and Vern jumped out of the car drawing their revolvers, then ran around the front side of the house. She was pretty sure that was the county DA's car already parked up close to Mom and Pop Linden's house.

Ignoring her high heels and the knife thumping at her thigh from within her apron pocket, she began running, bearing her weight on the balls of her feet. It had been quite a while since Ella had run full out, much less in heels, but she kept those heels as high off the ground as possible as she ran down the two-rut road that led to the Linden home. She whisked past Elizabeth and Ben's bicycles, haphazardly thrown on the grass at the side of the house, fear almost taking her strength. Not knowing why, she sped around the back side of the house, opposite to Axel and Vern's choice.

Ella slowed her pace and began a covert approach to the last corner before the side porch. She toed off her high heels even as she heard Axel warning someone to put down their weapon. Gaining the last corner now, she peeked out and what she saw made her whole being grow cold.

She'd heard of people saying their heart skipped a beat or had plummeted to their shoes, and taken no notice of what she considered an exaggeration. But she now experienced that sensation profoundly. The scene before her nearly drained her of consciousness. Their district attorney stood on the second step of the stoop fairly radiating anger; and on the ground, Lelah Linden endeavored to stand stock still with Vince's gun held flush to the back of her head. Facing the DA and his hostage, her family huddled before them about three feet away, eyes pinned on the catastrophe taking shape before them. Vince held a big manila envelope of papers in his right hand.

The old lady was trembling slightly, but otherwise stood bravely with shoulders back and focused countenance holding the attention of her family. Beyond them, Axel Arnette and Vern Starnes were carefully edging toward Vince. The DA's gun hand had begun to visibly shake. His visage emanated stark fear and hate. Ella could see that he was beyond unstable and that his attention was wholly taken up by his hostages and the approaching officers. His back was partially turned toward her and the screen door was between her and Vince, held open by his shoulder and part of his left arm.

"Get back," he husked at the officers. "Get back, now!" and he jerked his head at the two men while pulling back the hammer to cock the revolver. She noted quickly that he was left-handed and that a length of the arm holding the gun extended beyond the screen door.

Ella stepped quietly from her corner and began a stealthy approach to the threatening figure before her, praying that her family would not betray her presence by their expressions.

She saw Elizabeth and Ben's eyes widen through her peripheral vision, and then at the slight shaking of her head, the two settled back to watching Vince and Lelah Linden determinedly. She softly let out a breath, still inching forward, and pulled out the sharpened chef's knife she'd accidentally carried out of the house from the pocket of her apron. She turned the knife blade upwards. Holding her weapon in both hands, she prayed for strength, courage, accuracy and speed. Ella started low and brought it in a sweeping motion upwards, aiming at the wrist of Vince's gun hand. She made the swipe with all of the strength she could muster.

Everything happened in the Bible's "twinkling of an eye". As she met Vince's arm and thrust upwards, his finger squeezed and the gun fired. Simultaneously, Axel and Vern's guns blasted the quiet of the country afternoon. Grandma Lelah dove to the ground and both Art and his father jumped to aid her and subdue Vincent.

There was nothing to subdue. Vincent DeLand Caudell slumped backwards half on the stoop, half on the porch, the door caught over his knees and only partially opened now, his gun having fallen silent beside him. As quickly as the judge before him, he was gone.

The uproar that echoed through Freeman County was unprecedented. The papers and beauty shops were full of the hum of people sharing what they knew and supposing what they didn't. People came in for haircuts to local barber shops days early, came to church like it was Easter, and lingered outside longer than ever just to exchange stories. The GBI showed up the following Monday. They conferred with Axel and Vern, and called in the Lindens and Caudells. The bullet that Julian had hit Alex Harrington with had gone cleanly between any major organs or arteries, and was generally regarded by the locals as a miracle, along with Connie Caudell's reappearance. Alex had lost a lot of blood and had been transported to the local hospital by the funeral home's hearse; where he underwent surgery performed by Dr. Prescott. Allowing a few days to pass, the GBI visited the mending doctor with more questions. Alex produced a safety deposit key along with a lawyer's address and phone number—both in Tallahassee, and agents were duly sent out to question the lawyer and the PI as well as retrieve the safety deposit box contents. It contained all of the evidence

Alex's detective had uncovered in the last three years. It had information on the whereabouts of J.C. and Della Jensen who'd carried out Connie's kidnapping and imprisonment; evidence linking both Julian Connors and Vince Caudell with the Blue Heron and other nefarious ventures in and around Freeman County. It also connected the dots between Freeman County's Judge and DA to Connie's kidnapping through their involvement and payments to both Ed Norris and the Jensen's. They had phone records on long distance calls the Judge had made to the two apartments that Ed Norris and the Jensen's had rented. They had a dated picture the detective had obtained by happy accident. When questioning the neighboring apartment dwellers, a long-time renter remembered having a picture of Connie. He searched some albums and had produced a picture of his new car, a gleaming red Buick with the dealer sticker still on the window, which not only showed off his vehicle, a model now old, but in the background, a recognizable glimpse of Connie Caudell being escorted into the Jensen's apartment building by Ed Norris—and every bit of the body language of both Ed and Connie said, 'it was only by force'. "And yes," he'd be "glad to testify." *Never had liked those people; and had wondered about the illusive, quiet woman who never walked out unescorted; and had always seemed frightened.*

Jerry Bigham was arrested for collusion to hinder an investigation by violating a court ordered search warrant, as well as part ownership in the object of that search—a brothel/gambling establishment; along with Harve Whitcomb, and Dale Green, the supposed lone owner of the purported restaurant/motel. The information that Raynelle had gathered and been blackmailing them with, had cemented their probable stay in prison, and the information that Alex Harrington and Connie had provided, assured that it was not just probable, but their future residence for many years to come. In addition to all of this, a couple of the girls who had worked The Blue Heron were willing to testify for the state in exchange for leniency. Things began to settle down. A new DA and Judge were duly appointed for the interim until a special election could be held. The state was reconsidering Big John's sentence without knowing just who to pen Raynelle's death on. The governor in an almost unprecedented move, pardoned Big John, and he was released from prison. The local police reopened Raynelle's case. In subsequent trials, Jerry Bigham, and Dale Green were only too glad to besmirch the memory of the dear departed. They had alibis for the night Raynelle was murdered, but both managed to implicate Julian and Vince before they were silenced. The state concluded that Julian Parker Connors or Vincent DeLand Caudell, either singly or together, had planned and carried out Raynelle Anne Abrams' murder. They closed the case files. Big John reclaimed his old truck and after stopping in Barne's Store, he set out for Phenix City to get his children.

Alex Harrington was released from the hospital and encouraged to take it easy for a few weeks. He had developed a firm friendship with Dr. Prescott and his sister, Hannah, and was being courted as a partner for Dr. Prescott's practice. Alex had begun to think of it as a real possibility. He became a regular visitor in the Caudell home. He was the big brother that Connie always wished she'd had in Vincent; and their mutual respect and appreciation had engendered a solid friendship in the three years they had been gathering information on the Judge and Vincent. He was now 38; nine years older than Connie and two years older than Camille. Miz Eulee adored him, of course.

The Caudell household had been in deep mourning over Vincent. It had been a bitter thing to see such a life wasted, and Eulee Caudell had loved Vincent, and longed to mother him; but had settled on befriending him; and then been rejected at both. It was the one thing she had not been able to do for Rich. With the few words she and Rich had exchanged on the afternoon of his death, she'd made a heart promise and a verbal one to him, as well, that she would somehow "reach" her stepson; that she would continue to love and pray for him. And she had utterly failed at even having had him believe that she loved him. Rennie had finally had a talk with Miz Lee. "Miz Eulee," she had said, "Even God don't make folks choose Him. He up an' died for 'em, but He don't make 'em choose Him. You sho' can't do no better than Him at dat."

"Mr. Rich. He unnestand. He know now. I'm sho' he knew den, too. All you could do was love dat boy. An' you done dat. Now, Miz Lee, you leave it in God's hands. Dat's wat you do. He got it anyway. You let Him heal you up now, and you let go a dat burden. You got yo' *baby girl home*! Bless the Lord! It's time to rejoice. Dat's what I say. Rejoice! I know Mr. Rich is."

Mrs. Eulee Barton Caudell, had smiled then; and said as humbly as Rennie had ever heard her, "Rennie Girl. Thank you. I don't believe Rev. Archer could've put it any better. God smiled on us 'bodaciously' the day you first walked through our front door." And Camille overhearing Rennie's assurances had taken Rennie's words to heart, as well. She had been struggling with the same issues essentially that Mama Lee had been brooding over. Could she have done it differently? Should she have continued to turn the other cheek when he had manhandled her? A God given peace settled within her. It was covered. She knew. And, also, she knew that Vincent had never intended their marriage to be anything but a financial bailout. He'd seen her as a cash outlet and clung to an unfaithful lifestyle from the very first until the very last day of his life. She'd returned to her room and wept for the want of a father for her baby. One who would love and show their little one what a true man was. She wept and allowed God to begin to heal the long years of hurt. Vincent had injured so many people—not the least of which was his own sister.

Alex had begun to work with Miz Lee in the afternoons; stretching her leg muscles and exercising them. She'd found that she was able to resume some movement and had hopes of regaining some of her independence. He had shown Connie and Cammie how to do the exercises with Miz Lee and they were making great progress. Of all the things that had prompted Miz Eulee's efforts to regain autonomy, the biggest impetus was the return of her precious girl. She marveled every day at God's goodness.

Camille and Connie had become friends. Cammie had helped Connie with Ben's understanding of the time he'd been left without his mother and a belief that she was dead. He'd had such mixed feelings—great joy at having his mother again; anger at her letting him think she was dead; and confusion in trying to reconcile those deeply held feelings. He'd gone to Cammie and even to his Grandma as the days passed—trying to understand the things his mother had done and not done.

They hadn't told him about his birth. Connie thought that it was too much to handle. But at last, she had had to level with him about his beginnings and birthright. She had softened the blow by trying to lighten Ed Norris' character, but her son had been there with her and remembered the man. In the ensuing weeks, Ben had grown too quiet for a ten-year-old boy. They all worried and prayed for both him and Connie. Finally, one afternoon, Rennie had been baking sugar cookies and had asked Ben to ice and decorate them with her. He'd been just as quiet while he'd worked side by side with sweet Rennie. But he'd smiled during the decorating, and after a dozen or so had piled up on his side, he ventured. "Rennie?" and he paused with the butter knife poised above his cookie with the icing almost imperceptibly gathering to drip. Rennie ignored this and said, "Whachyoo want, Honey?"

"I wuz just wonderin'," and he'd paused again, seeming to be thinking something over. Rennie smiled and waited for the boy to think things through. "The preacher read a while back where 'the sins of the fathers are visited to the third and fourth generation on their children...' And it made me wonder some. That's all. If your Daddy hurt somebody, does that mean you're gonna pay for it; or does it mean you'll hurt somebody, too. Does it mean I'll—mmm—someone'll be just like him—his children will, you know?" He paused and turned his big, sad eyes on her questioningly.

Rennie held *her* knife in the air, now, not caring about the progress of the icing toward her clean table, either. She took her time, and the boy before her seemed not to mind. "Honey," she said finally, "It be some true that a natural curse do get passed on from fathuh to chile." Ben's face fell and the light in his eyes seemed to die out. "But, wait, Honey. Dey's more. See. De prophets in de Bible say dat dere would come a time when dat wouldn't be true no mo'. It was the diff'ence Jesus made, you see. Every chile born was chained to sin, almost like a genetic disease—our preacher done 'splained it like dat. You, me, Miz Cammie, yo Mama, Dr. Prescott, Mr. Linden, Miz Abby, Elizabeth—dudn't mattuh who. We all got it at birth. No matter how good somebody seem, dey's all sinned. Come into da wurl full up a self an' not carin' bout nobody but ourself and dead to da Lord. But when Jesus come and died for us, it wudn't necessa'ly true, no more. I mean, you could break da curse, see? All you gots to do iz ask Him to break it fo' you. He don't just forgive yo' sins, see Ben. He clean you up from 'em on de inside. He changes yo' heart. Sometime it take a long time for a body to quit sum a dem sins. Sometime, you be doin thangs to break his heart, an' you don' even know it. But He know all 'bout you. He able to make you a new man, see? Spite a yo Daddy. No mattuh who yo daddy or mama is. Ain't mattuh what coluh eithuh, Ben. God don't look at people like us people do. He see da heart. And when He's yo' Savior, He say, everythin' is clean. Everythin'—de past, de present, de futuh. De Bible done sayed, 'Dey's therefore now no condemnation.' Dat's what He done fo' us. You unnestand that, Ben? We free."

Ben thought a moment and then nodded at her and smiled. "Listen, Honey," she assured him, "don't matter who yo' Daddy wuz. Don't matter what he done. You got da chance to be a new person. Start a new family line. You be da first one to pass on a legacy." And she rolled that last word off her tongue like it tasted good or something. Ben smiled. There was nobody like Rennie. "And yo' legacy is dis—you live knowing Jesus got a great big love for you. Dat He knows yo name. Dat He care about you and what happens to you. Dat He's plannin' up good for you and your family. And when you gets a fam'ly of yo' own, why den, you introduce 'em to Him. Just like you would yo' best friend. Cause dat's what He iz, boy. Dat's what He is."

They finished icing the cookies then. Ben was still quiet. But it was a good quiet. He was mulling over what Rennie had shared and thinking about how in the world a boy like him could matter to God. By the time he'd iced his last cookie, he smiled at Rennie and thanked her for her 'splainin' things to him. He mulled over that speech for some time to come. But somehow it lightened up his worries. With every passing day, he got back a little more of the joy he'd begun to have here in this big old house. He was sorry that his uncle had never learned the things about the Lord that Rennie and Cammie had been teaching him over the past three years. He must not have known them, or he'd have been a different man. He knew that when he had realized that God loved Him and knew His name even, it had made a world of difference. One thing though, he didn't miss his uncle. The old place felt like someone had opened up all the windows on a spring day and let in warmth and light. He could see even his aunt changing before his eyes. And he had his Mama now! He still couldn't believe it.

The local paper had arranged for Ben and Elizabeth to meet with them together at Carl and Lelah Linden's home. They wanted to interview all four of them and Art and Ella Linden, too. The man who came to interview them, Ron Barnes, brought along Gordon Clarke, who worked for him a few afternoons a week doing odd jobs and some photography and developing. He wanted to know all about Elizabeth and Ben's finding both the secret papers and money hidden in the kitchen baseboard; but he made a big "to do" over their finding the papers and ledger that Raynelle had hidden under the house. Ron didn't ask them anything about that last day when they had seen Vince Caudell die. The Lindens had specifically asked him not to put the children through all of that again. Even the adults had had trouble with nightmares after that afternoon, and there were nights when it was hard for the children to get to sleep. It was beginning to recede for them and that's the way they wanted it.

The interview went well. The reporter had centered on the children's having found important documents that had helped to clear John Colton Abrams' name, and won him a pardon by the governor. He gave a little background on the interests of Ben and Elizabeth, who their parents were and their ages. He'd gotten Elizabeth's grandparents' permission to take a picture in the kitchen of the Abrams' home. He had Gordon take the picture; and had asked Ben and Elizabeth to pull out the little kitchen baseboard drawer. Then, Gordon had taken one more of the silver signet ring that Elizabeth had found and wore around her neck. When the article came out in Thursday's paper, they had used not only the picture of Ben and Elizabeth, but the smaller picture of the silver signet ring with the amethyst lion. There was a small write up on how Elizabeth had found the ring at the Abram's house and it's dating back to the eighteenth century by the British silversmith stamps on the inside of the ring.

Ben and Elizabeth were instant stars in their elementary school; but they both refused to talk about what had happened with Vince Caudell. Both Linden couples and the Caudells had gotten together at the Caudell home one evening just after the tragic day, and talked through much of what had happened during the traumatic events of that afternoon. They had prayed and sought each other's forgiveness where anyone felt they needed to do that. Mostly, Miz Lee had apologized for the hurt her son had inflicted; but the Lindens had expressed their sorrow that Vince was killed.

Chapter 13

"Funny thing about dust. It always kickin' up."
—Rennie Esther Jones Baker

S o, life seemed to settle down then. Elizabeth asked Ben on Thursday's bus ride home from school if he'd like to ride his bicycle around the neighborhood and help her deliver her Girl Scout Cookies. "Saturday morning," she'd added; then looked up to see Ben eyeing her with exasperation. He was just on the edge of saying "No!", when the thought occurred to him that so much adventure seemed to follow this girl. "Mmm," he'd stalled, while looking around to see if anyone had heard. "Maybe." he'd mumbled. She'd laughed then with understanding. "Oh. Sorry," she'd offered, and made a face at Pete Belden who'd turned around in his seat to stare at the both of them knowingly. Pete had red hair and an abundance of freckles and was in the same grade as both Ben and Elizabeth. He liked to laugh. He liked to laugh a lot. But Elizabeth didn't want to be the brunt of it. "Nevermind," she'd said firmly. Ben looked some relieved.

When Saturday came, Ben showed up at Elizabeth's house with his bicycle and asked if she still planned to deliver cookies. She'd nodded and then he'd asked, "Do any of them go to places where there are kids? Mmmm—kids in our grade?" She'd laughed and said, "Only a few, but I'll get Mama to take me to deliver to those, okay?"

He'd smiled then and relaxed. "Where to first?" and they'd churned up the dirt trying to beat each other to the end of the driveway. "Miz Gadsden's first!" she'd called after him.

It had taken most of the morning and Elizabeth had saved Miz Elise Parrish's cookies for the next to the last delivery. After Miz Parrish, there was only Miz Abby to deliver to. She'd had to wait until the young clerk had gotten off work at Barnes'—which would be just after the lunch hour. Elizabeth knew that she probably should have delivered Miz Parrish's cookies first as her neighborhood was where she had started, but she dreaded that drop off so much that she kept procrastinating. She'd acquainted Ben with the next delivery's name and the fact that the lady was a bona fide character.

She waited a bit and between puffing while she pedaled, she'd finally opted for honesty. "She's a pill," she'd confided. "She's *weird*." And then, she'd gone on to describe the way she looked to Ben.

Ben looked at her and said, "I think I might've seen her in Barnes once. She was squawking about there not being a Clarion in the newspaper bins." He paused and straightened, allowing his bike to coast a bit. "Maybe we should get your Mom to take us to this one?"

'Lizbeth looked like she was thinking that over some, but then announced firmly, "Naw, let's get it over with. I'm not going back there to sell nuthin' after this. She gave me the creeps." and then she felt a little guilty for talking about a customer like that. Her mother often said, "If you're afraid to say it to a person's face, don't get so brave behind their back."

They puffed over the pedals, playing at racing and let a little silence fall. Then Elizabeth said, "Her house is pretty close to yours. She lives in Dennis and Clara Hilton's garage apartment.

Ben looked surprised. "You mean she's the one drives that ol' red convertible Nash?"

"Yeah," and Ben noticed Elizabeth got a little soft-eyed. "Isn't it cute?" she continued and turned to him to get his response.

He thought this wasn't the time to critique a car she liked. "Shore," he said and stretched the truth some, but he really didn't want to hurt 'Lizbeth's feelings. "Okay," and he was pedaling along beside her now, "Well, let's just take it to her and stop by my house to see Granny. She's been sayin' she wanted to see you. Then we can hit Miz Abby's."

Elise Parrish had read and reread the accounts of the Judge and DA's demise. She'd begun to feel a little safer about the events of the past six months. Surely, no one would have any way of knowing that she had once been Raynelle Anne Abrams' sister-in-law. There were just a couple more "loose ends" to tie up. She smiled to herself and started the off-key humming again. In the background she could hear the incessant dripping of her kitchen sink. It seemed to be keeping time with her humming. She ratcheted up the squeezing motion on her old scissors, busily cutting out the picture of *HER RING* from the local paper.

Blasted little girl. What was SHE doing with it? She had planned to go back to Raynelle's house after the investigation was over and the trial furor had settled down and search for it. She knew that she'd lost it that night struggling with Raynelle. *What had poor little Jeffrey been thinking to take up with the likes of her?* Elise had seen the files at the Lafayette Facility where she'd been confined. She knew what those big words had meant that were written in her folder. So. She'd been diagnosed crazy, but *she* had more sense than to take up with a person like *Raynelle.*

Her humming warbled all over the place. *No, that's not how it went. It went up, there, didn't it?* She had always had trouble with that melody, but *she WOULD have found her ring.*

The snick snick of the scissors went out of rhythm as her vise-like grip tightened suddenly causing a "miscut" that escaped her eye. She knew that. *If it hadn't been for that Linden child. But I'll take care of it,* she thought to herself and continued her humming.

Footsteps sounded on the stairway to her apartment. "That must be Dennis Hilton." Most days, the woman enjoyed the solitude of her home. She pushed away at the quiet of the house with conversations when it got to knelling in her head too much. Looked like this conversation was going to be interrupted though. She frowned. *The footsteps were too light.*

"Oh, yes. It's the Linden girl with the cookies." In the process of placing her last clipping between the pages of her scrapbook, she looked down to see she'd slit the whole top corner off. Furrowing her eyebrows, she released a huffing breath and slid it between the black pages of the book. She put her packet of little black tabs and her scrapbook to one side and reached down for her purse.

She took her purse and the malicious looking pair of scissors to the counter. It ran the length of one of her tiny kitchenette walls to the doorway, was covered by a thin Formica veneer and sported chrome molding around its edges. The purse was set down at the edge closest to the doorway, and then she placed her scissors at the top of the middle compartment of the handbag. She pulled out the envelope with the exact amount in it for the cookies. *She did love chocolate mint.* Reaching into the envelope, she took out two dollars, placing it within the confines of her purse, then smiled. "There. That should get 'er in here."

Her apartment's front door opened to a small kitchen/dining room, and then led to a den. She stepped over to the kitchen sink and opened a cabinet. Elise pulled out an old paint drop cloth. She doubled it over the mat that covered her entrance and awaited their knock. Her doorbell wasn't working currently, but Dennis had promised to come over and fix it and her leaking faucet—this week. She could hear from the footsteps that the girl wasn't quite to the door. She walked over to the side window and peeked out to see if the girl's mother awaited her downstairs. There was no car, but there were *two* bikes. She scowled and thought on that for a bit. The knock on the door interrupted her.

Phenix City, Alabama

Lydia had called their family lawyer the morning after Annie shared about her biological father's death. Annie's aunt was so thankful that he was an old friend of her husband's and had often visited in their home in years past. He had volunteered, upon hearing the trembling of emotion in her voice, to come over after hours to listen and offer advice. And "No, no," he would not hear of "money changing hands on this occasion". She was to look at it as respect for both Frank and her, his dearest old friends.

So, she had swallowed her protests and thanked Preston, deeply grateful for his offer to help. Lydia had gotten a trusted neighbor to keep both Annie and Bo while Preston and she talked over her problem. The following afternoon he'd shown up at her door, and over coffee and cake, had listened to the story that Lydia repeated from Annie's telling.

At the end of it, she went a little further with the story than the child had been able to provide—offering details of Raynelle's life and two marriages, and then of the last year's events. At the finish, she offered one last piece of information. "Preston," and she'd fastened her eyes on his seriously, "Raynelle's first husband, Jeff Jr., had a sister. She'd had a lot of—trouble—from the time she was a child she'd been troubled. And she discovered her mother's d-death herself. She was alone at that big old house in Pineville—well, that's where the Perkins were from—Pineville, Louisiana, you see; well-to-do folks; lived on an old family plantation."

"Frank and I were acquainted with them because we'd lived there when we were first married. We heard about all this later, but the daughter, Elise, she discovered her mama's body. It was a suicide. At least, that's what they thought," and she paused in her story to run her middle finger over her thin lips. She took a deep breath then, and continued, "They never found a note. There was some talk about 'foul play', but nothing was ever proved, no charges were ever brought. And the girl, Elise Lee, she wasn't ever the same after."

"Like to have killed Jeffrey, Sr. At that time, she was his baby girl and only child, and she wouldn't even speak for months after. She didn't look like she heard what you said at all. Just kind of sat there staring off like. They said she hummed incessantly."

"He had in lots of psychiatrists and doctors. When she did come out of it, she'd mumble to herself a lot and then she started doing things—violent things. Well, I heard tell she showed tendencies toward that before the tragedy. Said they couldn't keep a pet because she was not to be trusted with them."

"Jeffrey made sure she was always supervised after she got worse, though. Finally, he and their family doctor took her to an asylum. Well, it was an unusual institution—it specialized in mental break downs and people with, mmm—mental health issues. It wasn't run by the state; it was a private hospital, and mostly 'rich folks' were there. Jeffrey Sr. went to see her often."

"He met a nurse there. Within the year they were married. A year after that, they had a baby boy. They named him after his father—Jeffrey Lyle Perkins. They were very happy."

"After some time, Jeffrey, Sr.'s daughter had to be transferred to a state institution because of repeated violence towards the staff and on one occasion, a visitor. I know all this because my sister, Nell Ann, and her husband, Ray, still lived in Pineville and kept us up with the news."

"But, Nell Ann and Ray's daughter, Raynelle; well, Preston, she was wild. She'd been spoiled. My sister and her husband, they gave her anything she wanted. Her first marriage with Jeff, Jr. didn't last any time at all. The only thing good came from it was Annie."

The lawyer was beginning to look a little bemused, wondering where the story was going. Lydia continued, "The thing is, when Annie told me about her real daddy last night; first thing this morning I called their family lawyer, back in Pineville, to see if Elise was still in an institution. We understood that the family business and any other family matters were being overseen through their old lawyer's firm."

She paused and sucked in a breath, "Jeff, Sr. and his wife are both gone now, and their lawyers wouldn't tell me anything because I wasn't family. But I have the 'uncanniest' feeling she isn't in confinement; and it's got me some worried."

"There are two things I need to know," she ended, "I need to know if Jeffrey's car and body are really in Hellman's Creek in Louisiana; and whether Elise is alive and sane, or still in an institution." She stopped and looked enquiringly at Frank's old friend.

John had almost made it to Phenix City. He was now driving through a lot of military traffic coming off of Ft. Benning, but after Columbus, would come Phenix City, Alabama and his babies. It almost felt like that first Christmas with his Uncle Burt. His stomach felt like a pinball machine had taken up residence inside it—but it was a happy kind of skittish. He was slowly letting go of the darkness—some form or another had been with him since the time he'd taken Raynelle as his wife.

Early in the marriage, he had realized that Annie was the best thing she'd ever done. She was the only joy in his home life, until little Bo had come along. He'd never known if Raynelle would be there when he got home or not. Sometimes back in Louisiana, she'd take Annie with her and that had always made him nervous, but usually, she'd leave the little girl at a neighbor's.

After they'd moved back to Georgia and Annie had closed in on six years-old, Raynelle had taken to leaving her at home on her own. She'd left her to look out for Bo, too, when he was just a baby. It had horrified John, the first time he'd found her there watching television by herself. She'd been eating crackers and had a Tupperware cup of grape drink that she'd made from tap water and a Fizzy tablet sitting on the coffee table. Bo was taking a nap in his crib.

The baby was closing in on two years-old, but Annie was way too young for that responsibility. He and Raynelle had had a horrible argument over what she'd done that night. He'd waited up for her and she'd trudged in after two in the morning, bordering on having drunk too much. She had come back at him with the fact that he had called her on his way home, and she knew he would be coming in about an hour after she left. She was sure that Bo would sleep that long.

He could *not* get through to her about all of the "if's" that hung over their children's heads with no adult in the house. She'd slammed the bedroom door and locked it. He could hear her falling on the bed while she yelled a warning at him to keep it all quiet unless he wanted the court to come in and take them away.

He'd wiped his face with his hand and turned away for their couch. He really didn't know what to do. Life with Raynelle had almost been like watching a movie with a train wreck coming. You just were stuck in your seat for the duration. Nothin' you could do about it. He thought about how he'd left off talking to the Lord about the same time he'd married Raynelle. He grimaced and shook his head back and forth, almost as if he were shaking out all the dross from the last five years of his life.

He smiled remembering the way Annie had said her aunt's name. She and Bo had had a special affinity for their Aunt Liddy. He thanked God for her. He wondered how the same two women could come from the same family. *The Lord was the One Who had made the difference.*

John's past kept him occupied all the way through Columbus and downtown Phenix City. He had come quite a few miles on the other side of town when he realized Aunt Liddy's house was just around the curve. He pulled up through a circular driveway lined by Live Oaks and Azaleas to stop in front of an old Victorian home encased in Sweet Shrub, Tea Olives and Ligustrum. Daffodils and Snowdrops encircled the beginnings of blossoming Violets and Marigolds and Sweet William, backed by Geraniums and Caladiums that ran the length of the porch on either side.

John remembered Raynelle saying how crazy her aunt had been about plants and flowers. He wondered if Annie had gotten to help her in her garden.

He stepped out of his truck and hardly took time for a needed stretch after so many hours of driving. He couldn't wait to see his babies. He strode to the door and rang the doorbell. He could hear laughter and footsteps; and then the door opened.

Liddy stood frozen and two small heads peeked out from behind her skirts, one blonde, one brunette. The two seemed to still for just a moment in time. Then Annie and Bo burst forth with "Daddy!" and he heard Liddy's

"John!" Liddy was in the process of opening the screen door to him when the two barreled into it throwing it back against the frame house with a loud clatter and stretching the springy coil that pulled-it-to beyond-its-former-furthermost boundaries.

It had caused John to jump back a foot in order to miss the wild sweep of the door to its banging climax against the side of the house. His children careened into his chest. He was kneeling now on their level and almost rolled the whole ball they'd become backwards off the porch.

He was never more thankful to *be* a big man; and his grin spread across his face like sunshine over a meadow. Aunt Liddy mirrored his feeling. "Everything was going to be alright now," she thought. Whatever God had done to release this big man from prison, she was rejoicing and praising Him. Two children had never needed a body more, she knew. "Come in, John. Come in. You're a sight for sore eyes."

Axel Arnette got a call from Baton Rouge, Louisiana about mid-day on a Wednesday—Tate Carson of the Louisiana State Police contacted him about what they thought was a five-year-old homicide that was connected to Raynelle Ann Abrams and, also, a search for a missing person, Elise Perkins, who had escaped from a prison for the criminally insane almost two years ago.

The conversation didn't last too long, but it cut up Axel's peace some. It had been a few weeks since Freeman County had been turned upside down by crooked officials and violent deaths, and the sheriff was counting on things settling down. He felt very possessive about his home place, and he liked it peaceful. Tate Carson had promised to send him the details of all their findings, but as far as Axel could understand—it spelled more trouble for his little town.

Raynelle's first husband had been murdered and his body hidden in a bayou in Louisiana. They had uncovered his car and what was left of his body only last week along with Raynelle's purse which still contained a legible driver's license with her picture and information. Further, said Jeffrey L. Perkins had had an older sister who'd been committed to an institution since adolescence. Past behavior indicated that she could be violent, this included the manner in which she'd made two escapes in the last ten years, and it was suspected that she had been involved with her own mother's death.

Raynelle's Aunt Lydia had alerted the Louisiana State Police through her lawyer. Little Annie had confided in her about Jeff Perkins' death, and from there the old lady had begun to wonder about Elise Perkins. During the process of the investigation, it was discovered that Elise had been using an alias—she was using the surname of Parrish with the first name the same.

Axel's first thought was to have Vern ask around about Elise Perkins and Elise Parrish. He was only waiting for a picture to be sent into his office. Armed with this, his deputy would hit the town grocery store, all four of the beauty salons, their two barber shops, and the diner and café located on Main Street. From there, he would talk to ministers, doctors, nurses, and check the town's one motel and all of the known rental houses in Carverville as well as Bennington.

He'd remind him to check the Western Auto, garages and banks and anything else he could think up. He jerked the telephone off his desk and pulled the Carverville Phone Book from beneath it. Axel reared back in his seat and opened the book to the "P's".

Abby Weston had made it home a bit early today. It was Wednesday afternoon and most stores back then took the afternoon off; clerks everywhere happily posting their "CLOSED" signs. The schools were out for Easter Vacation, too, and she was expecting Elizabeth Linden with her Girl Scout Cookies this afternoon. But that wasn't all she was expecting. She smiled absently to herself as she opened the side door to the kitchen. John Colton would be back in town today—at least she thought so. She prayed so.

Adam Linden, his old friend, had arranged for a vacation from his job in Macon, and along with some of their friends from the Bennington church, had begun to repair and clean up his uncle's old home across the street from the Linden's.

John's Uncle Burt had died while John was stationed in Louisiana. He'd come home for the funeral, but had to return quickly to his base. He'd been informed by his Uncle Burt's lawyer that he'd inherited his uncle's place. He'd managed to stay long enough for the reading of the will and probate, but then had to leave things as they were—only arranging for a high school boy to mow during the summers and check the outdoors on occasion.

When he and Raynelle had returned to Bennington, she would have no part of his uncle's old home. Said it looked unsafe, and that it was not modern. She'd agreed to live in the Linden's rental until he could either build or buy a more "fitting" home. This temporary stay had lengthened as John had tried to save for a down payment on a new home without much help from his wife. There were things a woman had to have she had frequently complained after squeezing too much from his check for things that he considered unnecessary.

He'd had to drive extra truck routes to make ends meet. It reminded him too much of his childhood with his parent's carelessness and had almost driven him crazy. He could never make her see that bills had to be paid first.

While Abby crowded through her kitchen door with a bag of groceries in tow, John Colton Abrams was even now heading home. He had managed to get a neighbor of Liddy's to drive his truck filled with her belongings and the children's things back to Georgia. He had driven Lydia Fleming's old Buick Sedan and it was full of three of the four people he counted most precious in his life.

Liddy had a radio in her car, but they mostly sang every silly song the kids could remember as the car and truck tucked away the miles between him and what he considered home.

He'd gotten Liddy to agree to live with him—at least for awhile, she'd said. But he had an eye to the future and counted on her being a part of his family for as many years as she could. He knew that she and Abby would love each other. He had bought a ring while he was in Phenix City and planned to stop at Abby's house before going to his uncle's home.

Alex drove to the Caudell home a little after twelve. He'd been invited for lunch. Cammie had invited him the day before when she'd kept an appointment with Dr. Prescott.

The doctor was pleased with her blood pressure and general health, but was a little concerned about the rapid weight gain she'd experienced. They talked about her diet and portions and whether she was still experiencing morning sickness. She asked if she should cut back on portions, but he assured her that what she indicated that she'd eaten was not too much.

Dr. Prescott said that he and Hannah would keep track of the weight, for her not to worry, "...just take those afternoon naps and eat sensibly, get reasonable exercise..." As she was walking out the door he asked if there were any twins in her family. *He certainly knew how to stop a body on a dime.*

Turning back to face him, she almost stuttered out that her grandmother had been a twin.

He scratched his chin and made a small noise underneath his breath, then offered, "Well, I was just curious. Probably not important. See you next month, then, Cammie. Kate will set up the appointment for you."

Cammie smiled. He always reminded her to check with his receptionist for next month's appointment.She saw Alex on her way out of the office. He picked up his gait to catch her as she approached the exit, and had reached around her now evidently increasing tummy to open the heavy door for her. They passed through together where he continued to walk alongside her as she made her way to her car.

He asked how she was doing, and if her visit had given a good report. She replied in the affirmative with a slight flushing of her cheeks. He cleared his throat and said that "that was good, that was good". She asked about his health and was relieved to hear that he almost felt back to normal.

It had taken Cammie a couple of weeks to understand the relationship between Alex and her sister-in-law. She had been surprised at the relief she'd felt when Connie spoke of how much he was like the big brother she had always wanted. And, then, Connie quickly apologized to Cammie, not knowing if that would hurt her newfound friend and sister-in-law.

Cammie assured her that she understood her feelings, and often yearned for Vince to be a different man than he was. She shared somewhat haltingly, that their marriage had been in name only for a very long time. And then catching Connie's thoughts about her obvious pregnancy, explained with much more reticence that her pregnancy had been an aberration due to Vince's drinking.

Before she had begun to show, Cammie had talked to Rennie about her pregnancy as they were working in the kitchen over a meal. It was not long after Vince's death, and Camille was still just beginning to realize that he was gone and that she had a baby of his to love regardless of all that had transpired between them. At some point in their conversation, Rennie had repeated the words God had given her to comfort young Ben, for they were some of the same things Cammie needed to hear now.

For over five years, she had been without a husband; only sharing a house—with no understanding or relations between them. That on that one night, out of almost two thousand others, a baby had been conceived only emphasized the fact that, despite what Vince had or had not been, or the way in which this child had entered her life, her baby was a gift from God.

Rennie had echoed her thoughts aloud almost verbatim.

Cammie stopped washing out a large pot dripping with suds, and looked at Rennie like she'd just heard a word from God. Her mouth frozen in a little "O" and suds dripping down her arms, she gasped, "Oh, Rennie, that is just what I was thinking—word for word. It's like a confirmation of the blessing of this baby."

They were both quiet for a moment then, the down at the nape of Camille's neck rising with this very personal assurance from the Lord. It was a memory she clung to over the next months.

Elizabeth and Ben were still talking about Miz Parrish's strange behavior. After speedily leaving her house, they'd stopped off to check in on his granny; and after calling 'Lizabeth's folks for permission, they'd had a short lunch with Ben's Grandma Eulee, his Mama, Cammie, Alex, and Rennie. They'd eaten in the dining room together, as Lee Caudell had succumbed to Alex and her family's persuasion to install a chair lift for the stairway.

She'd ridden down the stairs like a queen, then waved them all away after being helped out of the chair. Constance Eulee Caudell had clutched her cane determinedly and regally made her way to the old dining room table she and Rich had bought years ago. Alex had pulled back her chair and helped to seat her. His old school observance of southern amenities pleased her. The young doctor extended a manly courtesy to these ladies seemingly without thinking. It was a part of the way he cared about people, rather than an officious adherence to proper conduct.

As he slid her chair back under the table, Lee smiled, quickly cutting her eyes back and forth between Cammie and Alex. The slight air of excitement and a certain discomfort the two exhibited in each other's presence only added to her enjoyment. "Yes", she thought. "Things will be alright."

Connie caught her eye then and grinned knowingly at her mother. All the years that had passed during her kidnapping were as nothing. She felt an overwhelming joy at every meal she shared with this, her family. Her mother, her son, her sister-in-law—she couldn't thank God enough. That God had used a brother, who as long as she'd known him had troubled her heart, to bring her such a precious friend and sister was a source of wonder and great joy.

It was a pleasure to see the beginnings of a relationship between Alex and Cammie, too. The innate honesty between them and the kindness with which they treated each other was a reassurance of the validity and decency of love between a man and woman while Connie's own heart had time to heal.

Ben and Elizabeth ate with gusto and carried most of the conversation for the adults gathered around the table. Their meal was punctuated with laughter and lots of plans for their future entertainment. Children are a breeding ground for ideas that all start with "let's" and "why-don't-we". Before the meal had finished, they had secured several approvals for trips to the beach, a picnic at a nearby mill pond, and a trip to the Okefenokee Swamp in the fall. They had barely touched the surface, the two of them thought, but they dutifully thanked the cooks and excused themselves to make the last delivery of the day.

Just now they were pedaling toward the old Weston home in hopes of catching Miz Abby. They had two boxes of Girl Scout cookies to deliver and her promise to be there just after two. They pulled up at the grounds of the church they both attended. Most of Freeman County was flat, but their church sat on one of the few hills that graced this elongated county which touched the Atlantic Ocean on its eastern end and pulled back into swamp lands to the west. Elizabeth's granny often said, "the land was so flat, if they razed the trees, you could see all the way to Savannah".

They kept their feet on the pedals and balanced their bicycles by holding onto the white picket fence that surrounded the old church. Ben took the opportunity to wonder about "the Parrish woman".

"Elizabeth," he brought her attention back to his face which he twisted around to see her. They had their bikes parked one behind the other and he let go of the fence, swung his leg over and off his bike to engage his kickstand and talk seriously with her. Ben stepped back to her bicycle and continued, "You were right about Miz Parrish. I've never seen a woman act that weird—except maybe Miz Jensen. Something ain't right there. She made me nervous the way she seemed to make sure we stepped inside. I almost had the feeling she knew that money in the envelope wasn't enough. And what was that drop cloth over the door step about?"

Elizabeth was inclined to agree with him and said so, adding, "I was some worried, too, until Mr. Hilton showed up with the tools to make some repairs. And didn't she look mad, then. I was sure glad to get out of there!"

They had edged toward the door and around Dennis Hilton who filled the doorway. It had taken quite a bit of determination, and was only accomplished as he moved a little for them to squeeze through.

Elise Parrish had huffed her way past him, too, and called out after the rapidly retreating figures, "What if I need to get in touch with you today? Where will I call?"

Ben and Elizabeth had paused at the bottom of her stairway looking at each other quizzically—*what would she need them for?* Elizabeth had tried to answer politely, "We've just got one more delivery."

She turned and took another step to the ground only to hear the woman at the top of the stairs call down persistently, "But I'm thinking I might need some more cookies and I'd like to suggest some trips for your group. I need to talk to you today!" Miz Parrish's voice rang sharply in their ears, and Elizabeth watched as Ben's chin took on a definite firmness.

He turned slowly and said, "I know for a fact Miz Barnes would be glad to hear from you, Miz Parrish. She's the lady in charge of Elizabeth's troop. Why don't you call her? My granny is expecting us and after that we have to deliver Miz Abby's cookies. So, we won't be back. Thanks, though. Call Miz Barnes, or go by their store. She'd be there today." And he turned and fairly shoved Elizabeth toward their bikes. She turned her back to the obviously irate woman at the head of the stairs. She had to cover how amused she was at Ben's handling of Miz Parrish.

Still standing beside her bicycle, Ben sighed, and banged on her han-dlebars. "I sure am glad these two are the last boxes. The stuff that hap-pens to me when I'm with you! I'm just glad this last delivery is to Miz Abby."

"Yeah," Elizabeth agreed, "and she should be home now, too. Come on. Race ya'!" She spun up the dirt and laughingly took advantage of Ben's being off his bike. She only had a short glimpse of him dispensing with his kickstand and jumping on an already rolling bike. Neither one of them saw the little red Nash pulling on the other end of the church grounds.

By the time they'd pedaled into Miz Abby's, Ben had caught up to Elizabeth and passed her. He held up at the cattle gate and waited so they could both ride over together. They stared up the long drive and saw Miz Abby's Volkswagen was parked under the side portico.

Her house stood on what was one of the few hills in Freeman County. Ben always loved seeing her place because the land was so different than the surrounding flat lands. As they approached the old plantation home, they could hear her radio was wide open. It sounded like Shelley Fabares had a little help moaning over "Johnny Angel".

Ben dropped his bike on the ground near the front porch steps and grinned at Miz Abby's singing. "She sounds pretty good," he laughed.

"Hush, Ben," and Elizabeth made a face at him, "she'll hear you."

Claire and Janie had caught their younger sister miming "Born too Late" by the Poni-Tails in their living room one afternoon. She hadn't been playing it on their 45 phono too loudly. She'd kept it down just in case anyone came home. And boy, had they!

Claire and Janie had slipped in and enjoyed her act to the fullest. She was almost through the whole record before their laughter alerted her to her viewing audience. She hadn't been able to live down her "performance" yet. They were still ribbing her and getting laughs.

She turned back to Ben, "Come on."

Stepping up to the bell on the side of the front door, she rang, then knocked hard enough to be heard over Shelley's crooning. Pretty quickly, the radio lost volume and they could hear Miz Abby's high heels clicking toward her foyer. The door opened then and the sunshine that was Abigail Weston spilled over to encompass her visitors as she urged them to come on in.

They headed for the kitchen where she'd been putting a roast in the oven before Ben and Elizabeth had arrived. Abby had left her pocketbook hanging on the back of one of the dining room chairs and she walked over to retrieve it about the same time as Rennie tapped at the side door to the kitchen and opened it.

She poked her head in and grinned, her white teeth flashing against her warm chocolate face. "Hey," and she smiled at each of them, "Abby, I jest come over for some sugah. I fuhgot to get some on da way home from Miz Eulee's. Oh, and I plum forgot to bring yo' dogs with me. They were scratching at the door before you come home from work, and I let 'em in for a spell." This was said as she stepped in, set her cup on the table. and made a beeline straight for the window.

Persimmon was curled up there between the curtain and the window and when Rennie twitched the curtain, she mewed up at her. "I done seen dat woman what lives at Mistah an Miz Hilton drivin' up in yo yard wit dat funny little car she got." And she parted the curtain slightly to peer outside covertly while the three other kitchen occupants watched her.

Rennie had already shared with Abby how she had a bad feeling 'bout dat woman. *"LORD, HAVE MERCY!"* she cried out. "She comin' here—wid a *shotgun*! And to *DIS* side door!"

And she pointed a shaking finger at the door like it was the problem. Rennie sprang into action then and raced over to latch the door. Gathering up Abby's startled little tortoiseshell cat, she made for the children and Abby.

"Shoo out'a heah!" she hissed, shoving them out of the room.

Miz Abby looked aghast at Rennie, but allowed herself to be pushed from the kitchen along with Ben and Elizabeth. The cat, who loved Rennie, curled in calmly between Rennie's arm and body and amazingly hushed.

The two children were only too ready to believe Rennie's assessment of the situation. They had seen the Parrish woman in action only a couple of hours ago, and they urged Miz Abby to do whatever Rennie told her.

"She ain't *like* you, Abby. She *ain't like Mr. John.* I done seen dat in her eye—*long* time ago. She got a heart full a hate! Do what I'm tellin' you!"

Rennie ushered them to the landing above and grabbed the upstairs phone only to realize it was dead. "Oh, my Lawd. Hep us!" The words hadn't settled in the room before they heard what each one knew was the window in the side door being smashed by the butt end of a shotgun.

"Hsst! Abby, is dey anywhere up heah to hide? Dis a ol' house. Got to be somewhere."

As she heard the door downstairs thrown back against the kitchen wall, Abby started and began to realize she only had moments to take care of Rennie and Ben and Abby.

"Where are y'all?" singsonged a harsh feminine voice that rolled out from the kitchen.

"Follow me. Quick!" Abby led them to her room. "My Daddy told me about this passageway when I was little. Told me to keep it a secret in case I ever needed it."

She stepped hurriedly across the hall to the room opposite hers, threw back the curtains, and opened its window. Turning to retrace her steps, she ran smack into Rennie and the children huddled like three little ducks in her shadow. She motioned toward her door and followed their lead only pausing at the guest room door to lock it.

Abby quickly joined them within her room leaving that door open. They heard a step creak at the bottom of the stairs, and the three looked worriedly at their guide, then, followed her to her book case.

It was old, and had embellishments along the sides of the molding. The old shelf was made of a deep mahogany wood and reached to the ceiling. Sliding aside a piece of molding, Abby turned a small latch then slid the decorative piece of wood back in place.

She pulled the shelf quickly outward and it opened onto what looked like a dark hallway. She snatched at the flashlight on her night stand even as they heard Elise's steps at the top of the stairs. The woman had hushed and seemed to be stealthily searching for the house's inhabitants as she'd made her way up.

Abby silently urged them to enter the passageway. Once the four of them were within, she pulled the bookcase back in place, latched and bolted it from within. Abby turned on the flashlight and whispered for them to tiptoe behind her indicating that there should be silence. They couldn't hear anything out of Elise now, but Abby figured they'd eluded her by about five seconds. Thank God the woman had made her way up the stairs cautiously.

The little group followed Abby's light and her instructions with the stealth of Peter Gunn. Elizabeth could see Abby walking on the balls of her feet to prevent her high heels from clicking. She thought they had traversed the length of at least two rooms before Abby paused and bent down to pull up a doorway that covered an opening in the floor.

She pointed to a narrow staircase that descended to the first floor. Rennie took the stairs first, still clutching Persimmon to her side. while Abby held the light above her head. They could see Rennie's shadow magnified along the floor and casting strange shapes along the stairs and floor below. Elizabeth and Ben followed one by one. Lastly, Abby stepped down and closed the doorway.

She came down carrying the light in her left hand. They edged around the stairway and began to walk back in the opposite direction from the way they'd come on the second floor. Once again, Abby reached to open a doorway in the floor to another stairway. When they'd all made their way down, Abby had closed and locked the hatch covering the staircase. She walked over to a table that was standing at the center of the room, lay the flashlight on its side, and retrieved matches to light a large glass hurricane lamp that rested there.

Illumined now, the room revealed walls of brick on all sides with no opening or window. The floor was even made of the same brick. There was just too much to wonder at. Rennie and the children stared at their surroundings open-mouthed. Persimmon took advantage of their quiet to mew. Rennie set her down on the floor.

The small, square table was surrounded by four wooden chairs and underneath it a circular burgundy rug eased the harshness of the brick flooring. The little cat chose to curl up beneath the table right there on the soft rug. Ben and Elizabeth watched as her tail curled neatly around the mottled ball of fur.

A large chest rested against the back wall away from the stairway, and an old oaken wardrobe had been placed on the right wall next to the stairs. In between these two items of furniture, a yellowed pine corner cupboard was secured against the corner that connected both walls. Toward the middle of the left wall was a faucet and sink resting on a wooden cabinet. In the corner beyond the sink was a small closet, not too much larger than a phone booth.

Watching the children's eyes, Abby pointed toward it and said, "The shower and toilet. My Daddy had an old friend update the hand pump and 'thunder jug' that used to be here."

There was only one picture on the wall, and it seemed to be a very old map of Freeman County, and upstairs there ranted and raved a crazy woman with a shotgun.

Abby spoke first. "We don't want to get too loud, but this place is pretty much soundproof. She'd have to find one of the two doorways and then use an axe to get them open, because they're both bolted."

She paused for breath. "My father told me about this a long, long time ago. He made me promise never to tell, in case we ever needed it. I thought that was a great secret when I was little, and later I thought it was pretty funny. Even with the atomic scare a few months back and people building safe places, I still thought it was ridiculous. But I surely am glad he insisted now."

"Wonder what bee got up dat woman's bonnet up tha-uh?" Rennie asked.

"W-well,when we saw her today," Elizabeth offered hesitantly. "She seemed, um, kind of disturbed then. We almost thought she was *after us*. But for the life of me, I don't know why."

"We just took her by her Girl Scout cookies," Ben added. "Seemed like she just had to have us come inside her house. She was looking at the ring 'Lizabeth found at the Abrams' house, when Mr. Dennis Hilton shows up to fix her sink, and I thought she was going to have a hissy fit."

He rubbed the top of his crew cut then and looked up at the ceiling above them. "She turned plum purple when we wouldn't agree to come back and then got on our bikes instead. But I never thought she had anything in mind like this."

They heard the muffled sound of a gun going off somewhere upstairs. For Elizabeth and Ben, the shots re-surfaced the fear of weeks before with Ben's uncle.

Eyeing the four chairs around the table, Rennie motioned for them to sit, and after they did, she had them hold hands and began to pour out her heart to the Lord. They heard three more rapid fire shots. Rennie kept on praying. She prayed not only for their protection, but for anyone else's who came upon Elise stomping around with that gun. She prayed for the Lord to bring sanity back to the woman.

All seemed quiet upstairs when Rennie ended her prayer, but they had no way of knowing what was going on. Miz Abby began to talk about the passageway—more to keep the children from being afraid than anything else. Several more gun shots punctuated her story. She jerked a couple of times, but she, too, kept right on. "My Daddy said that passageway—" *BLAM!* "originally ran from the nanny's room to the children's." *BLAM!* "His great-great grandfather had a large—" *BLAM! BLAM!* "family, and loved to entertain. He made sure his children's nanny could get to them without any delay. No matter how many guests he had in the hallways, the nanny—" *BLAM! BLAM!* "could always have an unobstructed pathway to the children. The extra passage was added as an afterthought, so she could get downstairs without hindrance to the kitchen."

"Then, just before the War—" *BLAM!* "between the States, his great grandfather had the passageway sealed behind the bookcases, just in case his wife and children needed a place to hide. He had a ground level room bricked in under the house and then raised the dirt level under the house to cover the bricking. That's why we don't have to worry about making too much noise down here. Also, I closed the doorways that were put in to cover the stairs."

There was silence now since the last shot. The quiet was almost worse than the intermittent booming of the gun.

Abby spoke again, "You know, my Granddaddy said his oldest brother once told him there was a bricked tunnel from this room to the barn out back, but his brother had never shown him where it was. He made my granddaddy promise not to tell anyone—especially not their folks. My Daddy said *he'd* never found it; and had never heard his Daddy mention it before he talked to me about it."

"Strange, if it's true, that the two of them didn't know for sure. But my grandfather did say that my great grandfather's twin had fallen down the tunnel's stairs when he was just a boy and died later that night. I always thought they didn't want any other children to risk those narrow stairs after their war use. But, I'm really not sure; not even about the tunnel's existence."

Rennie spoke now. "If dey was a way to take a peek outside, I sho would like to. I'm some worried 'bout Earl. He rode over to Dublin to hep his brothers fix a car. He might be comin' home now. I sho' ain't want him to come in on dis! Lord, take care a dat man fo me!" And she rubbed her hand over her forehead and eyes, like she could scrub the fretting away.

"Well, let's look," Ben stated as he got up with Elizabeth following just behind him. "If your Granddaddy said it, there must have been one," he deduced. "That's not the kind of story someone would make up."

"Yeah," Rennie added, "da family prob'ly jess ain't wanted nobody to go down day aftuh what happen."

"It's got to be behind some of this furniture. That's how they did the other one," Elizabeth furthered Ben's cause while eyeing the large chest.

She bent to open it, and found a passel of old quilts. She and Ben looked to Miz Abby questioningly, asking with their expressions if they could empty the chest to check. "Sure," Miz Abby answered the two, nodding her head. "We'll all look—but quietly, okay? Don't forget to do it whisper soft just in case."

She and Rennie rose, too, and started turning around eyeing walls and furniture. Persimmon opened her eyes and quietly studied the strange behavior of her humans.

Ben and Elizabeth came to the end of the quilts with no hidden panel to show for it; plus, the chest moved fairly easily revealing nothing. They sighed and repacked it. Rennie walked over and pressed against the map to see if it covered an opening. She frowned and turned away to run her fingers over the bricks, pushing here and there, as she walked her way around the room. "Hep us, Lord," they heard her mutter.

Abby smiled. *If you had to be cooped up with a wild woman as your warden, she'd choose Rennie as an inmate every time.*

Ben and Elizabeth shoved at the old wardrobe, but it wouldn't budge. They sighed again and slumped down in the chairs at the table.

"Now, why wouldn't that move?" Abby wondered aloud. Stepping over to the bulky, reminder of a bygone era, she opened both doors, then absently wiped her dusty hands on the apron that was still tied around her waist. She stretched her neck to peer within and ran her fingers down the length of the right inside corner of the wardrobe. Finding nothing she followed the same search on the other side.

About midway down she ran across a small mechanism that seemed to give way when she brought pressure on what felt like a small handle. They heard a slight popping noise and a creak as the entire back of the wardrobe moved outward.

They were instantly crowded up to the opening oohing and wondering. Spider webs floated out from the edge of the door that had swung away from them. The air coming from what must be the tunnel smelled damp and stale as if it had settled there long, long ago. Abby pointed to the table and Ben retrieved her flashlight and blew out the hurricane lamp. He turned on the light and handed it to Miz Abby, watching along with Elizabeth and Rennie as she let its beam reveal another narrower set of stairs with just the merest hint of a small brick hallway.

"This has to be the tunnel," Elizabeth breathed.

"Thanks de Lawd!" Rennie's heartfelt exclamation echoed the feelings of each of them.

Persimmon chose this moment to jump into the wardrobe and make her way down the steps to the tunnel. She mewed and edged into the darkness away from them. Abby handed the flashlight to Rennie and gingerly stepped into the wardrobe and onto the first step of the staircase that descended further than their flashlight illuminated.

The staircase was more like an extremely angled heavy-duty ladder. The boards were made of what seemed to be a very thick oak planking, but where the light fell, you could see through the steps unlike the stairways before. The planks seemed to hold firm in bearing her weight and she reminded Rennie to close the wardrobe door behind them and to close its backing as well.

Abby motioned for the children and Rennie to follow as she slowly made her way down the steps. About ten feet down, their descent opened into a long, narrow hallway-like tunnel. They could hear Persimmon mewing somewhere up ahead. Rennie handed the flashlight forward to Abby who led the way down the old passageway. Indeed, it seemed not to have been used for many, many years. She began to think the old story about her great-grandfather's twin must be true as she swiped back the silken cluster of web before her with her flashlight.

The bricked and beamed tunnel stretched out before them and they walked quietly beneath the back yard of Abby's old home to a destination she was sure would be their old barn and horse stable. None of them could have said how far they'd walked later. There was just something about traversing a darkened, narrow spider-decorated tunnel that elongated distance. Ben would have ventured a half a mile. Elizabeth would've insisted it felt more like two!

The stables sat about two hundred yards from the old home and back in the day housed quite an array of fine horses. Abby's forbears had dabbled in some horse breeding and even some local racing; but all had loved farming and cattle and horse breeding; and all three had helped to sustain over five generations of Westons until the automobile had lured the Weston sons to industry over the agrarian and breeding interests.

The barn had been kept well in the years that passed with Archie keeping a small stable of horses for him and Abby and friends to enjoy. Archie had only sold the horses a year before his death as he'd been unable to support them. Abby began to wonder just what part of the stables their tunnel would lead.

She had always wondered why her great great great grandfather had chosen to wall in their barn with stones floated downriver from a quarry north of their small community. Now, she thought the tunnel may have affected his choice of veneer. It would certainly have a better longevity in keeping a secret passageway *secret*.

She could almost forget their dire circumstances in the exploration and wonder of their discovery; but thinking of Earl coming upon the woman inside her home chilled her heart. *Poor Rennie!* She began to pray again, asking the Lord to protect anyone who might visit her home. Suddenly, she thought of the very real possibility that John might swing by on his way home. Abby thought she had felt fear before, but it chilled her very soul now.

Oh, no! Lord no! She forced a lid on those thoughts, and instead poured her heart out to God for John, his babies—*their babies*, and Miz Liddy, and Earl, and whoever else might drive up. Surely those shots would alert someone. Deer season was over. She never shot anything. Earl always went with a buddy to his land whenever he hunted.

One of her neighbors would have to note the gunshots and wonder. It came to her then that that was all they would probably do. Think about it idly—never perceiving a cause for intervention.

"Oh, God. Help us." Abby whispered.

Not three feet in front of her she spotted a ladder-stairs to match the one at the other end of the tunnel. Motioning to the others for absolute quiet, she waited until they were all gathered up below the stairs and understood. Cautiously, she crept up the steps and brandished the light around what appeared to be a wooden hatch.

They could see Abby pulling back a bolt and putting her shoulder to the door. She lifted it up about six inches and shone the light around her. As quietly as she could lift a creaking door that had sat idle for over ninety years, she managed to raise it enough to step into the room without allowing gravity to slam it backward. She leaned it against the outside walls stone work, then motioned the others to stay put for a minute. Carefully she flashed the light on the stone masonry around her.

It appeared to be a hall-like, stone-enclosed room that ran the width of the stables. She scanned the walls for an exit. At its farthest end, there appeared to be a break in the stone of the forward wall. It looked like about three feet high and six feet long covered in heavy wood planking. She walked to the wooden part to examine the difference. It had a door and it was bolted from their side of the wall. She blew out the breath she'd been unaware she was holding and retraced her steps.

Descending the stairs, Abby smiled to see that Ben had retrieved her little cat and held her gently in his arms. She quietly described the opening above. They made plans then for Rennie to stay with the children while she checked out the stable and yard between it and the house. They would wait together within the barn, and at the first hint of gunshots or Elise, would take cover in the tunnel, bolting every lock that was provided as they went. Rennie didn't like this last part of their plan and said so, under her breath.

Ben agreed and Elizabeth wanted to know what Rennie had said. This was explained and they delayed their exit with some more palaver over what would be better than Abby's plan. Finally, they agreed that Rennie and the children would return to the tunnel and possibly the cellar room, but that they would leave the door to the barn unbolted, locking all the rest. The children still grumbled, but were silenced when they climbed the steps to the stable above them. The group silently made their way to the doorway within the wooden planking; Abby sliding back the bolt and cautiously pulling it open to the side. She squirmed through the opening and bumped her head about three feet up on what appeared to be a lid to a long box.

She pushed the lid with her shoulders, tucking her head to her chest in the process. The long lid opened, and as it was hinged to the side at the back wall, she eased it up until it was leaning against the stone wall and climbed out.

Their passage had led to the back horse stalls—this box having been made to take up most of the last stall. There was a lot of tack hanging around the small enclosure and Abby remembered that her grandfather had never used it to house a horse. She would have smiled again with the thought that her great-great-however-many-back granddaddy had been quite ingenious; but the graveness of their situation stifled it.

Abby crept out of the former stall and quietly walked the length of the stables. She eased the barn door open a crack. No one was in sight, there was no sound of footsteps and the Parrish woman's gun was silent. She bolted the barn door from the inside, then bolted the side entrance toward the back of the barn, and scurried over to the box she'd pressed through previously.

Abby waved the rest of her little army through the small enclosure. They retraced her steps to the door. Rennie was to remain with the children behind her like ducklings, stationed at the entrance to the barn, watching Abby's progress through the cracked doorway. Abby had pointed out the bolted side entrance to the barn on their way forward, so Rennie had instructed the children to watch the back of the barn in the unlikely case of that woman finding their tunnel or breaking through the side entrance.

Abby had made it up to the porch of the house now, and Rennie saw her start and crawl underneath a bed of azalea bushes surrounding a live oak, not ten feet out from the porch. Within seconds of the bushes stilling, Elise Parrish came strutting around the corner of the house her shotgun held close to her body, anger exuding from her every movement.

An explicative rolled off her tongue like a how-do-you-do. "People don't just disappear," is all Rennie could make out from her continued muttering. Suddenly, the woman leaned down and shot into the bushes that edged the porch. *Thank God, Abby done hid in them azaleas and not them porch shrubs!*

The thought had no sooner entered Rennie's head than the woman turned and lifted the barrel of her gun toward that very bed of azaleas. At the front driveway, the motor of a car approaching broke Parrish's concentration. She turned and quickly trotted over to the edge of the porch, then continued around the back. *She goin' to get whoever drivin' dat car!* Rennie's heart stuttered.

Her relief over Abby's safety was choked back by the thought that someone was fixing to get a barrage of bullets. *Lawd have mercy!* She watched incredulously as Abby scurried from the azaleas and followed Elise around the side of the house.

It was all Rennie could do to stay with Ben and Elizabeth. She wanted to scream at Abby to get her *scrawny, little self back over to this hyeah barn!* If she heard anything else, she was going to lock them chi'ren in that tunnel and go see 'bout her chile. She had always felt like she had four babies—that Abby was her youngest—ever since she promised her old friend to have a care for her. She knew Abby felt the same.

Elizabeth tugged at the back of her dress and whispered, "Rennie."

"Shhh. Shh," Rennie responded, patting the child behind her back without looking.

"Rennie. I remember something," Elizabeth persisted. Rennie turned to make sure no one had made their way behind them up the passageway. No one was in sight. She looked anxiously at young Elizabeth, and the girl continued. "That Mrs. Parrish—she looks like a man pictured with Miz Raynelle and Annie. I think the man might be Annie's real Daddy. That Miz Elise woman looks a lot like him."

Rennie shushed her again and thought about this new piece of information as she turned back to take up her watch again.

John was so tired he could taste it. Nevertheless, he made up his mind while he was still on the outskirts of Carverville, to turn Liddy's big Buick sedan toward Abby's house. There was no way he was going to walk his family into his old home for the first time without her by his side. He would take her home later, after nightfall.

They had agreed that they would marry as soon as they could do the blood tests and get a license. It would be a small ceremony in the church. He'd take her to shop for a dress, or maybe she'd prefer Liddy to go with her. Either way, he'd insisted that he wanted to buy her the dress, but they were still arguing through that one.

He laughed lightly, because the children were asleep in the back having succumbed to "road lulling". Liddy had even dozed off beside him. The right side of her head was sort of resting on the windowsill. With her mouth gaping open and head leaning over at the most bizarre angle, she looked like one of Norman Rockwell's cover illustrations for the Saturday Evening Post. He had been wondering on and off if he should try to ease his hand against her forehead and move her head back against the seat. He had been trying to decide that question for the last fifteen miles. He was afraid she'd have a crick in her neck.

He chuckled quietly. He had envied his children's right to call their Aunt Lydia, Liddy. He'd frequently referred to Lydia as Liddy to his children, but had not presumed to call her by her pet name until she'd insisted. He had never really experienced a real mother's love or even an aunt's. John had taken to Lydia as easily as his children and had respected her, as well. So, when she had urged him to call her Liddy, and explained that everybody she loved did, he had been so pleased; and instantly took her up on it.

He mused his way past Barne's and through most of Bennington until Abby's road caught his attention. He hung a quick right off the paved road that ran through their little community and unwittingly took care of the angle of Liddy's head. She stirred and eased back into her nap. Travelling down the dusty road that led past his old rental, he was glad the kids were resting, too.

That house held such a mixture of emotions for him, but mostly a dark time he was glad to have behind him. It felt good to John to just keep driving on down the road past the milestone of his troubled last years, and to continue down the little dirt road, headed toward a person who felt like a part of home.

It wouldn't be long now. There was less than a mile of this narrow road between him and Abby. He had to fight the urge to press down on the accelerator. And there was Abby's driveway. He let out a breath he hadn't realized he'd been holding and turned in, his lips spread over his teeth in a smile his uncle would have relegated worthy of a grand piano keyboard.

Lord. Thank you. Thank you. He pulled up behind a late model Nash.

It was nothing but a red puddle-jumper and he wondered who its driver was. Sure, it wasn't a man driving *that* little Jitney, he thought in relief.

Annie and Bo were just stretching and waking up. Liddy still slept. "Come on, spuds," he enthused. "Abby'll be wantin' to see you two."

Just a corner away from Big John and his "spuds", Abby was slowly making her way around the house to the corner where she'd seen Elise Parrish disappear. She was glad she'd raked the leaves on her day off because their crackling would surely have given her steps away.

Peeping out, she saw the woman kneeling not far from an old "mounting block" to take careful aim at someone in her front yard.

Abby had kicked off her high heels back in the azalea bed, and when she ran for the Parrish woman, she was almost as fast as when she'd leapt off the bus as a young girl and run for home to find her Daddy. Elise Parrish was taking aim on Bo, and the woman actually smiled as she muttered about there being one less bit of Raynelle on the earth.

Three things happened in rapid succession—Big John saw the woman and her intent, and sprawled across his two babies. Abby barreled into the kneeling woman, and Elise pulled the trigger.

Chapter 14

"Home is the best place. I found it with my Father and Rennie and now John and Annie and Bo. But always it has been in my Lord."
—Abigail Faith Weston Abrams

A xel Arnette got the call-out from the old Weston place. Rennie Baker had been almost incoherent she was so excited.

Finally, she'd given up trying to explain and fairly screeched, "Get out hyeah, fast, Mistuh Axel!"

He'd had no idea what to expect and herded up Vern along with their handguns and two rifles. Vern had driven, and used the bubble and siren. (In the deep south, this is routinely pronounced with a long i, long e—si-*RENE.*)

Axel smiled grimly as people pulled their cars to the side of the road and craned their necks to see which direction their sheriff was heading. Regardless of the ability of Freeman County to spread news like odor after opening a cold greens pot, he *loved* small towns. He loved *this* small town. It was his and he was dead tired of bad folks causing trouble.

Whatever was going on out there, they'd better not have messed with Abby Weston. Archie had been a particular friend of his, and he could think of no one kinder in their little neck of the woods than this young woman.

Vern shut off the siren as he turned off the main road and down the old dirt road to Archie's. The black and white police car, a long Galaxy 500 chewed up the miles before them, and cast such a swirl of dust down the sandy white road that it threatened to leave only the dark, rich, hard-packed dirt beneath it.

When he hung a left across the cattle gate that covered the entrance to Abby's house, Axel's teeth jarred together, and his hip slid smack up against the arm rest on the right side of the car. He smiled as his deputy gunned the motor up to the house then stomped on brakes at the last possible moment. He'd have to give it to Vern, if you said put a rush on it, he could gift wrap it for you.

The ambulance was just pulling in the road behind them. Other than the emergency vehicle's blaring siren and the dust they'd both raised, the scene before him looked fairly calm. There was a white-haired lady looking a little shaken and examining a busted headlight on her old Buick. Big John Abrams had Abby sitting on the edge of the porch with Rennie standing beside him on the ground. Rennie held out a small wash bowl, and Big John was dipping what looked like a white wash cloth in it and gently dabbing at a bit of crimson that seemed to be oozing from the side of Abby's forehead. He held her chin in his left hand while he cocked his head at an angle and focused on the cut. For a big man, he surely seemed to be good with his hands and some solicitous.

A graying, red-haired woman lay sprawled on the ground beyond them. She was tied up with what looked like clothesline rope, but she appeared to be unconscious.

The Weston house sported a wide wrap-around porch and a big swing that a tired man could lay down in at the end of a hard day. Just now, and the sheriff grinned wryly, it was full of children; who, typical of a passel of young'uns, had already found a means of great fun. A beagle was sprawled across two of their laps and appeared to care nothing about the fact that they were swinging back and forth with such vigor that the bottom of the swing flew part way beyond the porch and over the flower beds every time the "forth" was finished and the "back part" took over.

An aging bird dog, looked like Archie's old pointer, Blue, and a tortoiseshell cat were as far from the children's corner of the porch as they could get, but Axel could see the cat's tail twitch a bit as she watched the slightly wild swinging. Looked like the Linden girl, and Miz Eulee's grandson and John's two kids.

He hated that these four kids had been exposed to more violence. But they were giggling and holding on to each other and the swing "for dear life". Seemed like a good way to burn off stress and pent up energy to him. A part of him wished he could join them.

Sheriff Arnette was some reluctant to interrupt John and Abby, but he reckoned he'd better get to the bottom of the lady trussed up like a Thanksgiving turkey and laid out on the ground. He shoved his door open and stepped over to the elderly woman, who had by now stopped examining what he assumed to be *her* headlight since the car had an Alabama tag. She had turned her attention to the four children pumping the aged swing. She let them be as he addressed her.

"Mm. Ma'am. Howdy. I'm Sheriff Axel Arnette, and this is my deputy, Vern Starnes." Vern had shut down the car and by now was standing at his side. "We just need to see what happened here."

Vern tipped his hat and nodded to the lady, "Ma'am."

The old lady's eyes widened, and she cleared her throat before speaking.

"Sheriff. Deputy. I'm sort of John's Aunt. Raynelle was my niece." She paused for that to sink in. "We just made it in from Phenix City, Alabama where I've been keeping John and my niece's children, Annie and Bo. I was comin' to Bennington to help John take care of the children and we stopped by to pick up Abby before going to John's house." Here, she stopped to draw in a breath.

"I was asleep when we got here, but I woke to a gunshot. That lady— over there—the one tied up," she clarified, pointing an aging index finger in Elise Parrish's direction, "'peared to be tryin' ta kill somebody with a shotgun. John had Rennie lock it up in the house. He'll show you."

Here she looked over at John tending to Abby, and smiled, "Well. In a minute."

At this juncture the ambulance began to unload with Dr. Alex Harrington on hand and a driver. He hurried over to the lady lying on the ground and looked up to question the sheriff. It took a bit of sorting, but the woman on the ground was identified as Elise Parrish which did take the sheriff and his deputy by surprise.

Alex took Elise's vital signs before moving her. The still unconscious woman was untied and placed on a gurney; where the sheriff quickly added handcuffs to her accommodation, and assigned Vern to ride along with the ambulance explaining the history on Elise Perkins/Parrish.

Alex ordered Abby to come to Dr. Prescott's office, indicating that her cut needed stitches. He told John that a clean white towel would be sufficient to stop the flow of blood on the trip into town. Rennie and Liddy volunteered to stay with the children, and await the Lindens' arrival. After being phoned, Art and Ella were driving their truck over to pick up Elizabeth and Ben and their bikes.

Sheriff Arnette, piled into the driver seat of the police car with the intention of following the ambulance to the hospital. Rolling the window down, he hollered out at Big John and Abby that he'd be in touch for their account of the story.

John squeezed his big frame into Abby's little bug after helping her in the other side. They didn't want to drive Liddy's car so close to dusk with its broken headlight—which, of course, was where Elise Parrish's wild shot had hit. He grinned at the spectacle he made all folded up in the driver's seat, and saw that even his children were getting a big laugh over his scrunched-up form.

He reminded Abby to hold the towel to her forehead to staunch the bleeding, and hollered out the window at Rennie and Liddy that they'd be back as soon as they could. Turning to Abby he allowed his smile to have free rein. "Abby girl, I hope my knees don't knock me out on the way over."

As she looked at him, she wondered how in the world he was going to handle the clutch, brakes and gas, and switch gears, too. Ben, Elizabeth, Annie and Bo stopped their swinging to watch all the interesting events unfolding in Miz Abby's yard. As the VW drove over the cattle gate, they abandoned the swing and marched over to the two ladies. Focusing their attention on their "keepers", they began badgering them about the secret passageway.

All four of them felt the need to explore both the passageway and the tunnel *right this minute*. Annie and Bo *needed* to *see* it. *Surely*, Rennie and Liddy could see that.

"Dat's fo' another day," announced Rennie unrelentingly.

And Liddy smiled behind her hand at Rennie. They had both taken a shine to each other and were already talking so thick and fast, the children had to wait to get in a word without interrupting.

"I'll talk to Miz Abby, and she make it so's you can all go down together wit' her and Mistuh John. I done know she will."

The four left off their cajoling, marched back to the swing, and took up where they'd left off minus the beagle who "was nowhere to be found". Rennie and Liddy did, too, talking excitedly over the afternoon and thanking the Lord about every other breath. The Lindens hadn't made it to pick up Ben and Elizabeth before Liddy knew most of Abby's history; although, the children and John had given her a fairly accurate picture of that young lady's character.

Art and Ella rolled up not too long after the county's emergency vehicles had driven off. There ensued pandemonium again as the children and adults began to explain the day's happenings. At last, Art had quieted Ben and Elizabeth, and Liddy and Rennie got Bo to hush. Even Annie seemed stirred up and wanting to talk about the excitement.

The Lindens listened in amazement to Rennie and Liddy's tale. Every now and again, the children added in a bit of extra information. Throughout its telling, Miz Ella exclaimed intermittently, "YOU DON'T MEAN IT!" while Art just kept staring in astonishment. Finally, he said, "So this Parrish woman was really Raynelle's former sister-in-law?" Rennie and Liddy nodded heads in sync.

After a good deal more conjecture, the Lindens had parted with Elizabeth, Ben and their bicycles in the back of the truck.

Rennie and Liddy immediately herded Bo and Annie in the house and began supper preparations. Between the two of them, they knew it would be a welcome sight when John and Abby got home.

Liddy wouldn't have thought it, but she had begun to cozen to the idea of Bennington as home. She already held a good deal of respect and feeling for the handful of its inhabitants that she had met.

She could hear Rennie's sweet humming under her breath and thought she recognized "Great Is Thy Faithfulness". She started humming along then, not able to duplicate the intricate embellishments that Rennie was cradling the melody with, but so loving the praising of their Lord together.

Dr. Prescott sealed Abby's cut with eight stitches while Big John paced back and forth outside the door like it was one of his kids.

"John," Dr. Prescott finally called out, "you might as well come on in. That way my nurses can get through the hallway." John ducked slightly to enter the small office, and entered with a sheepish grin.

"Sorry, Doc," he'd offered. "She's some important to me."

And Abby almost busted her face with the smile that spread out over it. It would have made the ongoing suturing hurt, except Dr. Prescott had started with a couple of shots of Novocain. They left after a short chat with both Dr. Prescott and his sister, Hannah.

When John closed the door to the doctor's office, he'd immediately took her hand, like he'd wanted to do all those years ago, when she'd first caught his eye "lighting out" from the bus for her home. She had been just a wisp of a girl then, and truly, not much more now; but she held his heart in her small hands, and he'd more than a suspicion that he had hers, too.

They walked to the little car then; John lightly swinging Abby's hand, and she smiling up at him for all she was worth. Abby insisted on driving the little bug home. She'd had her fill of laughing at John all the way over to Carverville, and was now beginning to feel a little contrite at the trouble he'd gone through just to drive her to Doc's.

He pulled out another sheepish grin and agreed that it would be a lot easier if he just had to fight being folded up in the little thing without coaxing it to move in any way. She laughed outright yet again, and he joined her.

A hint of the warm summer evenings to come wafted through the windows as they sat in Doc Prescott's parking lot. Not for the first time, she admired John's ability to laugh at himself. It was a rare gift she thought, to hold oneself not too seriously. She smiled up at him again, her heart in her eyes.

He contorted his great form just a mite more and covered her lips with his own. There was such a world of longing and sweetness that passed between them. It had taken so long to come home to each other. She placed her hands on his cheeks, her fingers extending onto his temples to reach into the dark tousled hair.

A car pulled in beside them and John and Abby pulled back from the kiss, John twisting to face the front with a groan. Abby smiled and cranked up the little burbling thing, and headed for home.

By the time, they reached the Weston Home, the sun had dipped below the pines; and they could see the evening star hanging in the first blush of pink and blue that stretched along the horizon and upwards to its spot in the sky.

The moon was just peeking over the big oak at her bedroom window as she turned across the cattle gate and headed the VW down her driveway. She pulled up under the portico and shut off the bug. After John opened his door and extricated himself with a minimum of grunts, groans and grimaces, they immediately noticed the singing of crickets. In the distance, a whippoorwill's cry completed the promise of spring. He sidled up beside her and stole another kiss before they headed for the door.

Laughingly, John and Abby entered the kitchen door amidst Deacon's prancing about their legs, and Persimmon, on her windowsill perch, unblinkingly contemplated the big man who accompanied her girl. Abby was still ribbing him about the permanent accordion folds on his person, as he held her hand and squeezed in behind her.

The nightmare of the past days had been swept away, and it was just like Rennie had read to her as a child, "Weeping endureth for a night, but joy cometh in the morning."

All the windows in the house had been open when they drove up and they realized they'd been smelling an aroma that had been pulling them toward the door before they'd even made it out of the car. The kitchen was full of smells that enfolded a body like a warm hug.

John and Abby both recognized the rich, homey aroma of roast smothered in gravy with onions. It was the first time she'd had a thought for the meat she'd placed in the oven just before all the pandemonium and havoc had begun to fly. Thankfully, Rennie and Liddy had saved it.

Abby had put up a lot of vegetables last summer, and the ladies had made use of them to lay out a spread that could take your breath. There was creamed corn, rice and field peas, a squash casserole, fried okra and biscuits. Annie and Bo were seated at the table washed and looking like they hoped whoever said grace would remember the word and be merciful.

The oven was putting out the enticing smell of a blueberry pie, and Abby knew she had vanilla ice cream in the freezer. Earl called and said he'd be late home, but had begged Rennie to save him a bit of that dinner she'd described. They all laughed again at her retelling of their conversation as many hands carried bowls and steaming dishes to the table.

Then, suddenly, they were all seated around the table with a hush that even the children allowed to fall around them; and Big John reached out and started them all holding hands. He began to thank the Lord for being their Deliverer this day, and for being Hope and Light; for being their Shepherd through this world and the next; and he blessed the Lord, saying, "Say it with me now, "Bless the Lord, O, my soul, and all that is within me, bless His Holy Name."

The trailing high-pitched voices of Annie and Bo only widened the smiles of the little group around the table. And intuitively, they lingered over holding each other's hands, a deep-held Amen voiced together, too. As Abby began to pass the bowls, she was reminded of Rennie's sharing with her after the "Joy Comes in the Morning" passage, that there were some little noticed phrases in the Bible— "yet a little while", "in due season", "in the fullness of time", "and it came to pass". These she'd said were a reminder of the faithfulness of our Great God, His timing being perfect, His Ways past our understanding.

And then she'd quoted the words of Moses as he was preparing to leave the children of Israel. "There is none like the God of Jeshurun, Who rides the heavens to your help. The Eternal God is a Dwelling Place, and underneath are the Everlasting Arms." Surely, He had carried her through the darkness of the last few years; and even in the darkness there had been His peace and comfort and joy.

She paused to help Bo's plate with rice and peas; then cut up the roast beef she placed there next. He'd asked for a biscuit and some creamed corn, and she made sure he was satisfied before turning back to her plate and thoughts.

Big John was placing a serving of roast on Annie's plate. Abby smiled at the bunch of them all cozy around her father's table. Looking back over the short span of her lifetime, she could see, just like David had said, "goodness and mercy" had followed her all the days of her life. Thankfulness and praise resonated in her heart toward her Lord Who was full of tender mercies. "And it came to pass..." she thought and turned her attention back to the people she loved and the table so full of good things.

Even Liddy had already made a dent in her heart. Abby unfolded her napkin, placed it in her lap and looked up still a little shyly at her Big John. He was waiting there for her to meet his focus. John was smiling like he'd just seen the front door of home after a long truck run; and there was love in the gray eyes that met hers across the table.

Copyright

Made in the USA
Columbia, SC
08 December 2022

73053188R00129